BETRAYAL
PIRATES OF CRUXES

KELLI COOK

BETRAYAL: THE PIRATES OF CRUXES
Copyright ©2024 Line By Lion Publications
www.pixelandpen.studio
ISBN 978-1-948807-94-4
Cover Design by Thomas Lamkin Jr. .
Editing by Dani J. Caile

For more information, email www.linebylionpublications.com

LINE BY LION
PUBLICATIONS

For Dakota. I love you most.

TABLE OF CONTENTS

PROLOGUE

IN the twenty-three years that he had been a captain at sea, Ansel Brodier had never seen fog so thick. The weightless wall of white filled the world around the ship and was moved only in gentle swirls by the breeze skirting across the surface of the water. Standing on the bow, he couldn't see the stern a hundred and thirty feet away. Even the tops of the galleon's three masts were hazy to his eyes. He hated to think of how far behind schedule this would put him, but he'd had no choice but to order his crew to furl the sails and wait until conditions improved. The last thing he wanted was to run the Kingfisher aground on a shallow reef on the edge of Mariner's Rest or Southway.

Brodier's first mate, Charles Massey, joined his captain at the bow. They stood in silence for a while as they strained their eyes to penetrate the gloom. Massey was holding a lantern, and its warm, orange light bounced weakly off the fog around them. He shook his head in disappointment. "It doesn't look like it's going to clear anytime soon. Mr. Travert is going to dock our pay for this."

"Better that than the alternative," Brodier replied, and although Massey chuckled, there was nothing funny about the rumors of their employer's violent nature. If there was one thing that Brodier had learned over the two decades he'd worked for the man, it was to do everything in his power to stay on Landon Travert's good side.

A crewman's voice rang out from his lookout near the top of the main mast, startling them both. "There's something in the fog!"

Brodier's eyes scanned the thick cloud around him for any sign of what the crewman had spotted. Beside him, Massey muttered, "No one would be crazy enough to sail through this."

As if in direct defiance of that thought, a single mast and triangular sails of a small sloop materialized off the starboard side of the bow, pushing through the heavy mist that had concealed them. The smaller ship was so close that Massey could have thrown his lantern onto its deck from here, and Brodier cried out, "Sound for collision!"

A bell began to toll from its place near the helm, and the frantic ringing was distorted into a haunting sound by the fog. Massey leaned over the wooden banister that ran around the edge of the Kingfisher's bow and called out to the passing ship that they needed to turn hard to port. Brodier leaned over beside him, and as the mist parted and swirled along the deck of the little sloop, his eyes were able to pick out more than two dozen men. Their clothing was ragged and mismatched, and the gentle glint off their pistols and knives made Brodier's blood run cold.

"Fools," Massey growled. "They could have rammed right into us."

Brodier gripped the banister so tightly that his knuckles turned white. He said through gritted teeth, "This wasn't an accident."

The frantic ringing of the bell was suddenly drowned out by the deafening blast of cannons. The Kingfisher shuddered beneath their feet as at least six cannonballs tore mercilessly through her hull. Massey stumbled back from the banister in utter shock, and when he looked at Brodier, the weathered captain saw true terror on the younger man's face. He seized

Massey by the sleeve of his uniform and shoved him toward the nearest hatchway, barking, "Get men on the cannons! Hurry!"

Massey rushed off at a run to do so. All across the Kingfisher's three decks, crewmen scrambled to ready themselves for an attack that none of them had seen coming. Brodier bellowed orders, but even as he did, a large, four-pronged hook appeared over the starboard banister, and its metal claws dug deep into the wood there. To Brodier's horror, a second hook landed just a few feet away from the first, followed almost immediately by a third. At the same time, the cannons aboard the sloop sounded again, and the Kingfisher's hull was punctured with another set of jagged holes.

Brodier called for one of his cabin boys to bring him his pistol, and within seconds, a lad who couldn't have been more than twelve years old was placing it in his hand. The boy was trembling in terror, and Brodier felt that same degree of fear try to creep its way into his own heart. He pushed the notion aside and whirled to face the banister that was now peppered with metal hooks. As he watched, a man in a tattered vest and pants hauled himself up over the side. Brodier's gun barked fire in his hands, and the man tumbled off the far side of the banister with a pained shriek. Brodier took aim at the next man, but it was too late; more than a dozen pirates were clambering over the banister and onto the deck of the Kingfisher. Beneath them, the sloop's cannons lobbed a third volley of cannonballs into her side.

The pirates met Brodier's crew with pistols and knives that were hungry for blood. The roar of gunfire was soon joined by a chorus of screams as men were injured. Brodier fired his gun twice more before his shoulder erupted in a terrible, stinging sensation. He fell down to the deck with a grunt, and his pistol skidded across the fog-dampened deck. Brodier grimaced, pressing his hand against his injured shoulder, and when he pulled it away, his fingers were dyed red. He looked all around himself in a daze and found a nightmarish sight: members of his crew – some of whom he'd sailed with for years and considered friends – were falling left and right. The pirates showed no mercy.

Brodier clambered to his feet and raised his uninjured arm above his head, shouting, "We surrender! Lay down your weapons!"

The pirate crew let out a great cheer at that, and Brodier's men slowly laid down their own guns. The pirates ordered them to their knees, and Brodier found himself kneeling before a man who couldn't have been more than twenty-two years old. His skin was the color of roasted almonds. His hair was black and looked to be cut to the length of his shoulders, though it was tied back in a ponytail at the moment. He offered Brodier a cocky grin and asked, "Are you the captain?"

"I am," Brodier panted against the pain still searing in his shoulder. "The ship is yours. Are you going to sink her?"

The pirate glanced around at the corpse-strewn deck around them, and Brodier knew that it had been a useless question; he could already feel a gentle tilt to starboard as he knelt here. The Kingfisher had begun to list to one side. Brodier asked miserably, "What will you do with my crew?"

To answer that, the pirate's lips stretched into a cold and murderous smile.

CHAPTER ONE

JOURNEY opened the door to his father's study to find the man sitting at his desk, his elbows propped on its surface and his hands cradling his head. Landon's hair, usually slicked back with expensive oils, was a mess this afternoon. A dozen papers were scattered across his wooden desk, and an ink blotter had spilled over the edge to form a black puddle on the floor beside it. Journey decided to tread carefully from this point. He knew what could happen when his father was in this state. Landon said without lifting his head from his hands, "Come in, Journey."

He closed the door behind him. The study was as ornate and spacious as any of the other two dozen rooms in the sprawling mansion, and Journey made his way past bookshelves laden with expensive trinkets on his way to the chair that sat in front of Landon's desk. Once he was seated, Journey waited for him to speak. He eyed a few of the papers scattered around and saw that they were estimates for the value of the latest sugarcane haul. It was an impressive sum, but the joy that should have brought Landon was nowhere to be found.

Landon sat back in his chair. When he spoke, he was able to keep his tone at a reasonable level, but there was a tremble to it that Journey didn't trust. "I just received word that the Kingfisher has been lost. Burned wreckage washed up on Mariner's Rest. There's been no sign of survivors, and the cargo is presumed lost."

Journey didn't respond for a moment as he mentally added up the amount of money that this was going to cost them. He didn't like the total. Landon was waiting for his response, so he asked, "What do you think happened?"

Landon barked a humorless laugh and rocked back in his chair to stare up at the ceiling. "What do we think happened?" he asked the wooden beams above them. "The boy wonders what could have happened."

"The Ocean Sprite," Journey decided, and the words left a bad taste in his mouth. "She hasn't been sighted in almost a month. I was starting to hope that Romilly had given up and moved on."

"Captain Romilly is a thief and a coward," Landon declared, still speaking to the ceiling. "All pirates are. But they're also stubborn, and they don't give up on something that they can't have right away. When I put you in charge of security for the islands, I thought you understood that. Now, you've let down your guard, and we both have to pay the price. I admire your effort in commissioning the brigantine, but you've ultimately failed."

"With all due respect, the Jubilee has never failed us in action," he objected. "You wanted her ready to show off to the Horizon representative when he comes here in a few weeks, so I had to call her in early for routine maintenance. She's been anchored on the north side of Stonewell for the past six days."

Landon tore his gaze from the ceiling and merely stared at him. His hands were clenched fists in his lap, but he forced himself to relax them. Before he could say anything, Journey told him, "I can have her ready to sail again in a day or so. This isn't a total loss. I'll keep an eye on the markets in Kinsman Lane and Eastport. Romilly will try to sell the cane to Western Straights or Whitefish at a steal. I can use Trader's Law to get it back."

Landon raised an eyebrow. "And if he chooses to take the load north? Or West? You'll miss him in those markets."

Journey shook his head. "You're right about him being stubborn. He knows that the Twins have a lot more to offer than what he just took. He'll stick around to try to hit us again. Besides, now he'll be overconfident."

Landon was silent again, and Journey gave him some time to consider it. He watched as Landon's eyes searched him for something that he could only hope he'd find. Finally, Landon decided, "I'm going to trust you to fix this. We'll have to swallow the cost of the Kingfisher, but if you can get back even a portion of the cane, then we can move past this. Don't rush the maintenance on the Jubilee; I don't think Romilly will be back so soon."

"He'll hole up in a bottle of rum in a tavern somewhere and drink away his earnings."

Landon nodded. "That's my hope. We'll keep the Jubilee anchored and ready until we spot him again. Tell Captain Elbridge that he has three weeks from that day to sink the Ocean Sprite. If she's not on the bottom of the sea by then, he can consider himself unemployed. He'll be cutting cane before the end of the year."

Journey stood to go, but paused as Landon added, "I talked to Ansel Beaumont yesterday. He says that Caresse is hoping for a spring wedding. She and her mother are going to start interviewing dressmakers." He pointed a finger at him in warning and said, "I heard that the two of you had an argument last week. If you haven't patched it up yet, do it right away. Don't mess this up."

"It was a minor disagreement," he assured him. "I got a letter from Caresse two days ago, and everything's fine."

There was a knock on the door, and one of the mansion's butlers, Bromley, stuck his balding head into the room. There was a no-nonsense expression on his face that Journey didn't think he'd ever seen the man without. He announced in his dry, craggy voice, "There's a man from Kinsman Lane here to see you, Mr. Travert. He says it's urgent, but he doesn't have an appointment."

Landon flapped a hand toward the door to signify permission to allow the visitor to enter, and Bromley disappeared from sight as he went to fetch him. Journey took it as his cue to leave, and as he started for the door, Landon ordered, "Don't forget about what I said about Caresse, Journey. Fix it."

"It's already fixed," he reiterated, and then he was out the door before Landon could add anything else. As he stepped through the doorway and into the hall, he nearly collided with a man who was hurrying in the opposite direction. Journey didn't recognize the man, who was dressed in a humble, linen waistcoat and tweed cap. He kept his gaze firmly set on the door to Landon's study, and as he passed Journey in the hall, he didn't utter so much as a greeting. Journey felt a jolt of pity as he let the man pass by. The impoverished families of Kinsman Lane often sought financial aid from Landon, but in Journey's twenty years of life, he'd never known his father to give it.

As Journey stepped out of the mansion's foyer and into the bright sunlight outside, he paused to take a deep breath of salt-tinged air. Stonewell Island was an inhospitable speck of stone that jutted up from the sea, as if in defiance of the waves that lapped at its base, but four generations of his family had called it home. It hosted the sprawling mansion, a few offices, a row of four warehouses, and a small port for a handful of ships. It was the less impressive docks on the north side of the island, however, that Journey now started toward. It was a perfect day to make the trek: warm, but not too hot, with an occasional cloud drifting before the sun. It was a shame that news of the Kingfisher was bringing down his mood.

He followed the stone path around the corner of the sprawling mansion's east wing and into the garden, which was so full of blooming flowers that their fragrance choked the air all around them. From there, the path wound its way down a steep slope and eventually ended where the rocky shoreline kissed the untamed ocean. There were two wooden docks here, and as Journey stepped up onto the nearest one, he paused to look up and admire the ship that loomed above him. The Jubilee was a two-masted brigantine that measured eighty feet long and twenty-five feet wide at her broadest point. She was a true beauty, made of the finest oak and cedar that money could buy.

Journey carefully made his way up the gangway that stretched from the dock to the ship, and he was immediately greeted on the lower deck by a balding man with broad shoulders and a permanent scowl. Journey offered the man his hand, and he shook it with a hand that had been calloused by years spent at sea. Journey said, "Captain Elbridge, I'm sorry to stop in without warning."

"It's no trouble," Elbridge assured him, but that scowl and the curtness of his words made Journey doubt that. He glanced around the deck and found a dozen sailors working on various chores: restringing ratlines, replacing old ropes, and scrubbing the wooden planks that made up the deck beneath their feet. Elbridge swept an arm around at all of this and assured him, "We're still on schedule. She could use a good careening, but we still have plenty of time to do that."

Journey motioned for him to follow him, and they climbed the steps to the main deck. He led Elbridge to the tall, wooden helm, where none of the crewmen were currently working, and once they could speak in relative privacy, Journey told him, "The plans have changed. We've lost the Kingfisher."

The older man's face turned a furious shade of red in an instant. He asked through gritted teeth, "Was it the Ocean Sprite?"

Journey nodded. He understood his frustration. Elbridge and his crew had been chasing the sloop and her pirates around for months now. Twice, they'd gotten close enough to exchange cannon fire, but the Sprite had managed to slip away both times. Now her pirates had managed to take advantage of the Jubilee's short absence while docked, and the sailors aboard the Kingfisher had paid for it with their lives.

Journey told him, "We'll keep an eye out for the Sprite. She'll be back eventually. When she shows up again, you'll have three weeks to run her down and sink her. If not…" He didn't finish, but he knew he didn't have to.

The aging captain heaved a sigh and looked out over the open ocean to the north. As his eyes considered the expanse of calm waters, he said, "You've always been good to me, Mr. Travert. You've been good to all of your father's employees, to be honest. You've argued for better wages for us and changed his mind when he wanted to lay off half of the workers on Green Plot. I think you should know, though, that I'm not going to hunt the Sprite down because I think I owe it to you, and I damn sure don't owe it to Landon. I knew a lot of good men on the Kingfisher. If I send her to the bottom, it's going to be for them."

"And for yourself," Journey agreed. "Romilly and his sloop have been a thorn in your side for a long time now. I'd like nothing more than to see you put an end to that."

Elbridge took his gaze from the northern horizon, at last, to look him in the eyes. "I'll sink her," he vowed. "You have my word."

Journey offered to help Elbridge conduct a throughout audit of the Jubilee's cannons and gunpowder, and he accepted his help with thanks. By the time they were finished and Journey started toward the mansion, the sun was sinking low in the west. He made the trek back up the stone path in good time, and when he reached the gate to the low fence that ran around the garden, he spotted someone who had never failed to brighten his day: his mother. Jubilee's fiery, red hair was up in a fancy style, and her dark green dress contrasted her pale skin beautifully. She was sitting on her favorite bench in the midst of thick bushes that modeled crimson roses, and when she noticed her son on the path, she called his name. There was a book in her hands, and Journey didn't doubt that it was one of the tacky romance novels that she could never get enough of. She set it aside as he planted a light kiss on her cheek and sat down beside her on the bench. A look at the title on the cover of her book – Shipwrecked Desires – told him that he'd been right about the genre. She noticed his glance and said sheepishly, "You know it's my guiltiest pleasure."

"I won't judge you for it," he fibbed. "If you're not too wrapped up in it, we have time for a few games of backgammon before dinner. I might even let you win, this time."

She laughed at that, and the sound was as sweet and melodious to his ears as it had always been. She sobered, however, and said, "Your father sent for me a few minutes ago. I was finishing one last chapter before going inside to find him. He said it's important."

"He's in a mood," he warned.

Jubilee gave him a wistful look that broke his heart. "I know all about his moods, Journey."

A rush of questions threatened to clamber out of his mouth, but he'd never had the courage to ask her about the bruises and scratches before, and today was no different. Perhaps she saw the concern on his face, for she forced herself to brighten and said with a cheerfulness he didn't believe, "After dinner, Abigay and I are going to decide the new color scheme for the main guest room, now that the repairs on the ceiling are finished. Once we've done that, I'll take you up on your offer for a game or two before bed."

"You can invite Abigay to play, too," he suggested, and he was glad to see her forced smile turn into a more believable one. Abigay Laval had been his mother's dearest friend for as long as he could remember. She was technically one of the paid house servants, but Jubilee had always treated her like a younger sister.

He kissed her on the cheek once more before leaving her in the garden to use a side door to enter the mansion, where he was greeted by expensive oil paintings and luxurious carpet. A stairway and a long hall brought him to his bedroom door, and Journey let himself inside. He passed by the large, canopy bed that had been his since he'd outgrown a cradle and sat down at the wooden writing desk near the window. Afternoon sunlight shone down through it to fall across the sheaf of papers he needed to work on. They were cluttered with the clumsy handwriting of the foremen his father employed, and for a moment, Journey paused as he considered it all. Aside from Stonewell, Landon owned three other islands. Nymph's Rest and Green Plot – most often called the Twin Islands by the locals – hosted expansive sugarcane plantations. Travert's Fourth, which Landon had named in a stroke of unimaginativeness, grew cinnamon trees and brought in a sizeable fortune each harvest. One day, it would all belong to him. It was a daunting thought, sometimes, but also one that kept him on a straight and narrow path in life.

He bent over the papers to begin calculating some of the foremen's numbers, but was interrupted by a knock on his bedroom door. Journey called for whomever it was to come in, and he was pleased when Abigay opened the door. She offered the loving smile she'd reserved for him his entire life and held up a small, white envelope. Caresse Beaumont's handwriting spelled out his name across the front. Abigay told him, "Another letter arrived today. She must miss you."

"Thanks, Abby."

She crossed the room to set the envelope on the corner of the desk, and a whiff of his fiancée's favorite perfume drifted up from it. Abigay lingered beside him, and when Journey glanced up at her, she looked like she was expecting something. She asked, "Do you have anything to send back to her?"

Journey eyed the envelope, then the stack of papers from the foremen. After a bit of internal struggle, he said, "I'll write something to her before bed tonight."

Abigay gave him a frown, but offered no further scolding. She headed for the door, instead, and left him to it. Journey bent over the paperwork once again.

Chapter Two

JOURNEY arrived in the dining room at seven o'clock, just as he did every night, and found that he was the first one here. He took his place at the long, wooden table that dominated the room. Aside from his own, the only other settings were for his mother and father. They sometimes invited one of the captains of Landon's ships to join them, or the occasional business associate, but it was just the three of them, otherwise. The servants generally waited until all of them had arrived to serve the food, and by fifteen minutes past the hour, they were getting restless in the kitchen. Just as Journey was beginning to wonder if they'd ever show up, Landon threw the dining room door open and strode inside. He was a far cry from the composed state that he usually came to dinner in. His hair was in a worse mess than it had been earlier today, as if he'd been in the wind down near the docks, and his white shirt was stained with sweat. Journey nearly laughed at the sorry state of him, but decided against it when he saw the feral look in the man's eyes.

"Dinner can wait!" Landon announced. He was strangely jovial, as if excited about something, and he came to stand beside his son's chair at the table. He clapped a hand on Journey's shoulder, and he had to concentrate on not turning away from the stench of sweat. What in all the worlds had Landon been doing?

"I was starting to think you were too busy to eat," Journey told him.

"Dinner can wait," he repeated. "I have a surprise for you. It's important. We need to go to the north dock."

Journey considered him, wondering if he had gone crazy. "It's something that can't wait until morning?"

Landon didn't answer, but headed for the door he'd just arrived through. "Hurry, Journey. We're running low on daylight."

He decided to play along and see what the old man was up to. He followed him out of the mansion, and as they started past the garden to the path that would take them to the dock on the north side of the island, Journey asked, "Is mom in on this, too?"

"She knows all about it," Landon assured him, and then gave a high-pitched laugh that wasn't like him, at all. He clapped Journey on the shoulder again, however, as if welcoming him in on the joke. He wondered if the man was drunk, but he hadn't smelled alcohol on him. Then again, it was difficult to smell anything beneath that putrid scent of sweat.

For the second time that day, Journey made the trip to the north docks. The sun was hovering just above the horizon when they reached them. The Jubilee was still right where he'd left her, but Landon's private sailboat was now tied off at the end of the second dock, instead of being tucked away in its usual place in the boathouse. It rocked gently on the small waves that were lapping at the base of the dock. Journey asked, "Are we going somewhere?"

"Just you and me, boy," Landon agreed, and Journey wasn't sure why the hairs on the back of his neck stood up at that. As they stepped out onto the dock, Journey spared a look up at the Jubilee and noticed that the workers who had been getting her in pristine condition were now nowhere in sight. As if Landon had expected him to notice this, he explained, "I let them quit early today. They'll be back to work first thing in the morning."

"That was generous of you," Journey said, but only because he wasn't quite sure what else to say. He followed him down the dock. He'd decided that he knew what this was about, after all: Landon meant to take him out onto the water, where no one else could bother them, and chastise him some more about the loss of the Kingfisher. He might even threaten to cut off his allowance, although Journey hardly cared about that. Aside from the occasional trip to a tavern in Kinsman Lane or the impromptu gift for Caresse, he had little need for his own money. What he did care about was the responsibilities that Landon had entrusted him with and could easily take away. Being in charge of keeping the islands secure had given him a sense of purpose, and it was much better than sitting around the mansion all day, bored out of his mind and feeling useless.

A steady breeze took them away from Stonewell at a comfortable speed. Journey sat on one of the benches on the sailboat's stern and watched his father work the sail. He steered them west, away from the cluster of islands they called home, and toward the open sea. There was silence between them, interrupted only by the sound of the wind as it skated over the open water to catch in the sail. The waves were mild and the sky was cloudless. Journey watched the sun set, appearing to sink slowly into the ocean that was stretched out before them.

By the time Landon hove to, only the topmost crest of the sun remained above the horizon. There were already a few stars twinkling in the sky overhead, and it promised to be a beautiful night. Landon secured the sail so that the boat would stay put, then joined Journey at the stern. He sat down on the bench opposite his and took a cigar out of his pocket. Journey leaned back against the bench's backrest to await whatever speech his father was sure to give.

Landon lit the cigar with a match and then puffed on it for a while. Journey felt the man's eyes considering him closely, but pretended not to notice. After a long time, however, Journey grew tired of the silence and sat forward on the bench again. He studied Landon's face through the smoke from the cigar that was clamped between this lips. Landon didn't seem ready to speak, so Journey prompted him with, "You brought me all the way out here for a reason. What did you want to talk to me about?"

Landon drew deeply from the cigar, then exhaled a cloud of fragrant smoke. Once the ocean breeze had whisked it away, he said grimly, "All these years, I loved you. I know I was hard on you, sometimes, but I always loved you like a son."

Journey laughed – the sound escaped him before he could reconsider. He said, "I hope so, since I am your son. What's this about?"

Landon only stared at him, and the dimness of the dying day painted his face with a dark mask. The only thing that wasn't dark was the glimmer in his eyes that Journey didn't much care for. It made him shiver, as if the breeze coming across the water was skating over ice, instead. Journey dared, "Are you talking about disowning me? Over the Kingfisher? I mean, I've already given you my word that I'll do something about it. And you said that we could move past it..."

Landon reached behind his back and took something out from where it had been nestled in the top of his pants. When he brought it out before him and aimed it squarely at Journey's chest, Journey's brain refused to believe what his eyes were reporting: it was the gun that Landon usually kept in the top drawer of his desk. The last sliver of the day's light shone off its long barrel.

Journey stayed very still and found that he couldn't take his eyes off the gun. Landon growled, "Stand up."

"I told you I would get as much of the cane back as I could..."

"On your feet!"

He got to his feet as commanded, raising his hands in what he hoped was a calming gesture. His heart was hammering in his chest, but he forced himself to remain composed. "We can work this out, dad."

"Don't call me that!" Landon howled, and Journey shut his mouth so quickly that his teeth clicked together. He could see Landon's finger twitching on the trigger. All around them, the ocean reflected none of the panic that was in Journey's heart. The vast waters were as peaceful as he'd ever seen them. He wondered if perhaps this was all a dream. It certainly couldn't be reality.

Landon drew a sharp breath and held it. After half a minute, he let it out, and Journey was relieved to see that it had calmed him down a bit. When he spoke, it was with a monotone voice that chilled Journey to his core. "Once upon a time, my great-grandfather signed a contract that made Commercial Horizon his parent company. He only owned the Twins, at the time, and there was hardly a good row of sugarcane on either of them. But John Travert was a hardworking man, and he poured his sweat and blood into that soil. He hoisted the Travert family up out of poverty and set us on a path toward owning everything that I have, now. He did it honestly, Journey, and that's the same way that my grandfather did it after him. It's the same way my father taught me to do it. It's the same way that I've always tried to show you."

Journey didn't know where he was going with this recap of their family history, but before he could ponder that, something else caught his attention: a small scratch at the corner of Landon's left eye. He thought of Jubilee's empty seat at the dinner table, and his racing heart skipped a beat.

"Where's mom?" he asked, although his own voice sounded far away to his ears. Much louder was the sea breeze, although the rational part of his mind told him that it was barely blowing, now.

Landon continued, as if he hadn't heard him. "My father was hesitant to arrange my marriage to Jubilee. The Bazinet family wasn't poor, but they certainly had less than we did. Her father owned a small fleet of fishing boats." He gave Journey a surly look. "Fishermen, Journey. That's the sort of family she called from. But her father's cousin was in good standing with Horizon, and we thought that my marriage to Jubilee would look good. It would show our dedication to our parent company. I suppose it did, at the time."

"Why are you telling me all of this?"

"Because I'm not a fool, boy!" Landon howled. The outburst was so sudden that it startled a gasp from Journey's lungs. He stared at him, dumbfounded, as Landon spat, "The two of you might have fooled me for this long, but you should have known that the truth would come to light. All this time...all these years...I should have known. I should have suspected."

Journey only continued to stare at him, bewildered, and his lack of a response made Landon's fury boil over once more. His finger twitched on the trigger of the gun again as he demanded, "Where's my daughter, Journey? What did she do with her?"

"Daughter?" For a moment, it was the only word that his lips seemed willing to produce. The question was so absurd that he knew he must have heard him wrong. Landon was clearly waiting for an answer, so Journey asked, "What are you talking about? You're not in your right mind."

"My daughter," Landon insisted, as if he should have known what he meant. "What did she do with her?"

"You don't have a daughter." A million thoughts were whirling in his head, and that wasn't the only thing whirling – the boat felt as if it might be spinning at some unthinkable speed. Maybe the entire ocean was spinning around them. "You've only had one child: me. Why don't we go back to Stonewell and talk to mom about this? She'll help you calm down and think about it rationally. We can talk to her together."

"Jubilee is finished talking," Landon smirked.

Journey's stomach churned as his fears concerning the scratch near his eye were confirmed. His legs felt so weak that they threatened not to support him. His face twisted in heartbreak, and he breathed, "What have you done?"

Landon didn't answer, but that was answer enough. Instead, he raised the gun in his hands a little higher and growled, "The only thing left to take care of is you, whore's child."

The gun went off in a thunderous bang. Searing pain tore through the front of Journey's shoulder, just under the end of the collarbone. He stumbled back, and his legs collided with the bench behind him. His lower back landed painfully across the bench as he fell backward. Before his dazed mind could comprehend what was happening, his feet were above his head and he was tumbling over the side of the sailboat. The water swallowed him up, and the pain in his shoulder ignited further as the wound met saltwater. He let out a scream that was muffled by the water around him. Panic overtook him, and he began to thrash wildly. He lost track of the surface and realized that he didn't know which way was up or down. That scream had stolen most of the oxygen from his lungs. He was in trouble.

Jubilee's voice spoke up in his head, as clearly as if she had been speaking into his ear: Calm yourself, love. This isn't finished. The thought overrode all others, and it was enough to allow him to wrest control of the panic that had taken over. He'd lived his life surrounded by the sea, and he knew what to do. He stilled in the water, although his desperate lungs begged him to do anything but, and he loosed the last bit of air that they'd been holding. The bubbles rose toward the surface, and he followed them up.

As much as he wanted to gulp fresh air into his empty lungs, a cold, instinctual part of his brain reminded him that Landon would shoot him again if he saw him. Instead of breaking the surface right away, he found the hull of the sailboat with his hand, and he used what little strength he still had to swim toward the back of it. Once he had rounded its end and was confident that he was behind the boat, he inched his way to the surface. He had started to feel dizzy when the top of his head finally felt fresh air, and he kicked his legs once more to lift the rest of his head out. He sucked in sweet oxygen, but managed to do so silently. He stayed as close as he could to the back of the boat as he tried to listen over the sound of his hammering heart for any sign of Landon above him.

There was a thud that he recognized as the hatch to the cabin below the boat's deck being thrown open. It was hard to hear anything else over the lapping of the gentle waves around him or the sound of his own heavy breathing. He still felt dizzy, and he realized that he was going to pass out if he didn't get himself under control. The ball of agony that his left shoulder had become was threatening to lock up because of the bullet wound, and it made treading water difficult. Even so, he concentrated on slowing his breaths, and before long, the dizziness passed. He could think a little more clearly, and he knew that he was going to have to take his boots off if he was going to keep this up. They were impeding his ability to kick his feet fast enough, and his legs were getting tired. There was a small ledge that ran along the back of the boat that was there for decorative purposes and nothing else, but it was just wide enough for him to grip it with his fingertips. He did so with his right hand. Then he brought one foot up and reached for the laces of his boot with his left hand, gritting his teeth against the fresh pain it caused in his injured shoulder.

It wasn't long before he heard the hatch bang against the deck again, but he'd managed to take both of his boots off by then, and it was easier to move his legs. He listened as Landon's footsteps crossed the short distance between the hatch and the side of the boat. The back of the boat was too tall for Journey to see him from down here, but he could imagine that he'd gone down to fetch the oars. The wind had shifted slightly, and he was going to need them if he wanted to head back the way they'd come.

There was a loud splash on the same side of the boat that Journey had fallen off of, and for a moment, he thought that Landon had jumped in to come find him. But then he heard the man's footsteps on the deck again, and he had no idea what he'd thrown overboard. He didn't dare look around the side of the boat to find out. Instead, he stayed as still as he could without sinking, even as his fingertips began to ache from gripping the little ledge for so long. He listened as Landon did something with the sail. It seemed to take forever, and he was starting to feel cold. This area of the ocean was relatively warm, but this was the middle of fall, and the temperature of the air wasn't quite as high as he would have liked. Besides, he was relatively certain that he was suffering from some type of shock because of the wound in his shoulder. How was he going to make it out of here? The nearest island was Stonewell, and he couldn't go back there. A few miles west would bring him to a tiny spit of land that didn't have an official name on any map, but the locals called it Sandhill. That's all it was – a few lumps of sand and rock that stuck out of the water when the waves weren't too high. He wouldn't be able to survive there for very long, but at least he wouldn't drown. If he could make it that far.

He noticed a smear of red out of the corner of his eye, and he turned in the water to find something that made his heart want to stop cold: floating face down amongst the little waves that pushed and tugged her was Jubilee. Her long, red hair was spread out atop the water all around her head. She was still wearing the green dress that she'd had on when Journey had seen her in the garden earlier that day.

A small sound that was something between a sob and a gasp escaped his lips. He braced himself for the gunshot that was sure to follow, certain that Landon must have heard him. That hardly mattered. He couldn't take his eyes off of Jubilee's lifeless body in the water. It was moving slowly past the boat, and she was so close that he could almost touch her if he'd reached out his hand to try.

There were two splashes as the oars struck the water, and his attention was pulled back to the task of surviving. The boat lurched forward and away from him as Landon got it moving. Journey took in as much air as his lungs would allow and slipped beneath the surface. He kept himself just a few feet below the lapping waves and strained his burning eyes to try to make out the silhouette of the boat above him. The moon had come out, and there was just enough light up there for him to be able to see it. The shape moved slowly as Landon turned it around to face it in the direction of Stonewell, but then it picked up more speed as he started on the course he wanted. Journey needed to surface, but he knew that Landon would be facing in this direction if he was moving in that one...

His lungs couldn't hold out anymore. He swam upward, but aimed for the much smaller silhouette that was Jubilee's corpse. He surfaced just beside her, gulping air in as quietly as he could. Her body was between him and boat as it drew farther and farther away. He kept just his face above the surface and next to her head, so that her red hair laid limply across his forehead and cheeks. He squeezed his eyes closed as the tears came, and silent sobs racked his body. He stayed like that for a long time, weeping for his mother as the ocean's waves gently licked the tears from the sides of his face.

He didn't know how much time had passed, but when he finally dared to peek over Jubilee's back, the boat was gone. He supposed it wasn't as far away as he would have liked, but the darkness that the moon couldn't completely dispel had cloaked it. That was fine, as it would hide him, as well. He needed to get moving, however. He was already tired, and he hadn't even started the trek to Sandhill.

But he still lingered, setting his head against Jubilee's shoulder in the water. He'd thought the tears had passed, but here they came again, and the pain in his heart almost rivaled the pain in his shoulder. He didn't want to leave her out here, in the middle of the unforgiving sea, but it would be impossible to pull her along all the way to Sandhill. He had to let her go.

"I'm sorry, mom," he sobbed against her lifeless shoulder. "I'm so sorry. I love you."

He would have given anything to have been able to hear her say those last three words back, but Landon had been right when he'd said that Jubilee was finished talking. There would be a time to wonder what else he'd been right about, but Journey didn't currently have the luxury of pondering any of that. Instead, he forced himself to swim away from Jubilee's floating corpse. He headed west, toward the tiny specks of rock and sand that would save his life.

Chapter Three

IT was too far. That became clear after only an hour. Whenever he got too exhausted to keep swimming, he floated on his back for a while. He needed these breaks more and more often, until he was eventually spending more time resting than swimming. His speed and form were impeded by his injured shoulder, and he wondered vaguely if the blood would attract sharks. After a while, he also wondered if that wouldn't be better. If he was going to die out here, then he wanted it to be over sooner, rather than later. His tortured muscles and aching shoulder couldn't give him much more than he'd already demanded of them.

He turned onto his back, possibly for the last time, and stared up at the stars. They were beautiful tonight, shining brightly down on the open ocean. He wished that his mother could have seen them. He recalled her lifeless body bobbing up and down in the water and shut the image out of his head immediately. That was too much, for now. Instead, he thought of her in the garden the last time he'd seen her alive. He recalled her smile and songlike laughter. Could she truly be dead? Or was this all some heinous nightmare?

The agony his body was in assured him that he wasn't dreaming. His eyelids felt heavy, and he let them slip closed. He was cold – he was shivering all over and his teeth were clacking together. Sandhill may as well have been a million miles away, at this point. It was too far. He was too tired, too cold, too sore, too badly injured. All he desired now was rest, and that would come soon enough if he just allowed himself to fall asleep…

He heard Jubilee's voice once more, although it was only a memory, this time: This isn't finished. She was right. He forced his eyes open and gazed up at the stars again. They were twinkling fiercely, and whether they were cheering him on or laughing at him, he couldn't decide. It didn't matter. He couldn't give up, yet.

He turned in the water and began to dogpaddle, as it was all he had strength left to do. Every few minutes, his struggling legs would falter, and he would start to sink. Twice, his head slipped below the surface for a few seconds. His exhausted body managed a fresh shot of adrenaline each time, and he was able to get his head back up to the surface, but he knew that there would soon come a time when he wasn't able to do that. He was going to die.

He was so fixated on his sad plight that he nearly missed the rigid shape that appeared above the crest of a small wave twenty yards to his right. It was just a silhouette in the moonlight, but his heart gave a hopeful leap. He stopped swimming and treaded water for a few seconds, his eyes straining to see it again. He knew that there was a very good possibility that he had simply imagined it in his desperation, but refused to believe that. Then he saw it again: a black shadow that rode the crest of a wave and then disappeared in its trough.

Cramps locked up both of his legs, and he went under. He dug frantically at the water around him with his arms, but it wasn't enough. After a few terrifying seconds, the cramps subsided, and he was able to kick his legs again. He clawed his way toward the surface, his lungs screaming for oxygen, and found it at last. Water from a passing wave splashed into his mouth as he gulped air, and he broke into a coughing fit that only made things worse. Once he could breathe again, he started toward the last place he'd seen the shape in the water. As he drew close, he saw that it was another twenty yards away, now, still rising and falling on the waves. He reached down deep and used the last of his energy to pursue it. Every yard felt like a mile, and every passing second brought him closer to death.

But death wouldn't have him tonight. He reached the dark shape, at last. It was a ten-foot length of smooth, cylindrical wood. Large, empty notches along the sides of it told him that other things had once been attached to it, and he realized that it had once served as a ship's mast. A mizzen mast, most likely, although it was impossible to know for sure under these conditions. It wasn't important; all that mattered was that it was floating, and when he clung to it, it didn't sink. He cried out in relief. When he tried to climb up on top of it, it merely rolled in the water and dumped him off. His arms were too weak to be able to cling to the wood for long, so he used one hand to unbuckle and strip off his belt. He felt along the length of the mast until he found something he could use: a piece of metal, likely a nail, jutted out from the side of the wood. He slipped the buckle of the belt over it so that it held on nicely, then looped the other end of the belt around his wrist and pulled it tight. It pinned his arm over the top of the mast and kept his head above water, and that was the best that he could have hoped for. He was still freezing cold, but at least he wasn't drowning, and he uttered a laugh that could have easily been mistaken for a sob. In the miles and miles of open ocean all around him, the odds of him finding something like this were likely next to impossible. There was even a chance that it had belonged to the Kingfisher, and wouldn't that have been ironic. It was as if someone was looking out for him and had sent it to him. He recalled his mother's words once more: This isn't finished.

"You're right, mom," he croaked into the waves that were splashing against the mast. "I won't give up. I promise."

Chapter Four

HE slipped into a half-conscious daze that may have lasted hours or days, for all he knew. When he came around, the sun was beginning to rise. He couldn't recall steering the direction of the floating mast throughout the night, but he must have done so, for he saw that he had arrived at Sandhill. Three little lumps of sand and rock peeked above the surface just a short distance ahead of him. His right arm was numb from being tied over the mast for so long, but he managed to get the belt unhooked from the nail on the other side with his injured arm, cussing the pain as he opened the wound in his shoulder again. He pushed away from the mast and dogpaddled toward his salvation, although it was slow going. His right arm was still dead weight, for the most part, and his left shoulder kept trying to lock up on him. Despite this, he made it to the rocky edge of one of the tiny islands and hauled himself up onto the soft sand. He rolled onto his back and then simply laid there, too exhausted to move further. An occasional wave splashed over his bare feet, but he didn't have the strength to move them, anymore. Besides, what did it matter? He was alive, and just before he passed out in the sand, he looked up at the brightening sky above him and smiled.

When he woke again, the sun had crossed the sky and it was the middle of the afternoon. His flesh itched from the salt and sand that he was covered in. His wrist ached, and he realized that the belt was still tied around it and had made the flesh beneath it raw. He freed his wrist from it and cast the belt aside. Then he forced himself to sit up, despite painful objections from his sore muscles and injured shoulder. In every direction he looked, there was only ocean. He was terribly thirsty, but there were no rain clouds to interrupt the pristine blue sky above. The land he was one was only about thirty yards wide by fifty long, and there were no plants, aside from the dried tangles of dead seaweed that had been washed up here by the most recent storm.

But the situation wasn't completely hopeless. He reminded himself that Sandhill sat along a major shipping route. In fact, there had been talk for years of building a lighthouse here to warn vessels of the natural towers that just barely peeked their heads above the surface. If he could keep from dying from dehydration until a ship came close enough to spot him, he would be alright. And if not...? He decided not to think on that.

He spent the rest of that day on lookout, but he didn't see a single ship. Just after sunset, he thought that he spotted distant lights on the horizon, but even if there had been a ship, it was too far away to do him any good. The night passed slowly. Without the sun to warm the sand, it grew cold, and he spent an hour shivering in it before giving up on sleep. He perched himself atop a rock that jutted above the others along the edge of the island and began a long, lonely wait for the sun to rise.

By the time it did, he was so thirsty that his throat felt like sandpaper and the ocean water looked almost too good not to drink. He knew that was a recipe for death...but his parched body cried out for it, anyway. He ignored the urge and kept his focus on looking for ships. The morning passed without sighting anything, but just as the sun reached its zenith, a tiny dot appeared on the western horizon. He was careful not to get his hopes up, afraid that he may have been hallucinating, but he became more certain as it grew closer. It was a ship, alright: a square-rigged beauty with four masts. She was on a course that would take her right past his little island, and he knew that he wouldn't get a better chance than this.

He scrambled to find the belt that he'd tossed away and found it half-buried in the sand. The silver buckle was caked with sand, so he hurried to the rocky edge of the island to splash seawater over it. He dried and shined it with his shirt, then tilted it back and forth to see how much sun reflected off of it. There wasn't much, and he had no idea if anyone on the passing galleon would be able to see it from this distance, but it was the best he had. He climbed up onto the tallest rock again and held the buckle above his head, tilting it slowly to try to catch the sunlight.

His hopes began to dwindle as the ship kept going. She was close enough that he could make out the color and shape of her flags. The topmost one belonged to The Whitefish Trading Company. For a short time, she was parallel to his island, and he could even make out the cannon ports along her side. There weren't many – this was a cargo vessel, and not a ship of war – but they were there in the increasingly-likely event of a pirate attack. His arms ached from holding them above his head, but he continued to tilt the buckle back and forth, back and forth.

"Please," he whispered to any sea gods or force of fate that would listen. "Please, let them see me."

Perhaps someone or something had heard his prayer, for the ship began to slow. His racing heart sped up further, and when it became clear that they were stopping, a jubilant cry escaped his parched throat and lips. He continued to rotate the buckle, but they had seen him, and his rescue was at hand. This time, when he heard his mother's voice tell him that it wasn't finished, he believed her.

A longboat arrived within an hour, and as its wooden hull carved a narrow trench into the sandy shore, a man in a Whitefish Trading uniform hopped out. The insignia on his jacket said that he was a lieutenant. Journey had long since sunk to his knees in the sand to await their arrival, and the sailor looked him over with true wonder. He asked, "What in all the worlds are you doing out here, boy?"

Journey opened his mouth to respond, but caught the words in his throat before he could utter them. What could he tell them that wouldn't sound impossible or insane? The other two sailors had left the longboat and now joined their companion, and they were all waiting for an answer. One of the sailors asked, "Shipwreck?"

Journey still couldn't think of anything better, so he nodded. The three sailors exchanged nervous looks at that, and the first one ventured, "Was it pirates?"

"Pirates," Journey parroted. The word sank slowly into his dazed mind, and he decided to seize the suggestion. "Pirates attacked the Kingfisher. They shot me. The ship went down and I swam out of the wreckage. I barely survived."

The sailors shifted their gazes toward the open ocean all around the small mounds of sand out here, as if the very mention of pirates might somehow summon a ship into view. One of them urged, "We should get moving."

The lieutenant offered his hand down to Journey, saying, "You're lucky we spotted you out here. Let's get you aboard the Northwatch and back to civilization."

Journey took his offered hand with his uninjured arm and let him pull him to his feet. He sat in the back of the longboat as the sailors rowed their way toward the ship, and he watched the sand grow farther and farther behind them. Such a small, useless speck of land had been the only thing to save him from death. He supposed there was something philosophical to say about that, but he was still too stunned to consider what it might be.

Aboard the ship, Journey found himself standing on the deck before another man in a Whitefish uniform. He was an older, sea-hardened man with a grim expression that turned even grimmer when his lieutenant informed him of the pirate threat. He told Journey, "I'm Captain Leroux. Welcome aboard the Northwatch."

"Thank you for stopping to pick me up. There were pirates..." His words tapered off as he became dizzy, and Leroux grabbed his arm to steady him on his feet. He eyed the bloodstained front of his shirt with true pity.

"We have a doctor on board, and I'll have him take a good look at your shoulder. My first mate can set you up with a cot to rest on in one of the holds, and he might be able to scrounge up a pair of boots that'll fit you. Get some food and ale into your belly. You're lucky to be alive."

"You have no idea," Journey muttered. Leroux called for someone to fetch the ship's doctor, and as they waited for him to arrive, Journey asked, "Where are you headed?"

"Kinsman first, then Port Darry. We can drop you off at either of those for free. If you want to go with us all the way out to Jardin, I might have to charge you for food and drink." He shrugged his shoulders. "Company policy."

Journey waved this off and winced at the fresh pain it brought to his shoulder. "Kinsman is fine. I already owe you my life."

The doctor arrived, at last, and Journey went with him to have his shoulder patched up. He left the Northwatch's deck just as Leroux's voice rang out with an order to get the ship moving and for his men to keep an eye out for pirates.

CHAPTER FIVE

ANSEL Beaumont's house on Rose Street in Kinsman Lane was a colossal thing that towered over Journey as he stepped up to its front door. When one of the Beaumont family's house servants answered Journey's knock, he could tell by the grimace that came to the man's face that he assumed Journey was on the wrong side of town. Journey didn't blame him. His clothes were stiff with sea salt, his hair was a mess, and the front of his shirt was stained with blood. The man promptly explained that there was a charity shelter on Collins Way before trying to close the door on him. Journey stopped it with his foot, and although it took some convincing, the man finally recognized him as his mistress' fiancé. He brought him inside and asked him to wait in the foyer. Journey did so, and he was forced to bide his patience for the next few minutes.

Finally, Caresse appeared at the top of the staircase above him, and she hurried down the marble steps at the sight of him. She was wearing a lavish dress that was perfectly at home in such a luxurious house such as this, with its white, marble floors and expensive oil paintings on the walls. Her blond hair was pinned up in a complicated style, and to Journey, she'd never looked so beautiful. When she reached the bottom of the stairs, she cried out over the shape he was in.

"What happened?" she asked as she rushed to him to clasp both of his hands in her own. "Look at you! What happened to you?"

"It's a long story," he said, bringing the back of one of her hands to his lips to kiss it. "I didn't have anywhere else to go, Caresse. I need your help."

She eyed the blood on his shirt and the small hole in the center of it. "I'll call for a doctor right away. You need to lie down. Come with me."

He let her lead him deeper into the house. He soon found himself in one of the three guest rooms, and he didn't argue when she instructed him to take his filthy clothes off. He stripped down to his underwear and climbed beneath the soft blankets as Caresse left the room to send for a doctor. When she returned a few minutes later, she sat down on the side of the bed and leaned to plant a kiss on his forehead. Then she sat back and asked with a tinge of fear, "Pirates?"

"I'll tell you all about it soon enough," he said, but what was he going to say? That his father had disowned him and then tried to kill him? Even if he told her the truth, she would want details. He recalled hiding his face in his dead mother's hair as he'd wept in the water. There were things that he didn't think he'd ever be able to tell anyone about.

Caresse's servants brought him hot tea and a change of clothes, the latter of which they left on the nightstand beside the bed. Caresse explained that the clothing belonged to her father, so they would likely be a little big on him (Ansel was portly by anyone's standards), but he thanked her and assured her that he didn't mind. The doctor arrived within the hour, and Caresse excused herself from the room as he got to work on Journey's shoulder. She stood in the hallway outside the guest room and placed her hands over her ears to block out the sounds of the young man's screams as the doctor went on a search for the bullet. He managed to remove it, as well as the bit of fabric that it had drawn into the wound with it. Once his shoulder was clean and dressed, Caresse paid the man and sent him on his way. She returned to the room to find Journey asleep in the bed, and she drew the thick drapes closed over the windows and left him there to rest.

He woke two hours later as the door to the room was thrown open with enough force to bounce it off the wall behind it. Journey struggled into a sitting position as Caresse stormed in, a folded piece of paper held high in one hand. She screamed, "Out! Get out before I call the city guard, you murderous coward! You snake! You lying weasel!"

His groggy mind raced to piece together how things had taken this turn, but Caresse answered all his questions before he could ask them. She reached the bed and tossed the paper at him. It unfolded in the air and landed across his lap, and Landon's familiar handwriting stared up at him from its surface.

Caresse leaned over to get close to his face, and the pretty woman she'd been a few hours earlier had transformed into a hideous, howling beast. Her furious eyes were full of tears, and spittle flew from her painted lips as she spat, "Get out of this house, you filthy dog! Go!"

"Caresse, I can explain everything..."

She let loose her hand and struck him on the cheek before he saw it coming. The sound of their flesh colliding was loud in the room. He looked at her with wide eyes as a red outline of her hand began to form across his cheek. Caresse stepped back, as if suddenly frightened that he might retaliate, and demanded once more, "Get out of this house, Journey!"

He threw back the blankets, sending Landon's letter with them to the edge of the bed. As he dragged himself to his feet, however, Caresse retreated a few more steps, and he saw that fear now accompanied her anger. He raised his hands in a calming gesture, but she flinched away at the motion and retreated until her back was pressed against the wardrobe that sat against the wall.

"I'm not going to hurt you," he soothed. "I don't know what Landon said in the letter…"

"He told me what you did!" she howled. Her makeup had mixed with her tears to run down her cheeks, and a thin line of snot was starting to pool on her upper lip. "You murdered poor Jubilee! You killed her in cold blood, and when he confronted you about it, you threw yourself off the eastern cliffs of Stonewell."

"Listen to yourself, Caresse," he said, struggling to keep his voice relaxed. "That doesn't make any sense, alright?"

"You're a liar and a killer!" she sobbed. "I don't know how you survived the fall from that cliff, but I can't believe that you would come here and ask for my help. Landon thinks you're dead, and I wish you were!" To reiterate that point, she sucked in a deep breath and then repeated gravely, "I wish you were dead, Journey."

"You don't mean that," he told her, but the look on her face said otherwise. "I didn't kill Jubilee. Landon killed her and then tried to kill me. You have to believe me."

"Get out," she whispered, pointing a trembling finger toward the door. "You've been a fraud all this time. I can't believe I almost married you. I can't believe I was so foolish."

"Please," he begged, and made the mistake of taking a step toward her. She sounded an earsplitting shriek and took off for the door, calling for her servants to send for the city guard.

Journey stayed where he was, torn. There was no reason that he should fear the city guard. After all, he was innocent, and he needed to report Jubilee's real murderer. But Landon had already concocted a story that made him look guilty, and whom would the authorities side with? Landon likely employed half of their family members on his plantations.

His survival instincts kicked in once more, and he put on the clothing that the servants had brought him with frantic, clumsy motions. They were two sizes too big, but he pulled the belt they'd given him tighter, and the pants stayed up. He didn't waste time putting on his boots, but carried them with him to the window on the far side of the room. He threw back the drapes and shoved the window open, thankful that this room was on the first floor. He tossed his boots outside and then followed, and he didn't pause as one of the house servants arrived in the guest room and called for him to stop.

Journey spent the rest of that day hiding from anyone who even remotely looked like they might have been a member of the city guard. That night, he found himself behind a garbage pile in a dank alley on the north side of town. He sat amongst the discarded scraps of food and old, soiled rags. It began to rain, and the cool water soaked his borrowed clothes and washed the remaining salt from his skin. He drew his knees to his chest and rested his forehead on them, shivering and miserable. A stray dog wandered by and emitted a low growl when it noticed him, but Journey ignored it. The only light in the alley came from a window in the building he was resting his back against. Soft firelight danced on the bricks of the building on the opposite side, and he thought of Landon in the mansion, safe and warm before a fire of his own. His stomach would be full of good food from dinner, and he would likely be reading a book before bed. He would never have to spend a night behind a garbage heap in the rain, or worry that each set of passing footsteps on the main street might belong to someone who was looking to arrest him. He would never have to cower behind the corpse of his murdered mother, with her wet hair strung across his face as the waves bobbed her body up and down, up and down.

As he sat in the rain and stench of the trash, Journey realized that his broken heart was feeling something new: anger. No matter what sort of feud had transpired between Landon and Jubilee, she had been a good woman, a kind soul, a loving human being. Landon had taken all of that away. He'd snuffed her out, undoubtedly in some violent, painful fashion, and the world was an emptier, darker place because of it. He'd followed this with lies that shifted the blame to Journey, who had only ever tried to please the man. He recalled Jubilee's words once again: This isn't finished. That was still true, but it had taken on an entirely new meaning, now.

Journey Travert needed to get revenge.

Chapter Six

A month after Jubilee's death, Journey stepped off of the gangway of a hired sloop and onto a worn, splintery dock in Port Kelsey. A man in a short, dark coat that he'd most likely stolen from someone was waiting for him, and he held out his hand in expectation, saying, "Fifty marks, like we agreed."

Journey reached into his pocket and produced the requested payment. It was nearly all the money he had, but he didn't hesitate to honor their bargain and handed it over. The man responded with a grin and pointed a finger that sported black grime beneath the nail. "The tavern you want is the Hoary Witch. He was there an hour ago, but if he's already gone, that's not my fault."

Journey muttered his thanks and got moving in that direction. Despite the time going on ten o'clock at night, the docks were full of life. In the warm light of hundreds of lamps, drunken sailors stumbled to and from their ships, impromptu games of cards and dice were being held around overturned barrels that served as tables, and a chorus of eight men in various stages of drunkenness were singing sea shanties at the top of their lungs. Lively music was drifting down from a dozen taverns at the top of the seawall, atop which the town of Port Kelsey sat. Journey had never felt more out of place, although he supposed he currently looked the part. The sleeves and collar of his long, black coat were nearly as frayed and worn as the boots on his feet, and his cheeks were rough with unkempt scruff. It had been a long month.

In the place where the docks ended and the street began, he found an elderly woman resting on her knees on the hard cobblestone. There was an overturned hat in her hands, and lifted it toward Journey as he came to stand beside her. She was dressed in rags that were even filthier than his own clothes currently were, and judging by the gauntness of her cheeks, she was no stranger to hunger. She asked him, "Spare a few marks, sir?"

He took out the last few coins he had to his name and dropped them into the hat. She pulled it away quickly, as if he might change his mind and try to fish the coins back out of it. Journey didn't take it personally. He asked, "Do you know where I can find the Hoary Witch?"

The woman raised one eyebrow and tilted her head to the side as she considered him. "First time in Port Kelsey?"

There was no use lying, so he nodded. The woman offered her hand up to him, and Journey helped her stand. Once she was on her feet, she waved an arm around at all of the commotion all around them: a pair of drunk sailors squabbling loudly, a mangy horse pulling a wagon, a group of men howling laughter over a game of dice that they were playing right on the uneven stones of the street. The woman said, "There's no lovelier gem in all of Cruxes."

It was a joke, but Journey wondered if maybe this place had been beautiful once. The horseshoe-shaped port and town were guarded on three sides by steep mountain cliffs, and they were hulking silhouettes against the night sky. He could imagine the palm trees and native birds that may have once filled this tropical valley before the streets and buildings had replaced them. As if guessing his thoughts, the woman told him, "It was better before the war. Back when I could turn heads, there was still some class around here. Then the companies started their damned crusade to clear out the pirate ports. They blockaded this place for three months. A lot of people starved. The rest of us made it through to the end, but it's never been the same." She flapped one hand at him. "That was all before your time. As you can see, Port Kelsey is thriving again."

"Thriving at what?"

She gave him a cackle and a wink at that, then pointed down the street. "The Hoary Witch is that way. There's a sign out front with the name on it. Can't miss it."

Journey thanked her and got moving again. He skirted the group of dice players and made his way past storefronts that had metal bars over their windows. Halfway down the street, he found the wooden sign that the woman had promised. It sat before a two-story building that was made of stone and was currently exuding a ruckus of loud conversation and laughter from the patrons inside. Journey gathered his courage and stepped through the front door to join them.

The dim, musty interior matched the feel of the rest of the port outside. The first floor was one large, open room that hosted a long, wooden bar near the far wall and twelve tables that were currently occupied by drinkers, gamblers, and smokers. Two women in revealing dresses flitted from table to table, flirting with the men and advertising the services they undoubtedly conducted in the private rooms upstairs. Journey had no interest in any of that. Instead, he scanned the crowded room for the young man he was looking for. He'd started to fear that he'd already left when he finally spotted him at the bar. Journey could only see his back from the doorway, but he recognized him from the cobalt blue shirt he was wearing – a color he was rumored to be fond of. Otherwise, his attire was similar to the majority of other men in this place: black pants, worn boots, and an affinity for ugly jewelry.

Journey crossed the room slowly, not in a rush. He weaved between tables of drunken card players and desperate prostitutes. The barstools on either side of his target were currently vacant, and Journey made the one on his left his destination. The man didn't so much as look up from his ale as Journey sat down beside him. Journey took the opportunity to study his face, or at least the side that he could see from here. The stubble on his cheeks was in need of a shave. His black hair was tied back in a ponytail. And there was jewelry, of course: two thick, leather bracelets on his left wrist and a thin, silver chain on his right. Three of his fingers were adorned with silver rings. There were three necklaces around his neck, one of which was made of some type of twine and two that may have been real gold. At the bottom of the twine necklace was a two-inch-long shark tooth. Small, black earrings marched the length of his left ear, from the lobe all the way up the edge to the top. There must have been at least ten of them.

He took a swig from the glass on the bar before him, then said without looking around, "Am I the man of your dreams, or what?"

Journey was surprised to realize that he was speaking to him, and when the pirate finally looked at him, he grinned. Journey wasn't in the mood for antics; it had taken him four weeks to track this man down, and he was here to talk business.

"Are you Dallion Romilly?"

"Never heard of him," he replied, and took another drink from his glass. He let out a belch that earned a scowl from the bartender at the end of the bar. He ignored her glare and said, "Even if I had, he's not taking on any hands right now."

"My name is Journey Travert."

He must have known that name, for he finally looked at him, and there was a hint of alarm in his eyes. They were as blue as the sea and reminded Journey of Jubilee's. Dallion considered his shabby clothes and unshaven face and relaxed slightly. He grinned, "Yeah, and I'm the Queen of Carennac."

"Four weeks ago, you attacked and looted a ship called Kingfisher. She was a hundred-thirty-foot galleon carrying a load of unprocessed sugarcane from Green Plot. Ring any bells?"

The pirate shrugged, turning his gaze back to the ale on the bar. He said with a smirk, "I heard that galleon was sent under. And whoever's responsible managed to do it with just a little sloop."

"Not before you helped yourself to plenty of cane, which I can only assume has been sold on the open market, by now."

"If that's true, then you know the cane is gone, and there was no reason for you to come out here." He turned to him again, and there was a cockiness in his grin that Journey would have hated, if he wasn't here for his help. "It's your ship that's been chasing me around for months, now. What's she called? Jubilation?"

"Jubilee."

"She's quick. Faster than my own boat, if you want the truth." He leaned toward him, still grinning, and whispered, "But I'm a better captain than the old geezer you've got commanding her. That's why he hasn't caught me, yet."

Journey shook his head. "I'm not here to trade insults."

"Go ahead and make a move," Dallion goaded. "Six of my crew are watching us right now. Big guys. But from the look of you, I don't think I'll even need their help."

Journey doubted that anyone was paying attention to their quiet conversation at the bar, let alone watching to make sure there wasn't a fight. In a place like the Hoary Witch, fights were likely a nightly occurrence, anyway. At any rate, he had no need to fight him, and he said, "I've come here to make you an offer."

Dallion threw his head back and laughed in a carefree way that Journey envied him for. He raised his ale above his head in a celebratory cheers to the heavens, then finished the glass in a few deep gulps. He slammed the empty glass onto the bar and called to the bartender, "Matilda, bring me another one! This night keeps getting better and better."

Journey was looking at him as if he were trying to decide if the man was crazy, and Dallion told him, "That took a lot less time than I'd thought it would."

"What are you talking about?"

Dallion gave him a look that said he wasn't fooling him, but explained, "Once a pirate's been enough of a pain in the ass for some rich island owner, they'll offer him a salary to retire on. Basically, they pay him to give up the life and quit causing trouble. It means he's finally made it to the bigtime." He shoved a playful elbow into Journeys side. "I didn't think the Traverts would be so quick to cry uncle. I'm not going to take your offer, but it's nice to know I've really got your attention."

"I don't want you to stop attacking my father's islands," he said. Suddenly, he had his attention, and Journey said, "I want you to take everything he's got."

Chapter Seven

DALLION listened as Journey laid out his proposed plan. As he spoke, Matilda brought the pirate another ale, and he paid for one for Journey, too. With his interests perked, he left behind all the jokes and goading, and he was finally being serious. When Journey was finished speaking, Dallion sipped at his ale for a while, and Journey gave him time to think it through. Finally, after Matilda brought refills for their drinks once more, Dallion told him, "I'd have to be an idiot not to think this was some kind of trap. You know that, right?"

"It's no trap," Journey vowed. "I'll be on your ship the entire time. If anything happens that isn't part of the plan, your men can kill me."

Dallion studied him for a little while, then clapped him on the shoulder and stood from his barstool, announcing, "I need to piss."

Journey watched him make his way past the other tables on the way to whatever served as a toilet in a place like this. He had no doubt that Dallion was just stalling while he considered his options, but that was alright. They both knew that the offer was too good to turn down.

One of the women who had been paying visits to each of the tables stepped up to the bar and leaned against it to Journey's left. She pinched the lobe of his ear and gave it a playful tug, her red lips turning up in a practiced smile.

"Hi, doll," she crooned. "You're looking lonely over here by yourself. Need some company?"

"I'm broke," he said, his tone curt enough to tell her that this was the end of the conversation.

The woman snorted an ironic laugh and patted his shoulder. As she stepped away from the bar to leave him there, she muttered, "Ain't we all, kid."

Matilda came and asked him if he wanted another ale, but he turned her down, too. After a few minutes, Dallion returned and reclaimed the stool beside him. He propped an elbow on the bar and rested the side of his head on his fist. His blue eyes considered Journey, but he didn't press him for his decision, yet. Instead, they merely looked at one another for a few seconds, until Dallion asked him, "Why?"

Journey reached into the pocket of his coat and brought out a folded piece of paper. He opened it and slapped it onto the bar before Dallion with a little more force than he'd intended – it earned him one of Matilda's scolding glances. A sketch of Journey's face stared up at them from the paper. Dallion had seen enough posters like these to know that this one was from Kinsman Lane. In bold lettering across the top, it declared that Journey was wanted for murder.

"Landon Travert killed my mother and blamed me for it," Journey said, ignoring the slight waver in his own voice. "He's disowned me, turned my fiancée against me, and has taken away everything I ever cared about. The son of a bitch is going to pay, Dallion. Are you in, or not?"

The corners of Dallion's lips turned upward just the slightest bit, then slowly grew into a smile. He offered his hand, silver rings glistening in the dull light of the tavern around them. As Journey shook it, Dallion said, "You've come to the right man."

Dallion rented a room at the tavern and shared the night with one of the working girls there, but Journey hadn't lied when he'd claimed to be broke. He had funded his search for Dallion with odd jobs that he had taken in each place he'd stopped: sweeping a storefront, repairing a broken shutter, mucking a barn. He'd helped load a ship with bales of straw in Port Darry and spent a day helping a butcher slaughter sows on Courier Island just east of here. But he'd given his last few marks to the old woman near the docks, and his pockets were currently empty. His bed that night was the ground in a dark, narrow alley in the heart of Port Kelsey. It was something he'd become more or less accustomed to over the past month.

His clothes were damp and his body was sore when he made his way down to the docks the next morning, but his eagerness to get the new plan underway trumped all of that. Per the directions that Dallion had given him last night, Journey headed down to the far end of the docks, where he found the Ocean Sprite berthed between a pair of small schooners. Journey had never seen her up close before, and he decided that she was much less menacing than he'd imagined. The little sloop was all of forty feet in length and fourteen feet across at her widest, and her triangular sails had been patched so many times that he wasn't sure if there was any original material left.

As Journey reached the gangway that stretched from the dock to the ship, he found a tall, lanky man in his late thirties waiting. He was a lifelong sailor if Journey had ever seen one. His skin was so deeply-tanned that it had turned leathery, and there were lines around his eyes that had been left after years of squinting in the sunlight. As Journey reached him, he held out his hand in an offered shake and explained, "My name is Journey. Captain Romilly invited me to meet him here this morning."

The man didn't shake his hand, but kept his arms crossed at his chest as he considered Journey carefully. When he spoke, his voice was so deep that Journey didn't doubt it could carry across the deck in even the worst windstorm. "You're the Travert kid?"

He nodded. "I'm sure you've called me much worse things than that, though."

For a moment, he didn't think that his attempt at humor was going to work on this man, who hadn't given his words any type of response. After a few seconds, however, a grin slowly parted his lips, revealing the half a dozen teeth that still called his mouth home. He even allowed himself a small chuckle before saying, "I'm Lucien Cole. I'm the Sprite's quartermaster. When you're aboard this ship, my word is law. Got it?"

Journey gave him another nod and was relieved when Lucien started up the gangway. Journey didn't allow himself to hesitate to follow him. As he stepped onto the deck, he found a handful of pirates working to get the ship ready to sail. They looked exactly as he'd expected: stained and fraying clothes, windblown hair, and expressions of distrust when they caught sight of the newcomer. They hurried here and there as they prepped the Sprite's lines and carried out various other chores that they could likely do with their eyes closed. Journey followed Lucien across the old, worn planks of the deck and down through an open hatchway. His eyes took a moment to adjust to the dimness in the bowels of the little ship. A short, narrow hallway ended at a small door, and Lucien gave a cursory knock on it before pushing it open and stepping aside to give Journey enough space to squeeze past him and into the room beyond.

He found himself in cramped quarters that were hardly more than a closet, but afforded its resident some privacy from the rest of the crew. A bed took up the majority of one wall, and Journey was amused to see that its blankets were a similar shade of blue to the shirt that Dallion was wearing again today. He was seated in a chair before an overturned barrel that was serving as a table. There was a half-finished plate of scrambled eggs on it. Dallion set his fork aside as Journey came in, however, and he motioned with one hand for him to close the door behind him. Journey did so, then merely looked around the room with unhidden curiosity. There wasn't much to see, save for a crate full of crumpled clothes in one corner and a small, wooden chest in another. When his gaze made its way back to Dallion, both men took one another in for a moment, and Journey wondered if Dallion was trying to decide whether this was a good idea, after all. Journey certainly was.

If Dallion had any doubts, he was hiding it well, for he swept one arm around at the little room and announced, "Welcome to the Ocean Sprite. She might not look like much, but she's fast and sturdy. She's got eleven knots in her, if the winds are right."

Journey didn't bother to remind him that the Jubilee topped out at that speed, and Dallion had already confessed in the tavern that the Sprite couldn't keep up with her. Instead, he offered a polite, "She's a beautiful ship."

"Damn right," Dallion beamed. "A guy named Hager owned her first. He used to run rum between a few islands out west. Then a storm took him off course and he stopped off at Calico to make some repairs. I got a few friends to help me..." He considered for a moment, and Journey gave him time to come up with whatever words he was searching for. Finally, Dallion said, "We relieved Hager of his responsibilities."

"And his ship," Journey added with some amusement.

Dallion chuckled and leaned back in his chair to prop his boots up on the overturned barrel. One of them bumped the edge of the plate, nearly sending it and the eggs over the edge, but it somehow teetered without going over. Dallion didn't seem to notice; he was too busy considering Journey some more. He asked, "Do you know much about ships?"

"I had a hand in designing the Jubilee for my father. I know every inch of her. I've done some sailing and know my way around a deck."

"Good. I might put you to work on the way there."

Journey couldn't tell if he was joking about that or not, but before he could ask him, Dallion stood from his chair. He started for the door, motioning for Journey to follow him as he went. He led him back out onto the deck, and Journey had to wait for a few seconds for his eyes to readjust to the sunlight up here. Lucien was calling out orders from a place beside the helm, and Dallion started in that direction with Journey in tow. Crewmen passed them by, in a hurry to carry out their quartermaster's orders, and Dallion pointed a few of them out to Journey as they went by.

"That's Tawny Paul. He's been here for the past two years, now. The short guy over there is Wee Bit. I don't even know how long he's been around. The guys on the ratlines are Toasty and Venom." He rattled a few more nicknames off, each just as bizarre as the last, but Journey didn't catch them all. He suddenly found himself on the edge of panic. Perhaps it was the harsh sunlight or the brisk, morning breeze that brought him back to reality. Whatever it was, Journey became acutely aware of the fact that he was crossing the deck of a pirate ship, surrounded by men who would very likely kill him without a second thought. Something inside him struggled to accept that this was where the twists and turns of life had led him.

His feet continued to carry him after Dallion. Lucien was currently chatting with another man beside the worn, wooden wheel that served as the Sprite's helm, but as Journey and Dallion reached them, they fell silent. Dallion nodded to the man that Journey hadn't met, yet, and told him, "This is Pigeon. He's the sailing master, so he's in charge of getting us where we need to go. Pigeon, this is Journey Travert. When we get in close to Stonewell, he'll tell you how to get up close."

Pigeon's lips turned downward in a frown beneath his thick, blond mustache. He said to Journey, "I hope you know what you're doing."

"I do," Journey assured him, and wondered if he would soon turn himself into a liar.

Chapter Eight

ON their third night at sea, Journey sat at the bow of the ship with his back against the banister that ran around its edge. A light mist was coming down from heavy clouds that blocked out the moon and most of the stars. He wrapped a thin, ragged blanket around his shoulders to try to stave off the coolness of the night, but the mist soaked through it to coax goosebumps from his arms. He tried to ignore it and rested the back of his head against the wooden banister behind him, but before he was even close to falling asleep, he heard footsteps approaching from farther down the deck. He forced his tired eyes to open and found a man that he vaguely recognized from passing encounters over the last few days. He was stout and starting to bald, although he couldn't have been much older than thirty. He offered Journey a broad smile and squatted down next to him on the deck.

"You must like the rain, huh?"

He didn't; he'd been instructed by Dallion to sleep out here on the deck each night, and Lucien had scrounged this blanket for him from somewhere as an afterthought. Instead of telling him this, however, Journey merely shrugged his shoulders. The man nodded, as if he'd agreed with him, and said, "I'm Adam, but people call me Brain."

Journey wasn't in the mood to make friends on such a cold, miserable night, but he offered, "I'm Journey."

Brain turned his face up toward the weeping sky for a moment and let the water settle on his cheeks and forehead. He took in a deep breath of the salty air, then let out a bellowing laugh that startled Journey and a few of the crewmen who were quietly toiling away the nightshift around the mast and helm. Journey wondered if this man was crazy.

Dallion's voice sounded from behind him as he said, "Don't bother him, Brain."

Brain gave him a childish pout as Dallion appeared out of the gloom of the night and joined them at the bow. His shoulder-length hair wasn't in its usual ponytail, and he must not have been out on the deck for long, yet, because it was still relatively dry. His feet were bare and his blue shirt was unbuttoned to hang loose over his pants. Journey supposed he'd been in bed only a few minutes ago.

"Journey and I are just chatting," Brain told him.

Dallion jerked a thumb over his shoulder and in the direction of the nearest hatchway that would take him below deck. "It's after midnight. Go get some sleep."

Brain muttered something about enjoying the rain and didn't go anywhere. Dallion didn't seem annoyed by this, but turned to rest his lower back against the banister and rested his elbows on it. He looked down at Journey, who was still huddled in his wet blanket on the deck, and said, "We've been making good time. It won't be long until we get to your island."

"How much longer?"

Dallion glanced at Brain, who responded so quickly that it was as if he hadn't had to think about the answer, at all. "Two days, twelve hours, and thirty-six minutes. But that could change because the wind always shifts and Pigeon will probably make some course corrections. Lucien might want us to slow down when we start getting closer, too."

His tone was the sort that one might use to explain a complicated concept to a child, but Journey didn't mind. There was something about Brain that was hard to dislike, although he couldn't quite put a name to it. Brain seemed to consider something for a moment before blurting, "Tawny and Old Rube don't think we should go to your island, Journey. They think this is a bad plan."

"They can whine about it all they want, but there's already been a vote," Dallion said dismissively. He pointed to the hatchway again, and Brain accepted defeat, this time. He got moving in that direction, mumbling a goodnight to Journey as he left.

Dallion assured Journey, "He means well."

Journey stared after the man in question until he'd disappeared down the ladder in the hatchway. Once he was gone, Journey asked, "Was he guessing about the time?"

Dallion snorted laughter. "Brain doesn't have to guess about stuff like that. He always knows exactly how fast the ship is moving, how many miles we've gone since the last stop, and how long it's going to take to get to any place you can name. Point out any line or pulley on this ship, and he'll tell you how long it's been since it was last replaced, right down to the hour. He's a walking map, compass, logbook, and clock. He's some kind of genius, I guess, but a genius who can't spell his own name or remember how to tie even the easiest knots. He's a terrible deckhand, but nobody's better than him at the stuff he is good at."

"Your crew isn't exactly what I'd expected. Where did you find them all?"

Dallion looked down at him again, and Journey could almost see his thoughts turning in his head as he tried to decide just how much more to divulge about the inner workings of his crew. Journey chose not to press, but Dallion answered him, anyway. "Remember how I told you that I stole this ship with a few friends of mine? Well, none of us had done much sailing before, so after we stole her, we anchored her off the other side of the island and sent word around that we were taking on hands with some experience. A dozen guys signed up, and that was our crew. Lucien was the only one who had ever been out pirating before. He'd even been a captain once, but his crew had mutinied and marooned the poor bastard a hundred miles north of the Isle of Runes. I can't tell you how he made it all the way out to Calico, but he was working as a butcher when I met him. He was crazy enough to agree to come on when some clueless kids with crazy dreams told him they had a ship."

"And then you decided to start targeting my family's islands?"

Dallion shrugged his shoulders. "Not right away. I was nineteen and had no idea what I was doing as a captain. We barely managed to keep ourselves fed for that whole first year, until Lucien and I found ourselves running the ship with a skeleton crew that could barely keep a straight course. It was rough. We needed a new plan."

Journey waited for him to go on, but Dallion was watching him with eager eyes that were just begging him to press him for more of the story. Journey decided to take the bait and asked, "What did you do?"

"We lied," Dallion laughed. "Lucien went to Port Kelsey ahead of me by nearly a full month and spread rumors about an up-and-coming pirate who had spent the last year terrorizing schooners and brigantines belonging to all the biggest companies: Whitefish, Straights, Horizon, you name it. At first, no one believed it because they'd never heard of a Captain Romilly. But it got people talking about me, and before long, they'd all heard my name because they were all asking each other if they'd heard of me. By the time I got there, my reputation in Port Kelsey was good enough to have a line of men waiting to sign on. Lucien and I picked the best of them, and when we set off again, I had a loyal crew that knew what they were doing. Eventually, I figured out how to stop faking being a good captain and I actually started being one."

It was Journey's turn to laugh, and why not? He hated to admit it, but he liked Dallion. Until recently, he would have been pleased to see this man's head on a pike or his corpse dangling from a noose, but now that he had met him, he was glad that Captain Elbridge and the Jubilee hadn't been successful in catching him, yet.

Journey asked, "What did you mean when you told Brain that there has already been a vote about this trip?"

"The voting thing was Lucien's idea. Every crewmember gets a say in what we all do. If someone isn't happy about something, we just vote on it. That way, I don't have to worry about mutiny. If I say we're going to go do something and they don't think it's a good idea, then it doesn't happen. They haven't vetoed me very many times – just twice, now that I think about it – but the option is always there, and I think that keeps them satisfied. It also keeps me grounded, because I'm not going to suggest that we do something that isn't going to benefit us all. Lucien says that's important, and he's right. He calls it demotarcy, or something like that."

"Democracy," Journey corrected him, and he liked how refreshing that concept was. On ships owned by Horizon and the other companies, there was a strict chain of command, and anyone who didn't like it was whipped, locked up, or released from duty. According to the stories that Landon had told him of his time in the companies' war against pirates, this was doubly true for warships. But a captain who could only lead by the will of his crew, and was therefore careful to lead them well…It was something he had never expected from the uneducated cowards that he'd once thought all pirates were.

Dallion squatted down beside him and searched his eyes as well as the murky night they were enveloped in would allow. He said gravely, "I talked them all into this trip because I believe everything you've said, so far. But before we get any closer to Stonewell, I need to know for sure: you aren't lying, are you? This isn't some sort of trap?"

Journey peered coolly back into those sea-blue eyes. "My word might not mean much to you, but it still means something to me. Everything I've told you is true, Dallion. You're going to have to trust me."

"Alright," he decided, and clapped a firm hand on Journey's shoulder through the soaked blanket. "I'm glad you're not a liar, because if something were to happen that I'm not expecting when we get there, I'd have to spill your guts out around your feet."

Journey didn't respond to that. Dallion flashed him a grin and stood to head back to the hatch that would take him back toward his warm, dry bed. Journey watched him go and didn't doubt for an instant that his warning was sincere.

Roughly two days, twelve hours, and thirty-six minutes later, the Travert family's islands came into sight. They heaved to just out of sight of Travert's Fourth, the northernmost of the islands. They waited there for nightfall, and Journey knew that this would only work if the Jubilee was still anchored on this side of Stonewell. Landon had said he wanted her left there until they'd spotted the Ocean Sprite again, but if he'd changed his mind and Elbridge had her patrolling these waters...

But the Jubilee didn't show up, even as night fell and the pirates readied themselves for what was to come next. The moon occasionally peeked out from behind thick clouds, but the ocean was otherwise dark. Pigeon was at the helm, as usual, and he took the Sprite around the east side of Travert's Fourth to make straight for Stonewell. Journey stood to his right and waited as the Sprite slipped silently through the waters toward her target.

Dallion came to stand between him and Pigeon, and in a voice that was barely more than a whisper, he warned them both, "I don't like coming at it head-on like this."

"They won't see us coming," Journey said, and as if to verify this, Lucien called out over the deck for all of the lamps on the ship to be doused. Within seconds, the Ocean Sprite was a ghostly silhouette on a black sea. Journey's anxiousness was chased away by that darkness, and he was glad to find that all he felt, now, was determination and confidence. He only hoped that such things could be contagious. He whispered to Pigeon, "Keep her steady."

The deck of the Sprite was uncharacteristically silent as the crew waited. Just as Journey began to wonder if they'd somehow wandered off course, the clouds concealing the moon shifted, and the island before them was illuminated in its pale, white light. It was a half a mile off the bow, and Pigeon had managed to bring them perpendicular to the small bay that housed the north dock. There, revealed by an especially bright shaft of moonlight, the Jubilee still sat where Journey had left her a month ago.

Dallion tensed beside him and grabbed Journey's arm in a painful squeeze. Journey whispered, "Relax. She's anchored. There should only be a minimal crew on board right now – maybe three or four men. Landon's been keeping her tucked away until it's time to start chasing you around again."

Dallion didn't let up on his grip; if anything, it tightened. Journey reminded him, "I gave you my word. The Jubilee is yours, if you want her."

Dallion's grip softened at that, and the look on his face turned from alarm to hunger. Even in the shadows of the night, Journey could see it. He pointed to a sharp outcropping of rocks that reached into the ocean to the left to the bay and said, "There's a sandy beach on the other side of those rocks. It stays deep right up until the shore, so we can bring the Sprite in close. No cannons; there's no need, and we don't want anyone to hear it. The hill on the other side of the beach is steep, but you shouldn't have a problem. Make your way to the south side of the island, but be careful of the night watch by the main docks there. You'll come to the house, first. Remember: Landon dies, but none of the servants can be harmed. You're welcome to anything in the house, but the thing you're probably going to want most is his safe. He keeps it under fake floorboards in the cellar. Far left corner. The key is kept in the top drawer of the desk in his study."

"Sounds good," Dallion replied, but his gaze still hadn't left the Jubilee. To Pigeon, he said, "Slip around the other side of those rocks, like he said. You and Brain are going to stay here with Mr. Travert."

Pigeon obliged, and the bow of the Sprite turned slowly toward the rocks. Dallion clapped a hand across Journey's back, as if they were old friends, and the pirate's smile widened with each passing minute that his new prize drew nearer.

CHAPTER NINE

THE dark, sleepy mansion would have been an unfathomable maze of hallways and stairwells, if not for the clear directions that Journey had given him. There was a chorus of screams, shouts, and loud thuds coming from the floor below him as Dallion crept down a hall on the second floor. The candle in his hand cast a dancing, gentle glow on the painted walls and ceiling as he went. His boots were quiet on the expensive carpet beneath them. He counted the doors on the left side of the hall until he came to the fourth one, and the torchlight shone off of the metal doorknob. Dallion raised the candle to his lips and put out the flame with a puff of breath. He gave his eyes a few seconds to adjust to the darkness in the hall, then placed his hand on the doorknob and turned it slowly. The hinges were silent as he pushed the door open.

Landon must have been woken by the sounds of the first floor of his home being ransacked, for he was already awake and standing beside his bed. The match that he'd used to light a candle was still in his hand, and the candle's infant flame was barely enough to reveal the white bedclothes that he was wearing. He froze at the sight of the door opening, his eyes wide. A single, terrified word escaped his lips: "Romilly."

A grin stretched across Dallion's lips, and he took a single step into the room. Landon stumbled backward on the other side of the bed and bumped painfully into the armoire behind him. He squeezed the candle in his hands so tightly that some of the wax crumbled between his fingers. He cried, "Take it all! Anything in the house is yours. Whatever you want…"

"What I want is for you to know that Journey is alive and well," Dallion growled.

Landon gaped at him for a moment, but then a look of understanding crossed his candlelit face. His eyes shifted toward the drawer in a small table across the room, where he kept a gun, but Dallion was much closer to it than he was. Landon's shoulders slumped, and he said stonily, "I knew he was alive. I received a letter from Caresse Beaumont that said as much. Is that what this is about, then? Has the whore's child sent you to pay me back for cutting him off from his fortune?"

"He doesn't care about the money. This is about Jubilee."

Any hope of survival that Landon had been clinging to must have been stripped away by the mention of the woman's name, for he sank slowly to his knees and began to weep. A flood of pleading words poured from his mouth as he begged for mercy. Dallion had none to give him.

An hour later, with Landon's blood staining the sleeves of his shirt, Dallion stood at the dock on the north side of the island. Behind him, his crew was carrying their bountiful harvest toward the Ocean Sprite: fancy clothing, oil paintings, crates of food, expensive jewelry, and silverware sets that would fetch a good price on the black market. Dallion's only desire, however, was the ship he was currently taking in with greedy eyes. Lucien had already gone on board with two others to rid it of the sailors who had been left there on watch. For the moment, she was a ghost ship, hosting only a handful of corpses on her main deck.

Now, Lucien joined his captain on the cobblestone slab that sat before the wooden dock. He clapped the younger man on the back with a hand that was dyed red with dried blood. He teased, "You're a big boy, now, Dal. She's gorgeous. What are you going to do with all those sails?"

"Fly on the wind," Dallion breathed. The Jubilee was faster than anything else he'd captained. She had eighteen cannons – ten more than his sloop – and he estimated that there was room enough for a crew of a hundred, if he wanted that. She represented endless possibilities that a man as young as himself probably had no business being offered. He said to Lucien, "Keep as few men as you need to sail the Sprite and send everyone else over to me on the Jubilee. You can keep Pigeon. I'm going to take this beautiful gal out, myself."

"And the Travert kid?"

"Tell him we'll drop him off anywhere he wants. If he wants to go all the way out to Giverny, I'll take him."

Lucien looked at him, but the surprise on his face was faked, and Dallion knew it. They were in Journey's debt, after all. He had come in from nowhere with an offer that had paid off more than they'd deserved. If he wanted them to take him to the ends of the world, Dallion would oblige. Happily.

Chapter Ten

JOURNEY hadn't thought his future out beyond Landon's death, so he had no idea where he wanted Dallion and the others to take him. It was Lucien who suggested that he remain with them until he found a place he liked, and Dallion was alright with that. The crew voted to sell the Sprite, and although it broke Dallion's heart to see her go, he recovered from his grief as soon as he had the cash in his hands. Journey had helped him negotiate a good selling price, and an up-and-coming merchant sailed off with her.

Dallion allowed Journey to start sleeping below deck with the rest of the crew on the Jubilee, instead of out in the elements, and he was grateful. He spent the next two weeks trying to stay out of everyone's way, but while he was taking a nap in a hammock in the crew's quarters one afternoon, someone shook his shoulder to wake him. His groggy mind recognized the man as Wee Bit, and the pirate told him, "One of the forward ratlines came loose last night. Lucien says you need to help me fix it."

Journey was certain that he must have misheard him, but Wee Bit merely stared at him and waited for his response. He shook his head to dismiss the last of his sleepiness, then asked, "Are you sure he wasn't talking about someone else?"

Wee Bit gave an impatient huff. "He said, 'Go tell Journey to get his ass on deck to help you fix it.' So are you coming? Or should I tell him you aren't going to do it?"

"I'll help you," he answered, and set aside his confusion to follow Wee Bit up onto the Jubilee's main deck. If Lucien wanted to put him to work as the cost of letting him stay aboard, then he wasn't about to argue about it.

That was his mindset for the next few weeks, while the orders from Lucien kept coming. Journey trimmed the sails and sang shanties right along with the rest of the crew. He took his turns scrubbing the decks, volunteered for his fair share of night shifts, and got good at splicing rope. One evening, while playing a game of cards with Tawny Paul, Pigeon, and Old Rube around an overturned barrel on the main deck, Tawny asked him, "When are you leaving?"

Journey pretended to focus on the five cards in his hand as he tried to decide how to answer that. He could feel all three pairs of the other men's eyes on him as they waited, and he finally replied, "Whenever Dallion and Lucien decide they're tired of me."

Tawny Paul gave a nod of his head in approval of that, then played a card on his turn. Journey hoped that it would still be a long time before he had to part ways with this crew. Over the last few weeks, he'd come to realize that he was the happiest he'd ever been in his life.

He woke one morning to a commotion in the crew's quarters. He sat up in his hammock to find a dozen or so men scrambling to lace up their boots and arm themselves with various pistols and knives. Journey seized the shoulder of a crewman he recognized – a man who had somehow managed to avoid any nicknames to simply go by Thomas – and asked, "What's going on?"

"It's time for a fight," Thomas answered, and although there was a hint of nervousness in his voice, it was barely recognizable beneath his excitement. "Captain spotted a ship he likes."

Journey let him go and watched as he rushed after the other men who were on their way up the steep stairs that would take them to the main deck. Journey stayed where he was for a moment, torn. Scrubbing decks and trimming sails was one thing, but to actually take part in an attack on an unsuspecting ship was something else. He decided that he wasn't going to get involved, but Thomas cast a glance over his shoulder as he reached the stairs and asked, "Are you coming?"

Journey's body made the decision for him. He was leaving the hammock and jogging toward the stairs before the rational part of his brain could talk himself out of it. His heart was racing and every hair on his body was standing up straight as he stepped out into the bright sunlight spilling across the Jubilee's main deck. The sky in the east was still stained pink and orange by the sunrise. A dozen men were gathered near the bow, and as Journey joined them at the banister, he saw the small sloop that had seized their attention. The triangular sails on its single mast were taking it away from the Jubilee as quickly as they could, but there was no question about which ship was faster.

Lucien's voice rang out across the decks, calling for the crew to ready themselves. The men scattered. Journey left the bow and hurried to the helm, where Dallion, Lucien, and Pigeon were embroiled in conversation. There was an electrified light in Dallion's eyes, and Journey felt a stab of pity for the men aboard the sloop that he would soon overtake. Lucien was saying something about the starboard cannons, but Dallion turned his attention to Journey as he reached them. The seasoned pirate warned, "Last chance."

"For what?"

Dallion nodded in the direction of his ship's bow and the doomed sloop beyond it. "We're about to see what the Jubilee has in her, but you're no pirate. If you want to keep it that way, you should go below deck. You can help Brain watch for hull damage if they start firing back at us. We'll drop you off at the next port we come to after this is all over."

"Is there another option?"

Dallion's eyes narrowed, and there was something else in them, now – some sort of hope that Journey would take an offer. He replied, "You can lend a hand, if you want. But you know what that'll make you."

Lucien and Pigeon were watching him carefully as they waited for his answer, but Journey didn't take his gaze from Dallion's. He replied, "Just tell me what to do."

Dallion beamed with satisfaction as Lucien ordered, "Go fetch a pistol from Tawny Paul, then go to the starboard side and wait for my orders with the others there. There's no doctor aboard this ship, so don't do anything that'll make you regret that."

Journey turned on his heels and started for the starboard side of the ship, calling for Tawny as he went. Lucien asked Dallion with some amusement, "Do you think he'll survive?"

Dallion chuckled. "We're about to find out."

The Jubilee ran her down easily. The name painted on her aft end was First Prize, and Dallion bellowed laughter at how fitting that was. On his order, Pigeon brought the Jubilee up along her port side, and the cannons on the deck below his feet fired a volley of deadly iron toward their target. At this distance, it was hard to miss. Dallion's crew cheered as their cannonballs met the side of the Prize with explosions of shattered wood. The acrid scent of black powder followed close behind.

Journey stood at the starboard banister as the Jubilee shuddered with cannon fire beneath him. He may have commissioned her to defend islands against pirates, but the Jubilee was just as fit for something like this. He watched as the crew of the Prize scrambled across her small deck. She was barely half of the Jubilee's length, and judging by the flag atop her mast, she was partnered with Unique Investments. Journey wondered how badly the company would miss this little sloop.

All six of the Prize's cannons were on her deck, and the three on her port side roared to life. The cannon balls struck high up on the Jubilee's hull, and shards of wood flew in every direction. Journey pulled away from the banister instinctively, but the rest of the crewmen around him leaned over it to get a better look at the damage that had been done. It must not have been anything serious, because another cheer went up.

Dallion's voice sounded from somewhere else on the deck, calling for Pigeon to bring the Jubilee in closer. As he maneuvered her, Lucien appeared beside Journey and grabbed him by the shoulder. He raised his voice to be heard over the commotion all around them and said, "Get ready to jump."

Journey clutched his pistol to his chest and peered over the side and down into the space between the two ships. Far below, the ocean was raging between with white foam between the hulls. Fear seized his heart, and he had to battle against his mind's insistence that he'd made a terrible mistake. He had no business being here, in the middle of a bloody battle at sea. If he died out here, it would have only served him right.

As he watched, the space between the two ships narrowed. The gap was thirty feet across…twenty…ten. Journey thought that he would soon be able to reach out and touch the Prize, and judging by Lucien's words, that was exactly what he was about to do. The gap between the ships narrowed further, and just as it seemed like the two ships were going to crash into one another, Lucien shouted above all the other voices, "Jump!"

Journey was launching himself over the Jubilee's banister before he knew it. For a moment, there was nothing below him but churning water and certain death. Then he cleared the wooden railing that ran along the edge of the Prize's deck, and he landed with a painful crash. As he did, another round of cannon fire sounded from the Jubilee, and he felt the shockwave rumble through the deck beneath him. He clambered to his feet and found himself in the throes of chaos. The deck of the Prize was crowded with men struggling to kill each other. To Journey's right, a pirate named Venom fired his pistol a man standing only a few feet from him, and the man fell to his knees with a scream as he clapped his hands over the hole in his stomach. On Journey's left, Dallion swung a long knife with all his might, and the man at the other end of it crumpled at his feet. The air was choked with smoke and rang with the voices of men struggling to survive.

Journey got his feet moving toward the helm, where a member of the Prize's crew was trying desperately to steer the ship away from the Jubilee. He had to step around two fistfights along the way and somehow managed to dodge a bullet sent in his direction, but Journey kept his eyes on his target. The man at the helm saw him coming and cried out for one of his comrades to stop him, but no one was able to come to his aid. Journey stepped up beside him and leveled his pistol at the man's face.

"You don't have to die today," Journey told him, although he wasn't entirely sure that that was true. The man gave a frightened whimper as he stared down the short, black barrel of the gun. The Prize shuddered once more beneath their feet as another eight cannonballs plunged into her port side. That must have been all the convincing that the man needed, for he let go of the wooden wheel he'd been clinging to and scrambled away from it, his hands raised above his head in surrender. Journey seized the helm and straightened the Prize's course. From the bedlam that was currently engulfing the deck before him, Lucien called out for him to keep her steady.

Another voice rang out, and Journey didn't recognize this one. It belonged to a man who had climbed up onto one of the Prize's ratlines to be seen and heard by everyone else. Between deafening claps of gunfire, Journey could make out the word surrender. As he watched, the Prize's crew began laying down their weapons. Dallion, standing in the middle of the deck beside the ship's only mast, raised his hands and loosed a victorious cheer. All of the other pirates joined in, and Journey couldn't help but lend his own voice, as well.

Chapter Eleven

TWO months after the First Prize was captured and scuttled, Lucien called across the quarterdeck for Journey to meet him in the captain's cabin. He'd been rolling up a length of rope with Holey Head, and the man now gave Journey a knowing look, as if he was a child who had been summoned to the headmistress for chastising. Journey ignored this and made his way to Dallion's cabin, which was more than three times the size the one on the Sprite had been. Lucien was waiting for him at the door, and he led him inside. Dallion was seated at the small, ornate table that stood in the middle of the room, and there was a thick, leather-bound book sitting on it. Dallion's expression was uncharacteristically serious. Lucien crossed the room to sit down on the other chair at the table. Journey stayed where he was, suddenly concerned that Holey Head's look hadn't been all that far off, after all.

"We've been talking," Dallion told him, and Journey's spirits dropped further. He'd known that this time would come, but that didn't mean he had to like it. His best hope now was that they would still allow him to pick a place to be dropped off. He'd allowed himself to begin considering both of these men his friends, but as Landon had been fond of saying, business was business.

There was a small cabinet near the door that Dallion kept filled with boots, maps, dishes, and any number of random belongings. Journey sat against the top of it, crossing his arms at his chest and bracing himself for the guaranteed invitation to leave the ship. He asked with feigned indifference, "What's wrong?"

Dallion simply considered him in silence, but Lucien said, "You aren't signed."

"What does that mean?"

Dallion tapped a finger on the book before him. "Whenever we take on a new member of the crew, they sign on. It's basically a contract that says they'll follow the rules, won't fight with their shipmates, things like that. It's also an agreement that they'll get an equal share of all profits and an equal vote in all decisions. But you've never signed on. That's why you haven't gotten a share of anything we've taken while you've been here."

Journey shook his head, more confused than he had been when he'd first walked in here. "I don't understand. Are you telling me I can't stay on the ship because I'm not officially part of the crew?"

Dallion and Lucien shared a look at that. Lucien told him, "You never shirk your duties and you don't complain about orders. You were terrible with the sails, at first, but now you know what you're doing. The rest of the crew seems to like you. We know about the reading lessons you've been giving Brain every morning, and Pigeon says that he's been teaching you a few things about navigating. You've made some friends."

Journey glanced at Dallion, who almost certainly fell into the category. Nearly every night for the past few weeks, he'd invited Journey into this cabin to play backgammon at the very table he and Lucien were sitting at, now. They'd spent an untold number of hours passing the time together, while Journey let him cheat at the game and Dallion spun exaggerated stories about his pirating escapades.

He dared, "Are you asking me to sign on officially?"

Dallion chuckled. "Actually, we have a bet about that. Lucien thinks you're going to sign on."

"And you?"

He shrugged, but there was a goading grin on his face. "I think that rich, pretty-boy upbringing you had is screaming for you not to do it. You've spent your whole life hating pirates. It's in your blood."

"You don't know anything about my blood," Journey told him, and if there was a hint of sadness in his voice, the other two men didn't notice. "But I like Lucien a hell of a lot more than I like you, so I don't want to make him lose a bet."

Dallion howled laughter and opened the book as Lucien went to fetch a pen.

CHAPTER TWELUE

THE next two years passed in a whirlwind of thievery and reckless adventures. Crew members came and went, either because they were killed in battle or simply left to pursue fortune elsewhere. Holey Head retired after a particularly good payout from a Whitefish ship they captured. There were others who left, and even more who joined. Dallion increased his crew to seventy men and took on an experienced boatswain named Horus to shift some of Lucien's responsibilities off his hands. He chose Tawny Paul to be the deck officer to serve as Lucien's right-hand man. Then Dallion did something that came as more of a surprise to the others: he named a first mate. It wasn't something that was usually done in the pirate community, but the crew allowed it. Dallion offered the position to Journey, who accepted. He'd already been carrying out those duties, for the most part, and he wondered if perhaps putting an official title to it was Dallion's way of making sure the rest of the crew didn't grow jealous of their friendship. There was no doubt to anyone that they had become inseparable.

One night, as they sat in Dallion's cabin, playing what may have been their thousandth game of backgammon, Dallion told Journey, "I've been thinking."

Journey had come to know those three words for what they were when they came from this man: trouble. It meant that Dallion had something crazy planned. Nine times out of ten, he was able to convince the rest of the crew that it was good idea, and he hadn't let them down, yet.

Now, Journey moved one of his checkers on the backgammon board on the table between them and asked, "Are we attacking a ship or a port?"

"Neither. But I wanted your permission before I pitched this one to the crew."

Journey took his gaze from the board to look up at him, startled. As far as he had assumed, the word 'permission' wasn't part of Dallion's vocabulary. Intrigued, he said, "Alright, I'm listening."

Dallion rolled the dice and moved a sixth checker onto one of the points on the board, which was against house rules, but Journey didn't object. Dallion said, "There's a new president of Commercial Horizon."

"You know I don't keep up with that stuff, anymore."

Dallion nodded, but asked, "What do you think happened to Travert's holdings?"

Journey frowned. He didn't like talking about these things. A year ago, during a night of heavy drinking in a tavern on some obscure island, Journey had told Dallion the details about everything: his mother's murder, Landon's attempt to kill him, and all the rest. Dallion hadn't asked about it since, and Journey had been grateful. Now, he shrugged and took his next turn on the backgammon board.

Dallion pressed, "Guess."

"The company took over," he said testily. "Commercial Horizon was Landon's parent company, which means they had a contract that laid out the rules for how they would conduct business together. Horizon was required to pay top market value for everything he sold them and they would help him if his crops ever had a bad season. In return, Landon wasn't allowed to trade with other companies and he had to follow all of the company's bylaws. One of those bylaws states that the company inherits everything if an island owner dies without a male heir to pass everything down to. As soon as you killed him, all of his assets became the property of Commercial Horizon."

"Wrong," Dallion declared, and he slapped the top of the table with his palm, as if to drive the word home. It rattled the board and shifted a few of the checkers on it.

Journey sighed, unimpressed with his antics. "What are you talking about?"

"A lot of things have changed because of the new Horizon lady taking over."

"Audrey Dumont. She's been in the job since her uncle died six months ago, so I'm not sure she can still be considered new."

Dallion's eyes narrowed. "You said you don't keep up with these things, anymore."

"I don't. These are just rumors that I overheard in Port Kelsey during our last stop there. You know what Lucien says about that: anything you hear in Port Kelsey is a lie, and if it's the truth, it's by accident. What's your point, Dal?"

He'd lost all interest in the game, apparently, for he closed the backgammon board with a snap. The checkers and dice rattled inside. He pushed it to the side of the table, then laced his hands together in the place where it had been. Journey was familiar with this, as well. It meant that Dallion was about to lay out a plan.

"This Audra woman has been shaking things up. Did you know their captains earn almost a thousand marks a month, now? And for what? For sitting in a comfy chair while their lieutenants run everything for them?"

"Do you have a point?"

Dallion pointed a finger at him in warning. "Don't get an attitude with me, Prince. I'm trying to explain something."

Journey scowled. 'Prince' was something that the crew had taken to calling him over the first few months that he'd been with them. It had been a cruel way of reminding him that he hailed from wealth and privilege, unlike the rest of them. As time had passed, however, they'd abandoned that nickname for one he liked much better: Teach. It alluded to the fact that he had successfully taught twelve crewmen to read over the past two years. Brain was still struggling, but Journey had gotten him to the point of being able to write the entire alphabet, now, and that was something. Dallion was the only one who still called him Prince, and he only did it when he was trying hard to get under his skin.

Dallion continued, "Look, she's also changed some of Horizon's inheritance laws. Everything goes to the first-born in the family."

"That's how it's always been."

He groaned. "You're not listening. Everything goes to the first-born kid. Not son, but kid. It doesn't matter if it's a boy or a girl."

Journey stared at him in silence for a while as he considered the implications of that. Dallion urged, "Think about it. You told me that when Landon went crazy, he kept asking about what had happened to his daughter. You said that he never had a daughter, but what if he did? Maybe you have a sister out there that you never knew about."

Or maybe I was never Landon's son, Journey thought to himself. He stopped short of speaking the words, but it had been a possibility that he'd considered for the last two years, now. He recalled Landon calling him a whore's son and demanding that he stop calling him 'dad.' At the time, he'd thought that had been because Landon had decided to disown him, but the more he'd turned it over in his mind, the less he believed that was the case.

He said carefully, "If Landon and Jubilee really did have a daughter somewhere, I have no idea what happened to her or if she's still alive."

"Who might know?"

That gave him another pause. Surely, Jubilee couldn't have done everything on her own. She would have had to have birthed the baby without any help, which was possible, but unlikely. And then she would have had to surrender or hide her newborn without any emotional support from someone she trusted...

"Abigay," Journey said, somehow certain of it. "She had a friend named Abigay Laval. They were like sisters. If anyone knew all of Jubilee's secrets, it would be her."

"Where can we find her?"

Journey sat back in his chair, shaking his head. "I don't know where you're going with this. If the girl exists and is still alive, and if Abigay somehow knows who and where she is, what does that have to do with us?"

Dallion laced his hands together on the table again, and Journey braced himself. The plan was a good one, he would later admit, although it sounded ludicrous, at first. Dallion proposed that they track down Abigay and see if she had answers about the mystery daughter. If she was real and they could find her, then they would reveal her true heritage and the fact that she was the sole heir of everything that Landon Travert had owned when he'd died. They would convince her to travel to the Isle of Runes, where Commercial Horizon was headquartered. She would present her case and offer to allow Horizon to buy her out at a fair price, and the company would pay her for the cost of the islands and ships so that they could maintain ownership.

The pirates would initially strike a deal with the girl to get ten percent of whatever they gave her.

"Ten percent is perfect," Dallion assured him. "It's just the right amount to make her think that we're in this for a share of the money, but not so much that she won't agree to it."

"And what are we actually going for?" Journey asked, knowing him better than to think he'd settle for so little.

"All of it," Dallion replied. "Once she's cashed out and has the money on her, we take it, maroon her on the nearest island, and set sail for whatever beach our hearts desire."

Journey thought that it just might work, and wasn't there a vicious sort of irony in it? It seemed that he would have a share of Landon's riches, after all, if everything went well.

"And the best part," Dallion said, propping his feet up on the table and rocking his chair back comfortably, "is that this is easy money."

Chapter Thirteen

IT took some convincing, but they eventually got the rest of the crew to agree to the plan. A little over a week later, the Jubilee was anchored four miles off the eastern coast of Kinsman Island. They didn't dare to bring her any closer; she was known to be a pirate vessel in these waters, and drawing any closer to the island would attract attention that they didn't want. Pigeon and Horus – two men who hadn't taken part in the raid on the island two years before and therefore wouldn't be recognized by anyone – took a longboat from the ship and took turns rowing it for the hour that it took them to reach land. Per Dallion's instructions, they would stash it in thick brush just above the tideline and make the half-mile trek into Kingsman Lane on foot. From there, they could charter a legitimate boat to take them to Stonewell Island, paying the captain of the small vessel extra to not ask any questions.

Journey paced the main of the Jubilee while he awaited their return. He hadn't been this close to his old home since leaving it two years ago, and the knowledge that he might soon have word from Jubilee's dearest friend was getting to him. Lucien was nearby, trying to decipher a map that Pigeon had covered in annotations and scribbles. As he gave up on the map and rolled it back up, he grumbled, "Would you stop pacing? You're driving me nuts. Go see if Old Rube needs any help with the counts."

Old Rube was only fifty, but that was ancient, by pirates' standards. He was the supplies officer, and Journey knew without asking that he didn't need any help taking daily counts of their food stores. He took stock every morning and had Brain double-check his math, and Journey didn't doubt that the old man knew exactly how many eggs were on board the ship at any given time. He wasn't about to argue with Lucian, however, and at least bothering Old Rube would give him something to do.

When he came back up to the deck two hours later, there was still no sign of Horus or Pigeon. Journey helped Wee Bit and a few other hands with their chores, and the time passed by with torturous slowness. Finally, almost seven hours after the longboat had left the ship, one of the hands called out to announce that it had been spotted off the bow.

Horus and Pigeon were brought back on board and were summoned immediately into Dallion's cabin. Journey and Lucien joined them there, and they reported that there was no one named Abigay Laval employed on Stonewell, the Twins, or Travert's Fourth.

"You're sure?" Journey asked them. He was sitting against the writing desk in the corner of the cabin. Lucien and Horus were seated at the table, with Pigeon standing nearby. Dallion was laying on his back on his bed, his hands laced behind his head as he stared thoughtfully up at the ceiling.

Horus answered his question with, "We talked to the steward, himself."

"Steward?" Lucien asked.

He shrugged. Pigeon, who had once worked for The Whitefish Trading Company before turning to piracy, offered, "I think that Horizon appointed a steward to run the islands for them. He says he owns a bunch of other islands somewhere, but he's the steward of these four, and they're owned by the company. His name is Ansel Bowman or something."

"Ansel Beaumont," Journey corrected him, and he had to laugh a little at that. Why not? It seemed that Ansel's daughter, Caresse, had ended up in the mansion on Stonewell, after all.

Pigeon eyed him, unsure about what his laughter had meant, but agreed, "I think you're right. He said that he's usually back home, running his own islands, and leaves these four to his son-in-law to take care of. The son-in-law's laid up with a broken leg right now, though, so we didn't meet him. Saw the girl, though – Beaumont's daughter."

Horus gave a whistle. "Trust me, I want to be that son-in-law."

"Caresse," Journey said, his voice hardly more than a whisper. This time, they all looked at him.

"History?" Lucien pressed him.

"She was my fiancée," he answered, not meeting their gazes. Horus, who didn't know much of Journey's history, gave an amused snort, but the solemn looks on the other men's faces verified that it was true.

Pigeon rescued him by saying, "It wasn't a complete wash, though. We gave Beaumont a sad story about how I was Abigay's long-lost brother and I was trying to find my last living relative. He let us look through the old employment records from when the islands belonged to the Travert family. And guess what? It said she was a housekeeper for over twenty years, and then she was reassigned to cut sugarcane on Nymph's Rest. After that, the records were a mess – missing pages, water damage, you name it. We found her name again on a loose page toward the back. It said she'd quit not long after she got to Nymph's Rest. It didn't say anything else."

"Do you know where she would have gone, Teach?" Lucien asked.

Journey was surprised by how little he knew of the woman who had helped raised him. He offered, "I think she had family in Kinsman Lane. Her father died young, but she had a mother and a couple of uncles, if I remember right. Maybe a grandmother, too. She didn't talk about them much, though." He didn't add that the reason for that fact was that after over twenty years of service on Stonewell, the Traverts had become Abigay's family. It angered him to know that Landon had sent her to work in the sugarcane fields on Nymph's Rest...but it may have also been a sign that he'd been punishing her for something, and what would that something have been, if not keeping a dark secret for his wife?

Dallion, who had been silent throughout this entire conversation, now sat up on the bed and said, "Pigeon, Horus, you did a good job. You two should sit this next one out. Journey and I are going to go into Kinsman Lane to look for her."

"I don't think it's a good idea for me to get any closer to Kinsman than I already am," Journey objected.

Dallion shrugged. "Alright, don't go. But do you really think that this Abigay woman is going to be willing to talk about a secret she's kept for all these years to a stranger? At least she'll know you."

He hated to admit that he was right, but there was no escaping it. Lucien suggested, "You should go this evening. Ask around at the taverns. Kinsman is big, but not that big. Someone will recognize the family name, if they're still around."

Journey could only hope that they wouldn't also recognize him.

Wee Bit and Old Rube went with them so that they could stock up on some fresh food while they had the chance. It was almost eight o'clock when they stepped onto the streets of

Kinsman Lane, and Dallion and Journey left the other two men near the market. To Journey, returning here felt surreal. He'd sworn to himself that he would never again come anywhere near this place. If he had learned anything from his time with Dallion, however, it was that the man had a crazy way of leading him down very strange paths.

Perhaps it was coincidence. It may have been luck. To Journey, however, it felt like a twist of fate when they found someone in the first tavern that they went to who recognized the Laval family name. It was their timing that had assured this, as they had arrived on the day of the funeral for the family's matriarch, Adda Laval. She had been the oldest living person on Kinsman Island up until a week ago, when she'd slipped peacefully away in her sleep at the age of ninety. Such an age was almost unheard of around here, especially for a woman who had spent the majority of her life in poverty. The rumors that Journey encountered in the tavern that night said that the Laval family, or at least Adda and her youngest son, Manton, had come into a small fortune, by the standards of the common folk on the island. Manton had told anyone who asked that a rich uncle of his had passed away and left everything to him, but towns like Kinsman Lane preferred drama over the mundane, and so rumors had spread that he'd obtained it by more nefarious means.

Wherever the money had come from, it had been enough to purchase a house for himself and his aged mother closer to the southern end of town. Journey and Dallion paid for a carriage to take them there, and as they passed Rose Street, Journey didn't so much as turn his head to look down it; he had no use for the Beaumont family, anymore. The carriage arrived at the Laval home just before midnight, and although they'd expected everyone to be asleep, the windows were all lit with lamplight. They paid the carriage driver and were dropped off a few houses away.

Once the carriage was gone, the two men stood in the dimly-lit street and considered the house before them. It wasn't massive, especially compared to the houses of island owners and wealthy merchants that lined the rest of the street, but it was well-tended and respectable. There were horses and carriages on the street outside the house, as if there was a party going on, even at this time of night. Journey realized that it was likely a gathering for last respects following the funeral that had taken place earlier in the day.

Dallion started across the street, but Journey grabbed his arm to stop him and whispered, "We need a plan, Dal. Are you just going to walk up to the front door and knock?"

Dallion considered the house again, and Journey understood that truly had been his plan. He sighed. Dallion was dressed in his usual tight, black pants and blue shirt. He was wearing all of his customary jewelry, and he'd even brought his gun out here with him. It was tucked into the back of his pants beneath his shirt, but the bulge there was telling. Journey had donned a long, black coat for this expedition, and he now took it off to offer it to him, saying, "You couldn't make it more obvious if you hung a sign around your neck that said 'Pirate.' Put this on."

Dallion gave an unhappy grunt, but went along with it. He was broader in the shoulders than Journey, so the coat didn't fit as well as he would have liked, but it did help him look a little more reputable. Without prompting, he stripped off his rings and necklaces. As he handed the one with the shark tooth to Journey, he warned, "You lose this one, and I'll cut off a finger. Got it?"

"Was the shark a lost love of yours?" Journey teased, but even in the dim light on the street, he could see the seriousness on Dallion's face. He put the necklace and other jewelry in his pocket, making his movements slow and careful to set his mind at ease.

Satisfied, Dallion said, "I'll go in as a guest. You go around back so no one recognizes you. If Abigay's here, I'll convince her to come out back with me."

"If anyone realizes you shouldn't be there..."

Dallion flashed him a cocky smile. "I've got this. Don't worry so much, Prince. Everything's going to be alright."

"Sometimes I wonder why I haven't just turned you in for a bounty."

Dallion started across the street again, saying over his shoulder as he went, "That's pretty funny, coming from a suspected mommy-killer."

Journey didn't think he would have let even Lucien to get away with saying something like that, but he loved Dallion like a brother, and he was used to his harsh mocking by now. He watched as Dallion headed up the front walkway to the Laval house and knocked on the door. He was carrying a confidence that said he was right where he should be, and Journey envied him for that. Dallion had told him long ago that a person could go anywhere they wanted, as long as they acted like they were supposed to be there, and Journey had found this to be true. He just hadn't been able to master the audacity it took to be successful at it.

The door opened, although Journey couldn't see by whom. Dallion said something, and after a moment, he stepped into the house and out of sight. As soon as the door was closed behind him, Journey crossed the street and slipped into the shadows between two houses, heading for the back of the Laval home.

Inside, Dallion found that the house wasn't decorated quite as lavishly as he'd expected it to be. It seemed that Manton Laval's inherited fortune had been large, but not that large. The doorman who had let him in offered to take his coat, but Dallion declined. The short hallway he was in opened to a sitting area, where a fire was burning in the fireplace. There were a dozen people sitting around in there, sipping tea and speaking in low voices. Two women were weeping. A poorly-painted portrait of an elderly woman sat atop the mantle above the fireplace, and there were heaps of flowers on either side of it.

The doorman told Dallion that Mr. Laval was currently upstairs resting, but would undoubtedly be down to tend to his guests again soon. Dallion feigned disappointment at this, then imitated the man's polite, succinct manner of speaking to ask if Abigay Laval was here.

"Miss Laval is in the kitchen," the doorman replied. "Would you like me to fetch her?"

"Just point me in the right direction, my good man," Dallion replied, patting his arm in a way that made it all the more awkward. The doorman gave him strange look, but motioned toward a doorway a short distance down the hall. Dallion left him there with a curt thanks and stepped into the kitchen.

She was alone in here, he was glad to find. The smell of fresh bread and brewing tea filled the air. Abigay's back was to him as she wiped up a puddle of spilt tea from a long table against the far wall, but she said as she heard the door open, "It's almost ready. I'll have it out soon."

Dallion closed the door behind him, looking around the place. It was as sparsely decorated in here as the sitting room and hallway had been. He asked, "Abigay Laval?"

She turned to face him, and he saw that she was relatively pretty for her age, which he judged to be somewhere around forty. She was wearing a white apron over a blue dress that had seen better days. To Dallion, she looked more like a servant than a member of a family who could afford to live in this house. There were dark circles under her eyes, but she offered him a gracious smile that took a few years off her face.

"Were you a friend of my grandmother's?" she asked.

"No," he confessed. "Sorry for your loss. I'm here to see you."

"Me?" she asked. Her eyes considered him from the soles of his old boots to the tan lines around his neck where his necklaces usually rested on his skin.

He saw her look of doubt and said quickly, "I have a message for you."

She seemed to relax at that, and she didn't give any indication that she was nervous as he approached her. He came close enough to be able to whisper to her, but hesitated, not having a plan for what to say. She was waiting, her brown eyes full of curiosity, and he decided to take a chance. He said, "Journey Travert hopes you're well."

She recoiled, as if he'd physically sent a shock through her. She searched his face for any sign that this was some sort of joke, but Dallion found what he needed to see in her gaze: a flicker of hope. She glanced toward the door behind him, but it was still closed. She breathed, "Is he here?"

"He's around," he agreed. "He needs to be careful in Kinsman Lane."

"Take me to him!" she blurted, and he was surprised by the tears that were welling in her eyes. "If he's here, I need to see him."

"Is there a back door to this place?"

She started across the kitchen in answer, drying her hands on her apron as she went. There was another door in the wall to the left, and he followed her through it and into a hallway. They passed three closed doors before she opened the fourth, and he found it to be a sort of storage room filled with crates and barrels. There was a heavy, wooden door in one wall. Abigay opened it to lead him out into a well-tended garden that was bathed in moonlight. Dallion closed the door behind him, then hefted a small, stone bench from its place between two nearby rosebushes and set it against the door to keep anyone else from coming out here. That done, he turned and scanned the gardens for any sign of Journey. There was a five-foot stone wall that surrounded them, but it wasn't tall enough to have kept him out. Dallion made a low whistling sound with his lips, and after only a second or two, a silhouette he recognized appeared from behind a tree near the far corner of the garden.

Abigay had been waiting beside Dallion with her hands clasped before her in excitement, but as soon as she saw Journey's dark shape in the shadow of the wall, she hurried to him. They met in the middle of the flower-laden garden, and she wrapped her arms around him in the tightest of hugs. He hugged her back as a hundred memories of this woman flitted through his head: Auntie Abby telling him a bedtime story when he was six, tending to a scraped knee when he was nine, laughing gaily in the gardens with him and Jubilee when he was twelve. She hitched against him a few times as she began to cry, her face planted squarely against his chest. He held her, whispering that he had missed her, and noticed Dallion's gaze from where he was still standing near the door. There was an exaggerated look of adoration on his face, but Journey ignored him.

At last, Abigay pulled back to look at him. She placed both of her hands on the sides of his face, as if to hold him still so she could study him closely. He was glad when the smile he offered her was returned, and she said past her tears, "I knew it wasn't true, Journey. They said that you'd run off and turned to pirating, but I didn't believe it for a minute."

He didn't have to respond to that; the look in his eyes told her the truth. She pulled back, suddenly furious, and let her right hand fly. It caught him in the cheek with a sharp slap that sounded very loud in the otherwise silent garden. Near the door, Dallion's hand twitched toward the gun tucked against his back out of reflex, but he didn't take it out.

"You have!" Abigay cried, pulling away from him. "It's true!"

Journey put both of his hands together in a pleading gesture. "We need to whisper, Abigay. My life is in your hands right now. If anyone finds out that I'm here..."

"You'll be hanged as a pirate in the square," she hissed, but at least she had lowered the volume of her voice. "And you'll have earned it, Journey. Tell me differently!"

He couldn't tell her any differently, and she knew that. Instead, he said, "I wasn't the one who murdered Jubilee. You have to believe me."

She waved one hand at him in dismissal. "I'm no fool. I know you wouldn't have hurt her if someone had put a gun to your head and demanded it. Her blood is on Landon's hands, rest both their souls." Her eyes narrowed. "But you brought the pirates to Stonewell, didn't you?"

"Abigay..."

"They killed Landon and ransacked the house. They battered the servants, Journey. Poor Bromley had a gash from the top of his head to his eyebrow."

"I was told that none of the servants were harmed," he said, his gaze moving past her to focus coldly on Dallion. He wiggled a hand in the air in a so-so gesture, and Journey scowled. He asked Abigay, "Did they hurt you?"

"I wasn't there," she said. "Your father had sent me to Nymph's Rest just before he...just before your mother died." Journey took both of her hands in his and was glad when she didn't try to pull away. He said, "Abigay, I need you to be honest with me. I need you to tell me what happened between my parents. I want the whole story."

Her eyes flashed in the light of the moon at that, but she said, "I don't know everything..."

"My entire life turned upside-down that day. I need to know the truth about what happened."

Now, she did try to pull her hands from his grasp, but he held them firmly. She was silent for a moment, clearly struggling to come up with a way – any way at all – to avoid answering these questions. Journey pressed, "Please, Abigay. You might be the only person in all of Cruxes who knows the full story."

She held out for a few seconds longer, but finally confessed, "It was a terrible idea. I didn't want her to go through with any of it, but Jubilee insisted. She knew that your father...Landon..." Before she could find the words he so desperately needed, the door behind Dallion banged against the stone bench as someone tried to open it. A man's voice called out from behind it in annoyance, and although his voice was muffled from behind the door, they all made out Abigay's name in it. She clung to Journey's hands for a moment longer, and the fear in her eyes was countered only by her love for the young man she'd helped raise.

Dallion started in the direction of the back garden wall, whispering to Journey as he passed him, "Time to go."

Abigay cast a glance back at the door, which was being banged against the bench repeatedly. When she turned back to Journey, she told him, "Meet me at the docks in a few hours. I'll come to you after Uncle Manton is asleep and all the guests have left. I'll tell you everything you want to know, but you need to get out of here, now. Go!"

She didn't have to tell him twice. He took off at a run on Dallion's heels. Abigay went to the bench at the door, but paused before moving it to make sure they were out of sight. When she turned around, she caught just a glimpse of one of them as they disappeared over the wall. Then she was alone, and she answered her uncle's angry howls with soothing words as she dragged the bench out of the way.

Chapter Fourteen

THE docks in the harbor of Kinsman Lane were old, sagging things that had served fishermen and traders alike for more years than anyone around here could tell. Under the heat of an afternoon sun, they reeked of old fish, but at three o'clock in the morning, the smell wasn't quite as terrible. Most of the docks were currently hosting dark, sleepy ships of various sizes, and the only sounds coming from any of them was that of small waves lapping gently against their hulls. Journey and Dallion had selected one of the few docks that were void of ships, and they stood at the end of it, silhouetted in the moonlight shining down. Its silver reflection in the water around them was a ghostly image that may have been eerie to men who didn't spend so much of their time on the water.

Journey paced in circles at the end of the dock, but Dallion had sat himself down on a wooden crate that some sailor had left behind. He watched Journey pace for a long time before saying, "Maybe she forgot."

It was a joke, but Journey found no amusement in it. Before he could tell him that, his eyes caught movement at the other end of the dock, and he stopped pacing to focus on the newcomer. The figure was clad in a heavy coat that concealed all features, but as the person grew closer to them, the moonlight illuminated their face. Journey breathed a sigh of relief.

Abigay reached them, but didn't pause. Instead, she passed them both and stood at the very end of the dock. Journey waited with all the patience he could muster as she crossed her arms at her chest and stared out over the peaceful harbor. Dallion opened his mouth to say something, but Journey shook his head immediately, and he stayed quiet. Journey was thankful for small wonders.

After a long time, Abigay began to speak, and neither man dared to interrupt. "Jubilee and Landon's marriage was...difficult. He was a violent man. Jubilee would usually make up stories about where her bruises came from, but I knew better. I don't know how much of it you ever noticed, Journey, but I'd always hoped you wouldn't realize what was happening while you were younger."

"I suspected," he answered quietly. "I was afraid that it would get worse for her if I ever said anything about it."

She nodded. "It probably would have, but I still feel like a coward for not trying to help her. No matter how terrible he was to her, all she ever wanted was to please him. They tried for years to have a child. Landon needed a male heir to pass the family fortune to. He didn't want Commercial Horizon to take everything his great-grandfather had built up. Jubilee told me that he was considering divorcing her so he could remarry and try for a son with someone else. She was terrified. It would have left her destitute and alone."

"What changed his mind?"

"Landon received a letter from Commercial Horizon that said he needed to go fight in the war against pirates. He didn't have a choice. The day before he left, Jubilee told him that a miracle had happened: she was with child. I was happy for her. She said that Landon seemed pleased, but also said that he'd told her that it had better be a boy. She mentioned that so nonchalantly, as if it was an ordinary thing for a husband to tell his wife. I wasn't brave enough to ask her what she was going to do if the baby wasn't a boy. I didn't want to worry her, and it was the first time

I'd seen her truly happy in years. I wish I'd pressed her harder, now."

Journey dared to ask the question he already knew the answer to. "Was it a girl?"

Abigay offered a wistful smile out toward the quiet waters before her. "What did Landon tell you?"

"Very little. He said he had a daughter and implied that I wasn't his son. Did my mom have an affair to have me?"

Abigay scoffed at that, and in all the times she'd scolded him as a child, Journey couldn't recall ever hearing such anger in her voice before. "Is that what you think happened? You think Jubilee betrayed her marriage vows? That woman was many things, but she wasn't the type of person to do something like that. It isn't your fault that you don't understand, because we were very careful to keep the secret for so many years, but you need to know that everything Jubilee did for you and Landon, she did out of love."

"I'm trying to understand, Abby. I need you to help me."

She didn't respond to that as she stared out over the moonlit water for a while in silence. Journey gave her more time. He used it to wonder over all of the terrible knowledge this woman had held onto for so many years. Finally, Abigay took her gaze away from the open ocean before her and turned to face him. He found guilt in her eyes that he hadn't expected as she explained, "Landon went off to war. While he was gone, Jubilee gave birth to a baby girl. She was healthy, beautiful, and everything that a new mother could ever ask for. But Jubilee knew what Landon would do when he found out that he still didn't have a male heir for his fortune. I stood next to her bed that night and watched while she wept over her newborn baby. My heart broke for her. I had to do something, so I told her that my grandmother helped run the orphanage here in the Lane. I didn't even realize how bad of an idea it was until I'd already blurted it out. Jubilee couldn't be talked out of it after that. She thought she'd found the perfect way to save herself and her marriage. On top of it all, she'd be rescuing an unwanted baby from a life of poverty. She said that doing such a thing couldn't be considered evil, no matter the reasons behind it. I couldn't say no when she asked me to go to the orphanage with her. That's where we found you."

Journey felt as if someone had punched him in the stomach. He'd managed to accept the fact that he wasn't Landon's flesh and blood, but the possibility that Jubilee hadn't been his real mother had never even crossed his mind. The reality of it hit him so hard that he felt lightheaded, and he swayed on his feet. The dock felt like it was tilting beneath him. In an instant, there was a firm hand on his arm, and he realized that Dallion had stood from the crate he'd been sitting on. He tugged Journey's arm to guide him to the crate, instead, and he sat down heavily on it. He peered up at Abigay in astonishment as Landon's words echoed through the months and years to be heard once again: whore's child.

"Your real mother was a prostitute," Abigay confirmed through her tears. "According to my grandmother, she died in childbirth. You didn't have any other family on the island, so you were placed in the orphanage. You were only a few days old when Jubilee held you for the first time. As soon as you were in her arms, she lit up with pure joy and love. That's how she looked at you every day after that, Journey. You were the light of her life. Landon came back after the war ended four years later. By that time, you were walking and talking. You didn't take to him very well, at first, but you eventually grew to love him. For a long time after that, everything was fine. Jubilee and I had sworn to take the secret to the grave, and Landon had no idea what had happened. You even looked like him: hazel eyes, brown hair, similar height. There was no reason for him to suspect that you weren't his son."

Journey had a million questions, but this throat wouldn't allow any words to pass through it. He stared dazedly down at his hands in his lap, instead. Dallion came to his aid by asking, "How did Landon find out?"

"On the day that Jubilee died, a man came to Stonewell and told Landon a story. The man said that his mother had run the orphanage in the Lane for more than twenty years, and now that the old age disease was ruining her mind, she had started letting things slip out of her mouth that should have been left unsaid. The man was..." She took a deep breath to gather her courage to admit the next few words, but Journey had already put it all together, anyway. Abigay said, "The man was my uncle, Manton Laval. He demanded money from Landon to keep him from tattling to Commercial Horizon. He said it would look like Landon had been trying to fool the company for all those years, and he would lose everything if they thought that. Landon agreed to pay him the money, and then he wrote a letter of his own to Horizon. Landon had Uncle Manton sign it as a witness. It said that Jubilee and 'her adopted son' had lied to him. It cleared Landon's name and painted Jubilee and Journey as liars and frauds."

"And then Landon murdered her," Journey muttered. He recalled the strange man he'd seen in the hallway outside Landon's study on that fateful day and wondered how he'd never suspected something like this before. It was remarkable to have so many more pieces to a puzzle that had been incomplete for his entire life. Nearly the whole picture had come together, now, except for one final detail. He asked Abigay, "What happened to Jubilee and Landon's daughter?"

Abigay shook her head. "I don't know. Jubilee begged the midwife who delivered her to take her away. She agreed to do it. She said that she knew someone who wanted a child, but couldn't have one. She took the baby away that night. Jubilee couldn't bring herself to watch her carry the baby off."

"Do you know the midwife's name?"

She thought about it, and Journey gave her time, his heart sinking. After twenty long years, what chance did they have that she would remember it? She surprised him, however, by saying, "Winnie. I don't know her last name. She was from here, in the Lane. Jubilee and I never spoke of her after that night, but she looked after my cousin, Clara, when she was with child. That was ten years ago, now. The last I knew, she lived somewhere near Coldwater Road."

Journey and Dallion shared a glance at that. Abigay saw this and warned, "Don't try to track her down. She probably doesn't know the truth about her heritage. It's best to let sleeping dogs lie. Information like this can wreck a person's life. Of all people, Journey, you should know that. You should also know that some bonds are stronger than blood. It's true that Landon wasn't your father, and it's also true that Jubilee didn't give birth to you. But I don't care what Landon told you or what anyone else has to say about it. You were Jubilee's son. No one – not Landon, not Commercial Horizon, and not any pirate – can ever take that away from you."

He stood from the crate and wrapped his arms around her in a hug. He told her, "Thank you, Abigay. Thank you for helping my mom when she needed it the most, and thank you for helping me, now. Don't worry about me, alright? I'm going to be okay."

She squeezed him back as tightly as she could. "I'm going to worry about you, anyway. Jubilee wasn't the only person who always loved you like a son."

Chapter Fifteen

JOURNEY and Dallion waited out the last few hours of the night. They could have taken a room at a nearby inn, but decided against it. Journey knew that sleep wasn't something that he'd find tonight, anyway. Instead, he felt like he could have run a mile. The shock of the things he had learned from Abigay had worn off, and it had been replaced with a newfound determination. Landon and Jubilee's daughter was likely somewhere on this island, perhaps only a few miles from him, now. With any luck, the midwife would be able to tell them where to find her in the morning, and it would be the first step in their plan to secure all of the riches that Landon had once promised him. There wasn't enough money in all of Cruxes to make up for the abuse and cruelty that Landon had put Jubilee through, but he supposed it was the best revenge he would be able to get for her, all the same.

They were on the move with the rising sun, following directions that Dallion had obtained from a working girl in town. Coldwater Road wasn't difficult to find, but it turned out to be more of a trail than a road. It dipped between hills and cut through a small stand of woods as it wound its way out of Kinsman Lane toward the western side of the island. A half an hour by foot brought them to a small homestead. Its dilapidated cottage was surrounded by a picket fence, and there was an old, wooden swing hanging from a tree just outside it. In another fenced area, a milk cow and three goats were snacking on a few tufts of grass. A curl of smoke was rising from the cottage's chimney. To Journey, the place looked like a drawing out of a book of fairytales that had come to life.

They stood outside the fence's front gate and took in the sight. Someone was home, judging by the smoke, and with any luck, it would be the midwife they were looking for. Dallion reached for the latch on the gate, meaning to open it so they could start up the path of broken stones to the front door, but he paused as there was a noise from around the corner of the cottage. After a moment, a young woman appeared around it, carrying an armload of firewood. As soon as Journey saw her, he understood that all the remaining pieces of the puzzle had fallen into place in an instant. They may have come here seeking the midwife, but they no longer needed her help. The girl at the corner of the cabin was wearing a brown dress that was stained and worn. The hemline around her ankles was frayed. The flesh on her arms and face was fair and flawless, however, and her high cheekbones graced her with a beauty that nearly took Journey's breath away. But it was her hair that gave her away – a shock of red that was tied back to keep her untamable curls out of her face. This was Jubilee's child, and he would have laughed in the face of anyone who claimed to have doubts.

She noticed the two men at the gate and paused, considering them over the stack of wood in her arms. Dallion offered her his most charming smile and called across the small yard, "Good morning!"

The young woman dumped the load of wood onto the ground at her feet, then took a few steps toward them as she wiped her dirty hands on the apron she was wearing. She only crossed half of the yard, clearly wanting to keep the rest of the distance between herself and the two strangers. She called back, "Can I help you?"

Dallion gave Journey a glance that said he expected him to take over from here, but Journey was speechless. He hadn't thought they might find her here, and now that he had, he felt as if he were seeing a ghost. Dallion elbowed him, and that brought him around a little bit, but he still couldn't think of a single word to say.

Dallion took back over by asking, "Is there a woman here by the name of Winnie?"

She cocked her head to one side in an endearing way. "Why?"

"Someone in town told us we could find her here. She's a midwife, right?"

A sly smile touched her lips, and it melted the hearts of both young men before her. She approached the gate, at last. As she drew near it, she said, "I'm just guessing, but I don't think that either of you are with child. If there's a lady in your lives who is, I'm afraid you've come to the wrong place. You'll need to go back the way you've come and find the house with a red wagon in front of it. That's Lace Carnet's house. She's a midwife."

"Alas, there's no lady in my life," Dallion sighed. "And even if there was, I'm sure she wouldn't be half as beautiful as you."

She gave a dramatic roll of her eyes at his charm. Journey finally found his voice and asked her, "Who's your mother?"

Her brow creased. "It's not every day that someone shows up to a person's own home and asks them who their mother is, but I'll play along. Winnie Moore was my mother. She did live here, but she passed away five years ago."

It may have happened five years ago, but judging by the pain in her eyes at the mention of it, the loss was still fresh. Dallion must have understood Journey's suspicions, at last, because he stuck his hand out over the gate, saying, "It's nice to meet you, Miss…?"

"Saige Moore," she replied, and placed her hand in the one he'd offered. He lifted it to his lips and placed a gentlemanly kiss on the back of it.

He didn't let her hand go right away, but smiled at its owner and said, "Have we got a story for you, Saige."

"This is the craziest thing I've ever heard, and I think you've both lost your minds."

Saige's response wasn't a big surprise to Journey. After all, as he and Dallion had recounted the tale to her, it had started sounding impossible to his own ears. She had allowed them into the yard, and the three of them were now sitting in the soft grass in the shade of a calabash tree. It had taken less than ten minutes for them to explain everything to her – her true heritage, Jubilee's decision, the ensuing lies – but it had apparently been long enough for her to come to the conclusion that they were insane.

Journey said, "I understand that it's a lot to take in. It was hard for me to believe at first, too. But I wouldn't have come all the way out here to tell you this if it wasn't true."

A lock of red hair had escaped its leather tie to rest against her forehead, and she stuck out her bottom lip to blow it away from her eye. Journey found himself wondering what it would be like to brush that hair behind her ear with his fingers, but he pushed the thought from his head as soon as it arrived. She asked him, "Have you guys been to Toma lately? I've heard there's this bug there that can make you go crazy if it bites you. You start seeing things that aren't real…"

"We're not crazy," he assured her. "Actually, Dallion might be, but not about this."

Dallion merely shrugged in agreement. It brought a smile to her face, and they were glad to see it. Still, she insisted, "Twenty-two years ago, Winnie Moore gave birth to a healthy daughter and named her Saige. That's me. She had the baby lines on her belly to prove it. My father's name is Francis, and he'll be home any minute, now. When he gets here and finds two men that he doesn't know pestering his daughter with some crazy, make-believe stories, he's going to tell you both to leave, and he isn't going to be nice about it."

Dallion huffed, clearly losing patience, but Journey tried another tactic. "Which of them gave you your red hair?"

She frowned. "Nice try. My mother said that my great-grandmother had red hair like mine. Sometimes it shows back up in a family again a few babies later. It's not magic. Now, I can't say this hasn't been fun, but I wasn't kidding about my father. You should both get out of here before he gets home."

Dallion tipped his head away from her to conceal the look that he gave Journey, and he understood what he was trying to say with just a lift of his eyebrows and a shift of his eyes in Saige's direction: they could make her come with them, whether she wanted to or not. Journey gave his head the slightest shake, however. Instead, he pressed, "You're giving up a great opportunity, Miss Moore."

She heaved a sigh, but didn't tell them to leave again. Not yet. "Alright, I'll bite. What kind of opportunity?"

"When your real father, Landon Travert, died two years ago, there were no known heirs to inherit his fortune."

"His big fortune," Dallion said, leaning toward her to whisper the words. "I mean, before this guy died, he probably had enough money to pay someone to wipe his ass for him."

"He was ass-wiping rich?" she asked, amused. "Tell me more."

Journey explained, "His parent company was Commercial Horizon. When he died, they claimed all of his assets. They took ownership of his islands, ships, crops, and everything else. Now, if a viable heir were to show up, Horizon would have to surrender all of those things back to him...or her."

Something changed in her at that, and a quick look around at this place made it easy to understand why. The property wasn't in terrible shape, but it was clear that it had been a few years since it had last seen any real maintenance. The cottage's roof was beginning to sag on one side, and most of the shutters had fallen off or were contemplating doing so. The cow and goats looked well-fed, but the fence holding them in was in disrepair. It was a miracle that they hadn't escaped, yet. Considering all of this and the worn state of the dress that Saige was wearing, she and her father could have used the money.

Her tone was only half-joking when she said to Journey, "Let me get this straight: you find out that you're not who you thought you were, your father cuts you off, and after he's dead, you come out here to tell me all about this money that rightfully belongs to me. You're doing it all out of the kindness of your heart. Is that about right?"

Dallion held up a finger. "Hold on a second – no one ever said anything about kind hearts. We want twenty percent of everything you inherit. Think of it as a finder's fee."

She threw her head back and laughed, and both men struggled to take their eyes off of her. When she looked at them again, it was with an expression that said she'd figured them out. "I was wondering when this was going to turn out to be some sort of scam. I can't believe I gave you the time..."

"This isn't a scam," Dallion argued, but Saige pointed at him, her laughter drying up completely.

"You're a pirate if I've ever seen one," she declared. To Journey, she admitted, "You're a little harder to figure out, but if you're working with this fool, then I can only assume you're a swindler, too. Now, if the two of you aren't off this property in the next thirty seconds, I'm going to start screaming for help. The nearest neighbors are within hearing range. It's Mr. Houseman and his three sons, and they'll come running with shotguns. Got it?"

Journey raised two calming hands. "That isn't necessary."

"Prove it," she dared. "Leave."

Dallion got to his feet, cussing the young woman under his breath, and started for the gate. Journey stood, as well, but said, "We'll be staying at Carla's Place in town. It's near the docks. If you change your mind before noon tomorrow, you can find us there. Please think about it, Miss Moore." He paused, then corrected himself. "Miss Travert."

She pointed at the gate, and the stern look on her face ensured him that their conversation was over. Journey followed Dallion out of the yard, but he silently vowed to come back and try again tomorrow. For the first time in two years, he heard Jubilee's voice speak up in his head: This isn't finished.

Chapter Sixteen

FRANCIS Moore returned home an hour later. Saige had been watching for him through the window of their home, and when he rounded the end of the fence to pass through the gate and into the yard, she noted how pronounced his limp was today. He was sixty, now, and accident three years ago had left him with a hip that didn't always want to work quite right. It tended to act up whenever rain was on its way. One glance at the darkening clouds in the west told her that his old bones were right, as usual.

Saige opened the door for him when he reached it, and he thanked her as he shuffled to the table in the middle of the kitchen. He collapsed onto one of the chairs there with a grunt, then pulled a handkerchief from his pocket and wiped his forehead with it. Saige let him catch his breath for a little while as she went to the stove in the corner and fetched him a bowl of soup from the pot there. As she set it on the table before him, she leaned down to kiss his cheek. That coaxed a smile to his wrinkled face, and he gave her a loving pat on her shoulder. Saige sat down with her own bowl of soup, but she merely stirred it with her spoon, instead of eating it. She asked, "How did everything go?"

"Fine," he answered. "Mrs. Bloom is going to send some wool out here in two days, and I've arranged for three chickens to be delivered to replace the ones the fox got last month."

"He took another one last night," she said, not lifting her eyes from the soup she was still stirring. "I found her this morning."

Francis frowned. When he saw the sadness on his daughter's face, however, he forced himself to brighten and said, "I saw Edgar Shaw while I was in town. He asked me to send you his best wishes."

Saige didn't answer as she continued to stir her soup. Francis added, "He's still unmarried, you know. He's looking."

"We've already talked about this. If I were to leave and get married, you wouldn't be able to run things around here on your own. Not with that hip of yours, anyway. Besides, I can't stand Ed Shaw. Most nights, he gets falling-down drunk at Carla's Place and starts trying to talk every woman he sees into going home with him."

Francis didn't reply to that, and Saige immediately regretted how sour her tone had been. She muttered, "I'm sorry. I'm sure Ed is a good man."

"Don't worry yourself over it," Francis told her kindly. He began telling her a story about something else that had happened while he'd been in town today, but Saige was hardly listening. Her soup had cooled so that it was only lukewarm, now, and she still didn't eat it. She had no appetite. Her spoon made slow, delicate circles in it. Her thoughts were on the young men who had visited her earlier…and some of the things they had told her.

"Saige?" Francis asked. "Are you even listening?"

She looked up from the soup, an apologetic look on her face. "I was lost in thought, daddy."

"What are you thinking of?"

She knew better than to tell him that she'd sat and chatted with two men she suspected of being pirates. Instead, she asked him, "How old was momma when she had me?"

"Oh, I don't remember," he answered, and she didn't think it was her imagination when his eyes shifted slightly to the left to avoid looking at her. "You know I'm no good with things like that. Why do you want to know?"

"No reason," she lied. "I was just curious."

"She was always so proud of you," he said, and that stung her heart. She decided to put the things that the pirates had said out of her head for good.

"Eat your soup, daddy," she told him. "There's more if you want it."

Journey and Dallion retreated to the nearest tavern, where Dallion proceeded to drink more than he probably should have. Journey merely stared into his cup and let himself contemplate everything that had happened lately. He hadn't realized how much he had missed Abigay until he'd seen her last night, and he was glad he had. He regretted the fact that her uncle was treating her so poorly, but it was a miracle that Landon hadn't killed her when he'd learned that she had known Jubilee's secret all along. He wondered what she would think if she knew that Jubilee's daughter had been living so close by this entire time. Perhaps Abigay and Saige had even passed one another on the street in Kinsman Lane, at some point. The Realm of Cruxes was incredibly vast, but it sometimes felt surprisingly small.

They took a room that night at Carla's Place, just as Journey had told Saige they would. Dallion pulled rank to claim the bed. Journey stretched out on the floor with a blanket that Dallion tossed to him, but he still didn't feel tired. He kept thinking about Saige and her melodic laughter. As he stared up into the darkness around him, he could almost see the pretty curls of her hair and the easy smile that had touched her lips when she'd laughed. Sleep wasn't coming to him anytime soon. Finally, he gave up on that and spoke, shattering the silence in the room with a whisper. "Dallion?"

He hadn't really expected him to be awake, but he responded with, "What?"

"What's the story behind the necklace?"

Dallion didn't answer, at first. He had demanded that Journey return it and the rest of his jewelry back to him as soon as they'd arrived at the docks last night, and the shark tooth on the necklace in question was currently resting on his shirtless chest. Just as Journey decided that he wasn't going to tell him, he said, "My father was a drunk who only ever knew how to talk to me with his fists. My mother wasn't much better, but at least she didn't hit so hard. Anyway, I spent a lot of time away from home when I was a kid. There was this girl who was a year younger than me. Her name was Katria. Her father had died when she was a baby, and her mother had fallen in love with some sailor and took off with him. So Katria only had her older brother and their grandmamma. I spent a lot of my childhood in the woods around their house, playing with Bo and Kat. Eventually, Bo went and took a position on a Western Straights ship, and then it was just me and Kat."

There was silence for a moment, but Journey didn't push. After a while, Dallion continued, "When I was fourteen and she was thirteen, her mother came back. The sailor guy hadn't worked out, but she'd found a man who had some money and she'd married him. She wanted to take Kat away with her so they could all live together as a family. Kat didn't want to go, but she didn't have a choice. The morning before they left, I sat with her on the beach and we watched the gulls flying around, and I told her that I loved her. Not just that kid kind of love, either, but real love that you're just not sure how to deal with at that age. She reached into the sand and pulled out the shark tooth, and we saw that it had a little nick in the side, so it didn't look like most teeth. She told me to keep it with me always, because one day, when we were older, we'd find each other again, and if we didn't recognize each other, I could show her this tooth and we'd both know."

He fell silent again, and although there was more to the story than that, he didn't want to share it. How could he put into words what he'd felt for Katria on that day? How they had held each other closely in the sand as they'd listened to the nearby gulls crying out to the sea, or how she had whispered his name in his ear, or how she'd sworn to love him forever, no matter how long their parting was…All these long years later, he could still see her when he closed his eyes. He could still smell the salt of the sea and feel the warmth of the beach beneath them.

"Is that why you decided to leave and become a pirate?" Journey asked from the darkness.

"No. I started pirating because I'm an asshole who likes to steal other people's things."

There was a second or two when neither of them said anything, and then they both broke into laughter.

Chapter Seventeen

SAIGE woke with a start at the crack of thunder just above the cottage. Her heart was racing and the bedsheets were in a tangle around her legs. Her cheeks were wet with tears. She couldn't recall the terrible dream she'd been having, but she knew that it had had something to do with the young men who had visited. She couldn't explain why, but she'd woken with a heavy feeling of regret, as if she had missed out on something truly remarkable.

It was dark in the pantry room that doubled as her bedroom, as there was no window, but she didn't doubt that lightning was illuminating the entire island outside before each deafening crack of thunder. The wind was howling around the sides of the house, and she could hear the pattering sound of water as the roof leaked somewhere in the next room. She detangled herself from the bedsheets and slid her hand along the top of the wooden crate beside her bed to find the candle she kept there. There were a handful of matches beside it, and she grasped one of them in the dark and struck it. The warm glow of the tiny flame was a welcome thing. She lit the candle with it and fetched her shawl from the hook on the wall near the door, putting it on over her nightgown. This room was cold, but not quite as cold as it should have been, and she understood why when she saw the soft light of flames in the kitchen's fireplace dancing through the gap between the bottom of her door and the floor. She opened it and stepped out into the kitchen to find that the fire was, in fact, roaring. Francis was sitting at the table in the middle of the room, clad in his nightclothes. There was a cup of tea before him, but it was mostly untouched. He started as Saige came into the room, but he offered her an apologetic smile through the pain written across his face.

"I didn't mean to wake you," he said, straightening in his chair a little in an attempt to hide how badly his hip was hurting. "I couldn't sleep, so I thought I'd have a cup and wait for this storm to end."

"The storm's what woke me," she said, looking around for the leak she'd heard. She spotted it not far from the door, but Francis had already placed a bucket beneath it. That was fine, then, and she could have gone back to bed...but she still felt haunted by her dream. She joined her father at the table, sitting down on the opposite side of it, and set her candle down in the middle. In its light, Francis looked older than he already was. The dark circles beneath his eyes certainly didn't help, but when he noticed her look of concern, he waved it off with one hand.

"The pain isn't that bad," he fibbed. "I could sleep through it, but this storm..."

As if to prove his point, thunder cracked outside again, and Saige thought she could feel the cottage shaking with the rumble. She drew her shawl tighter around her shoulders. Her arms were covered in goosebumps, despite the warmth of the nearby fire. She hesitated for a moment, but the hidden truths that she so desperately needed to learn pushed her to finally say, "Two men stopped here to visit. They came while you were in town."

Francis had been about to take a sip of his tea, but now he paused, eyebrows raised. "Oh? Who were they?"

"I don't know. They didn't mean any harm, but..." She shrugged. "They told me an interesting story."

Francis set his cup aside, clearly concerned by the nervousness in his daughter's voice and the way she wouldn't meet his gaze. He demanded, "Were they vulgar? What did they want from you?"

"It wasn't like that," she clarified, but didn't know how to proceed. She was once again tempted to forget all about it and go back to bed, after all, but the feeling that her dream had left behind was too powerful to ignore.

She gathered her courage and asked in a small voice, "Am I really your daughter?"

Thunder crashed again outside, but she didn't think that was the reason for the slight widening of Francis' eyes. He looked away, but not before she saw the truth in them. He reached for his cup of tea and nearly knocked it over with an unsteady hand. He managed to lift it to his lips and took a long drink from it in a stall for time. When he finally set the cup back down, he gave her a tight laugh that she didn't buy and said, "I don't know why you would ever ask a question like that, Saige. It's insulting, to be honest."

"Lying is an insult, daddy," she said. Her heart was racing again, but she told herself that there was no reason to jump to conclusions, yet. "Even if it's done to protect someone you care about."

"I have no reason to lie to you about something like that," he said, but Francis was an honest man, and he'd never gotten the knack for telling falsehoods. He finished the rest of his tea and then set the cup down before her. "Be a dear and get me some more."

Saige didn't move, and when Francis' eyes met hers, she saw raw fear in them. He told her, "I don't know where all this is coming from, Saige, but it's ridiculous. Your mother and I raised you, cared for you, and loved you. We did everything that good parents could be expected to do."

"I've never doubted that you love me," she said. A few tears that she hadn't expected rolled down her cheeks, but she ignored them. She pressed, "I just want to know why it was a secret that you two weren't my real parents."

He opened his mouth to argue further, but he couldn't seem to find the words to do so. Instead, he simply looked at Saige and she at him. The storm continued to rage outside, but neither of them were paying it any attention. The seconds spun out, and there was a tight feeling in Saige's chest that was either sadness or excitement. She couldn't tell which.

Francis' face twisted into a mixture of shame and sorrow, and Saige was surprised when he began to cry. Tears spilled from his eyes and his chest hitched beneath his nightshirt. He offered one hand to her in the middle of the table, and she grasped it with loving firmness.

"You were never supposed to know," he sobbed. The flickering light from the candle reflected prettily in his tears. "Your mum didn't want you to find out, and I swore to her that I'd never let you know the truth. She was so worried that you'd think we loved you less or that you might go looking for your birth mother."

Saige shook her head slowly, desperately trying to grasp all that he was saying. Her grip on his hand was so tight that it was painful, but neither of them let go. She breathed, "Who is she?"

"I don't know," Francis said, and she believed him; there was too much pain and fear in his voice for her to doubt him. "Winnie never told me who she was. She brought you home one day, out of the blue. We'd had a child some years before, named Ivy, and she had been the world to us. She got sick with the red welts before her second birthday, and we lost her. We were devastated. We tried for years to have another, but it never took. I'd thought we'd both given up on it, but then your mother came home one day with the most beautiful little baby I'd ever seen. She told me I could never tell anyone that you weren't really ours. I was afraid she'd stolen you from somewhere, but I couldn't send you back, even if that was the case. I took one look at you and I fell in love. We raised you as our own, and as far as I'm concerned, you are our child. You may not be my daughter out of flesh and blood, but you're mine by love, and that's always been good enough for me."

Saige left her chair and came around the table to put her arms around him. Francis sobbed against her shoulder as she leaned to hug him, and he put his arms around her waist. They held one another for a long time as the storm continued outside. Now, there was another storm, and it was in Saige's heart. A part of her wished the pirates hadn't sought her out to tell her the truth. Another part yearned for more of it.

"You know I love you, daddy," she whispered. "And you know I loved mum with all my heart. But this is very important, and I need to know the rest of the story. The men who came to see me were certain that my birth mother was a woman named Jubilee Travert. Do you recognize that name?"

He nodded against her shoulder, and when he spoke again, she was glad to hear that he had started to settle down, now. "The Travert family owns the Twin Islands up north. But I don't know if the Travert woman…If she was your real…" He sighed.

"Please, daddy," she urged. "Think back. In all those years, mum never gave any sort of clue about it?"

"There's a letter," he whispered, and her heart leapt. "Winnie wrote a letter right after she brought you home. It was never to be opened, unless someone came asking about you and accused us of kidnapping. I've never read it. Winnie sealed it right away and told me never to touch it."

"Where is it?"

He let her go and stood, groaning at the pain in his hip. Saige felt a sudden wave of exhaustion overtake her. Her whole life had just been turned on its head, and she felt dizzy. She sat down in the chair that Francis had just left and waited as he limped his way into his bedroom. After a little while, he returned, holding a sealed envelope. There was nothing written on the front of it. Francis offered it to her, but before she could take it from him, he warned, "Whatever you might read, you need to remember that your mum loved you dearly. We both did. We never wanted anything but happiness for you."

Saige nodded, and he let go of the envelope. She tore it open and pulled a single page of paper out of it. She unfolded it to find Winnie's flowing handwriting. There weren't a great many women on Kinsman Island who could read, but Winnie Moore had always believed in educating her daughter. Saige read the words on the page, her heart racing faster with each sentence.

I, Winnie Stephens Moore, am writing this to protect myself and my family in the event that the pedigree of our daughter is ever questioned. My husband and I are not kidnappers. Although we did not come to adopt our daughter, Saige, in the most usual of circumstances, her birth mother surrendered her to us to raise as our own, albeit without the knowledge of the father. The two witnesses who can testify to what happened are Mrs. Jubilee Travert (birth mother) and a servant girl under her employ, Abigay Laval. They can testify on my behalf, if necessary.

It was signed with Winnie's name. There was a date at the top of the page, and Saige saw that it was the same year as her birth. The paper was yellowed and brittle from over twenty years of sitting in a drawer somewhere. As she read it a second time, a tear fell onto the page and soaked through it, smearing the word daughter.

Francis had gone to the fireplace to add a piece of wood from the pile beside it, but he stopped what he was doing as Saige left the table and joined him there. She grasped both of his hands in hers, and through teary eyes, she said, "There's something I have to do."

Chapter Eighteen

BY sunrise, the storm had diminished and there was nothing more than a gentle shower outside. Journey and Dallion ventured downstairs for breakfast, which turned out to be eggs and cabbage. Considering the cheap rates at Carla's Place, they hadn't expected anything better. A woman who couldn't have been more than eighteen or nineteen flirted with them while she served it. Dallion played her game, but Journey was too distracted for such things. He ate a little, but ended up simply pushing the eggs and cabbage around on his plate, lost in thought. Dallion had to say his name twice to get his attention, and Journey realized that he hadn't heard a word he'd said to him in the last ten minutes.

Before he could confess such to Dallion, the front door of the tavern banged open, and the figure that stood in the doorway was a wetter, more desperate version of the young woman he'd just been thinking of. Saige's long, red hair had come loose from its leather tie and now hung around her shoulders in wet tangles. Her dress – the same one she had been wearing yesterday – was soaked with rain, and mud from the road dripped from the bottom of it. The handful of other people who were eating breakfast in the room spared her a glance at the sound of the door opening, but they dismissed her after only a moment. Journey couldn't have done that if he'd tried. In her soaked, out-of-breath, almost frantic state, she looked like some beautiful, feral creature that he'd never dared to dream of. Dallion turned in his chair to follow Journey's gaze, and he brightened at the sight of the young woman in the doorway. She noticed the two men at the table, and a look of relief caressed her face. She approached their table, and Journey wondered if she was aware of how easily she could have commanded him, if she tried.

As she reached them, Dallion shoved an empty chair out from beneath the table with his foot. Saige sat down in it and unshouldered the small, leather pack that she'd brought with her. She set it between her feet beneath the table, then considered the two men in turn: Journey to her left, Dallion on her right.

"Change your mind, doll?" Dallion grinned, and Journey kicked his ankle under the table. They needed this girl to trust them, and making her angry wasn't the best way to do that.

She didn't seem all that annoyed, however. Instead, she looked nervous. She set her hands neatly on the table before her and said, "Eight."

"Eight?"

"Eight percent. You said yesterday that you want twenty percent of anything I inherit. I think eight is fair."

Dallion grinned. "Ten."

She nodded, sticking her hand out to him, and Dallion shook it. Her flesh was cold from the rain outside, but her grip was firm. When he let her go, he asked, "What made you change your mind?"

"That's none of your business," she answered, her curt tone daring him to press her on it. "All that matters to you is that I'm here, and I'm willing to go with you to the Isle of Ruin, or whatever you called it."

"Runes," Journey offered. "Commercial Horizon is headquartered there. They're the ones who took ownership of your father's wealth." It was still strange to refer to Landon as her father, instead of his own.

"And you're okay with all of this?" she asked him. "I've spent the morning wondering why a man who lost a fortune might be so willing to surrender it to someone else. You really don't feel cheated?"

"Of course not," he said, but neither she nor Dallion were fooled. "It's all yours by blood. I just don't want the company to keep it all, when there's a viable heir who could use the money."

Dallion slapped the table, making Saige jump. "So," he grinned, "daylight's burning. Let's get moving."

It wasn't until Saige was trailing behind them a short distance on their way to the shore that she became aware of how vulnerable she'd made herself. Here she was, trekking across an uninhabited stretch of the island with two men whom she barely knew and suspected to be pirates. What had she gotten herself into? Francis had practically begged her not to go through with this, and he didn't even know most of the details. If he'd known where she was right now, the poor man's heart would likely have given out.

She took a deep breath and reminded herself that Journey and Dallion hadn't done or said anything unseemly to her, so far. They were speaking in low voices ahead of her as they walked, occasionally laughing at something the other had said. They appeared to be good friends, despite Journey's more educated way of speaking and Dallion's crass attitude. She felt drawn to like them both, but wouldn't admit that, even to herself. She'd never associated with pirates before, but she knew for certain that they couldn't be trusted. There were plenty of local stories about murder, theft, and rape that had convinced her of that.

They reached the shore, where Dallion introduced her to Old Rube and Wee Bit. They were sitting before a small campfire and looked miserable in wet, muddy clothes. Wee Bit was angry that they'd had to stay out here in the storm with nothing more than an overturned longboat to keep them sheltered, but his irritation was soothed when Saige introduced herself to him. She was embarrassed by how deeply she blushed when Wee Bit gave her a dramatic bow and kissed the back of her hand. Journey and Old Rube readied the longboat, and once all five of its passengers were inside, they rowed her out into open waters. Saige gripped the edges of her bench so hard that her knuckles turned white, and when Journey asked if she was alright, she confessed, "I've never been out on the water before."

"The ship isn't far from here," he assured her. "If you start to feel seasick, look out at the horizon. That should help."

She didn't feel sick, but she fixed her eyes on the horizon, all the same. Eventually, the island was out of sight, and there was only ocean around them. She asked anyone who would answer, "Aren't there sharks out here?"

Dallion leaned to peer over the side of the boat. "I've never seen a shark on land, so where else would they be?"

Her eyes narrowed, but she stayed quiet. Before long, a ship came into view, and Saige brightened at the sight of it. It was beautiful, made of rich wood that must have cost a respectable fortune. The figurehead on the front was a regal-looking woman in a flowing dress. As they drew closer, Saige breathed, "What ship is this?"

"She's the Jubilee," Journey answered, and Saige was surprised to recognize the name as her birth mother's. Her curiosity concerning the men she was with deepened, but she bit back her questions, for now, and focused on the ship that would bear her toward her promised fortune.

They were hauled aboard the ship by several crewmembers. Saige peered around the deck with unconcealed awe as she watched men scramble to ready the sails. Lucien met Dallion and Journey nearby, and Dallion clapped his old friend on the shoulder in greeting. Lucien eyed Saige for a moment before saying, "Everything went according to plan, I see."

Dallion nodded toward Saige. "Lucien, this is Saige Moore."

"Travert," Journey corrected him. Saige seemed not to have heard them; she was far too distracted by the massive, white sails that were being lowered directly over her head.

Dallion cast a glance around and found the ship to be in the same shape they'd left it in, but asked Lucien, anyway, "You made it through the storm alright?"

"It wasn't pretty, but there aren't any damages that we can't repair while sailing. I set up an area in one of the stores below that the girl can stay in. It cost you a blanket from your cabin, but she needed something to sleep on. It'll be better for her to sleep there, instead of in one of the hammocks in the crew's quarters."

Journey considered the few crewmen who had paused in their work around the deck to gawk at the woman they'd brought on board. He suggested, "We should lay down some rules..."

"I've already done that," Lucien replied. "No one is going to touch her, and if she complains that anyone has hassled her, there'll be hell to pay."

Journey didn't doubt that for a second. Lucien didn't often need to threaten the crew with physical punishments, but with something like this, the man wouldn't have hesitated.

Dallion didn't bother with introducing her to any of the crewmen, but had Lucien get the ship underway immediately.

Before long, her sails were full of wind and they were making good time. Journey accompanied Saige to the small corner below that would be hers for the voyage. She held up the lantern he'd given her to get a good look at the blanket she was to sleep on. It was nestled between the hull and a row of wooden barrels, and although she let a disappointed sigh escape her, she forced herself to say, "It's wonderful. Thank you."

"I'm not sure I'd call it wonderful," Journey grinned as he leaned against a nearby barrel, "but it beats sleeping out on the deck. Trust me."

"How long will it take to get to the Isle of Runes?"

He considered. "Seven days, as long as the wind doesn't put up a fight. Maybe six and a half, if Lucien really pushes it."

She sat down on the blanket and arranged her dress so that it was spread out around her. Journey started to leave, but paused as Saige told him, "I've never been away from home before. Not off of Kinsman, anyway. And I never thought I'd step foot on a pirate ship."

He didn't comment, so she pressed, "You can stop pretending that you aren't pirates. You know I guessed that the first time I saw you. Besides, I may not have ever been on a ship before, but I'm not completely clueless. The Jubilee isn't flying any flags. Something tells me that she's not registered in any ports, either."

Journey merely shrugged, but there was an edge to his voice when he spoke. "You already knew what we are, Miss Travert. Don't act surprised about it, now."

"I'm not," she said, and she gave him a sly smile that made him want her. "But if anyone finds out that I'm associating with pirates, I'm going to say that you kidnapped me."

"You can try, but Dallion's likely to sell you out as the captain, if it'll save his own neck."

She laughed, and the sound sent a pleasant chill down his back. He decided that he needed to stay away from this girl as much as he could – there was too much about her to like. She sobered after a moment, and asked him seriously, "Am I safe here, Journey?"

"From what I understand, Lucien has already laid down the law about you. No one should give you a hard time. Besides, Dallion's crew isn't as cutthroat and savage as a lot of the stories you hear about crews like this. They're mostly just decent men who are trying to make enough money to retire on so they can go back to their families."

Her gaze was piercing in a way that made him uncomfortable. "And what about you?"

"I'm just along for the ride," he replied, and they both wondered how true that was.

CHAPTER NINETEEN

WEE Bit and a crewman they called Quick Bill took turns bringing meals down to Saige for the next two days, but by the end of the second, she felt like she might go insane if she remained cooped up any longer. She'd hardly had any visitors down here, aside from her meal deliveries and Brain, who was fascinated to have her aboard. She found him a delight to be around, despite (or perhaps because of) his awkwardness toward her. He came down to see her a few times each day, and she would tell him stories that she had heard from other seafarers who had put into port in Kinsman Lane. He would listen for nearly an hour at a time, until Lucien would send someone down to fetch him for some other task he had been shirking in order to spend time with her.

Finally, Saige headed up to the deck. The fresh air met her like a warm embrace, and she let out an audible gasp at the sight of the sunset on the western horizon. She couldn't recall ever having seen anything so beautiful in her life. Most of the pirates were finishing up their work for the day, and she retreated toward the bow of the ship to try to stay out of their way. Wee Bit spotted her and asked if she needed anything, but she assured him that she'd only wanted a little bit of air. She ignored the stares and lustful glances from other crewmen whom she didn't know and opted to let her attention return to the breathtaking sunset off the port side of the ship.

Someone appeared beside her, and she was pleased to find that it was Dallion. He leaned against the banister she was standing at, a rogue's smile on his face. "I was wondering how long you'd keep to yourself down there. Lonely?"

"I missed you terribly, Dallion," she teased. "I couldn't get you off my mind."

"I have that effect on women," he agreed. He admired the shine of the dying sun in her hair and wondered fleetingly if Lucien's 'don't touch her' rule also applied to him. He pushed the thought away and told her, "You should have dinner with me in my cabin tonight."

She shot him a look of suspicion, and he clarified, "It won't be just us. And it'll be strictly business."

She had doubts that anything with this young man could be strictly business, but she told him she would be there and watched him as he made his way down the length of the ship to the helm. There, he spoke with the helmsman, and Saige's gaze returned to the sea. The sun was nearly gone, now, swallowed up by the unending water. She wondered if her father was doing alright on his own and realized that she needed to decide if she was still going to call him that. It took her only a few seconds to decide that yes, Francis had been and always would be her father, whether by blood or not.

After a while, as the skies grew dark and heavy with nightfall, a bell tolled somewhere on the ship. She assumed that it meant that it was dinnertime, and she wasn't wrong. There were a few men still on the deck – what she didn't doubt was some sort of night crew – but they paid her no attention as she made her way to the captain's quarters. She knocked on the door and immediately received a call to come in.

She entered to find a rather lavish room, compared to the rest of the ship. The varying shades of blue were pleasing to the eye. The large, canopied bed had been pushed into a corner, and a long table had been brought in here from somewhere else on the ship. It currently dominated the center of the room. She was glad to see that Dallion hadn't lied when he'd said that they wouldn't be alone in here. Aside from him, there were four others sitting around the table and serving themselves from dishes that had been lined down its center. A delicious aroma hung heavy in the air, and she knew it wouldn't be the same salted meat and hardtack that had been served for almost every meal she'd had on this ship, so far.

The men had been in the middle of a conversation, but they all fell silent as Saige entered. She recognized Dallion, Journey, and Lucien, but the other two were strangers to her. One of these latter stood and politely moved a chair for her. It was near Dallion's chair, which was at the head of the table, and across from Journey's. Saige thanked the man and sat down.

"Help yourself," Dallion invited, sweeping an arm over the feast on the table. Dishes were heaped with fish, cabbage, boiled eggs, olives, grapes, potatoes, and some sort of meat that Saige didn't recognize. Her stomach grumbled at the opportunity to have real food again. As she loaded her plate with some of it, Dallion motioned to each of the men at the table in turn. "You already know Journey. He's my first mate. I think you've met Lucien. He's the quartermaster. Then there's Pigeon, the sailing master, and Paul, the deck officer." To the men he'd just introduced, he said, "This is Saige Travert, and this little feast is to celebrate all the money she's about to earn for us."

"I wouldn't say that there's a lot of earning involved," she admitted. "I'm going to ask someone at Commercial Horizon for what's mine. Hopefully, they'll say yes."

"They'll say yes," Dallion assured her. "But we need to talk about the plan from here. Obviously, we can't take the Jubilee too close to the Isle of Runes, so we'll need to charter a boat somewhere to take us the last leg of the trip."

"Why?" Saige asked between bites of potato.

Dallion gave her a look that said her question was a stupid one, but Lucien clarified, "Horizon knows this ship for what she is. We can outrun their galleons without a problem, but it would be suicide to get too close to their home port."

She nodded to indicate she understood, though she wasn't sure what the difference was between a galleon and this ship, aside from the fact that this one was apparently faster. She was amazed by the fact that, although she had grown up in a port town, she knew next to nothing about the vessels that roamed the seas.

Pigeon suggested, "Claymill could be an option."

Dallion had already thought of this. Claymill was a small island southeast of the Isle of Runes that housed a half a dozen factories that produced various pottery and porcelain goods. Some of the finest porcelain on this side of the Great Trench came from Claymill, and it was a popular trading stop for multiple companies. The people who called Claymill their home, however, were not beholden solely to them, and they were most often willing to turn a blind eye to suspicious ships, so long as the money was good. It would be easy to find a trade ship there willing to take a few passengers to the Isle of Runes. Dallion pointed a finger at Pigeon in agreement. "Claymill's our ticket. Lucien, you'll stay with the Jubilee after dropping me off on Claymill. Saige, Journey, and Tawny Paul will come with me. We'll buy our way onto a merchant ship to take us to Runes. Saige, you'll take over from there. They'll probably want proof that you're a Travert brat, but you're just going to have to let your charm and good looks convince them."

"I have proof," she said as she took a helping of the mystery meat from the platter it was on. "I have a letter that my mother left behind. It explains what happened."

"Letter?" Journey asked, his eyes sharp. "You didn't mention that before."

She paused in eating to reach into the pocket of her dress and brought out a slip of paper that had been folded into a small square. She handed it across the table to him, and he snatched it from her a little too quickly. She watched with a degree of curiosity as Journey withdrew from the table to go sit on the foot of the bed, unfolding the paper as he went.

Dallion ignored all of this. To Tawny Paul, he said, "When we get to Claymill, you'll be in charge of getting us disguises. We need to look respectable."

"Is that something you're capable of?" Lucien teased, but Dallion ignored this, as well. When he was on a roll, it was hard to distract him.

He told Saige, "Ask for everything in cash. As soon as they hand it over, we'll catch the next ship out of port and make our way back to Claymill."

"We'll be waiting for you there," Lucien promised, but Dallion shook his head.

"Meet us there five days after you drop us off. I don't want the Jubilee hanging around any ports that close to Runes in the meantime. Make yourselves scarce, got it?"

He was speaking to both Lucien and Pigeon at this point, and both men nodded in answer. Saige asked, "What if we aren't back on Claymill in five days?"

"Then it probably means you've been found out and hanged," Pigeon replied, and no one tried to argue that. They knew he was right.

Dinner was washed down with generous amounts of rum, and it wasn't long before Saige's head was swimming. She tried to conceal that fact, but the relaxed and contented look on her face gave her away. Eventually, Tawny Paul excused himself to go to bed. Lucien wasn't far behind him, off to check up on the night crew above deck before heading to bed, himself. That left Journey, Dallion, and Saige, and both of the latter two were drunk. Journey had only sipped his share of the rum, and although he'd returned to the table since finishing his third read of the letter that Winnie Moore had written so long ago, he hadn't participated much in conversation with the others. Instead, he'd fallen into a state of pensive silence, barely even speaking when asked a question directly.

Once Lucien was gone, Dallion left the table and collapsed onto his back on his bed, stretching out to somehow take up most of the space on a mattress made for two. Saige asked him, "What's the difference between a galleon and the Jubilee?"

"Size, for one thing," he answered as he turned onto his side to look at her. "A galleon is bigger. A lot of them have three masts, but some have more. The Jubilee is a brigantine, so she's smaller, but she's faster. She can turn deeper into a headwind, too. Then there are schooners and sloops. They're even smaller, and they're usually fore-and-aft rigged, instead of square."

She hadn't understood half of what he'd said, but she didn't want to admit that and risk taking away some of the joy that explaining such things had clearly brought him. Instead, she asked, "How did you come to be a captain?"

"Hard work, lies, and luck. How'd you come to be a beautiful woman in the midst of filthy pirates?"

"Just lucky, I guess."

Journey managed to pull himself out of his pensiveness enough to tell them, "You're both drunk and I'm tired. It's time for bed." He stood from his chair, but Saige's smile disappeared, and she reached a hand out over the table, as if hoping he would take hold of it.

"Stay," she pouted, and although it was childish, he found it endearing. He didn't hold her hand, but he did sit back down. Satisfied, she explained, "I haven't had anyone to talk to except Adam for the last two days. I could use some more company for a little while."

Dallion nearly asked her who Adam was before realizing it was the first time he'd heard Brain referred to by his real name in years. A laugh escaped his lips before he knew it was coming, prompting Journey and Saige to share a knowing look. He'd been right to call Dallion drunk. Saige asked him, "What's with all the blue, Dallion?"

"It's one of the only colors I can see," he said, but she dismissed this as folly. He saw this on her face and explained, "I'm not bullshitting. Everybody's always talked about all these colors in the world – red, purple, orange – but it's all the same to me. Gold is different, but pretty much everything else is a shade of yellow or brown. Blue is the only thing that really stands out."

"I'd always thought it was some sort of calling card," Journey said, surprised that he hadn't learned this about his friend sooner. "Like a branding technique to make yourself more recognizable."

"I'm not that clever," he assured him, and this time, Saige laughed. Dallion noticed the look of unhidden adoration on Journey's face as the young man took in the young woman before him, and he said slyly, "Why don't you kids go on out and get some fresh air? Daddy's got to get some shuteye."

"Sweet dreams," Saige quipped, and Dallion pretended to shudder to a delightful chill running down his spine.

She headed for the door, but as Journey downed the remainder of the rum in his cup in preparation to follow her,

Dallion told him, "If Old Rube's still up, have him send a couple of guys to clean up this mess and get the table out of here."

Journey agreed that he would do so, then followed Saige out the door and onto the deck. There wasn't much of a moon tonight, but the stars were out in the millions, and they both paused for a moment to admire them. Suddenly, Saige swayed, and Journey reached out to steady her, his hands on her shoulders. She laughed, recovering, and said with some embarrassment, "I still haven't gotten used to being on a ship."

He suspected that it had more to do with the booze in her body, but didn't say so. Instead, he took something out of his pocket, and she saw that it was Winnie's letter. She took it from him when he offered it and put it back in her own pocket. Journey said, "It wasn't because Jubilee didn't want you…"

"Yes, it was," she objected, but there was no anger or sadness in her voice. "It's alright. I ended up with a family who loved me, and I wouldn't trade that for the world. Besides, she rescued you from growing up as an orphan. It worked out for everyone, really."

He recalled Jubilee's lifeless corpse in the ocean and couldn't bring himself to agree that it had worked out so well for her in the end, but he didn't argue with her, either. She took a deep breath of the sea air, then said, "I should get some sleep."

"I'll help you…"

"I can get there, myself," she said matter-of-factly. "I might be drunk, but I'm not helpless. I can take care of myself."

"I believe you," he agreed, and was that a blush that rose in her cheeks, or just a trick of the moonlight?

He watched her make her way across the deck toward the hatchway that would take her below deck. Once she was gone, Journey leaned against the bannister at the edge of the deck and looked out on the nighttime ocean, breathing deeply and letting his thoughts turn as they would.

Chapter Twenty

THE next few days passed quickly enough. Saige spent most of her time on deck, watching with admiration as the crew went about their daily activities with precision and a certain degree of grace. One had to be graceful, at least, to scurry up the ratlines like they did, or to get anywhere near the top of the masts. Even the more mundane tasks, such as washing the deck, were done with a sort of practiced elegance, at least to her eyes. Eventually, however, boredom drove her to ask Dallion if there was anything that she could do to help out. He sent her to Old Rube, who put her to work helping to make dinner each night for the crew. She was appalled to learn that the mystery meat she'd enjoyed in Dallion's cabin on the night they'd finalized their plans was sea turtle. It wasn't unheard of as a meal on Kinsman Island, but she'd always found turtles too beautiful to want to eat them. Tawny Paul and Pigeon invited her to play cards each night, and she was secretly glad to find that Journey was a part of their usual group, as well. He didn't object to her joining them, and it took only a few minutes into their first game for them to be laughing and joking with one another.

Just after noon on the seventh day of the voyage, someone called out from the perch atop the main mast that land was in sight. Saige hurried to the bow to get a good look at what was still a tiny dot of land on the distant horizon. Journey was already there, looking out at the island through a spyglass. As she came to stand beside him, he asked, "Excited?"

"Of course," she agreed, but she hadn't expected to hear the tinge of sadness in her own voice. Journey had heard it, too, for he took the spyglass away from his eye to look at her, surprised. Saige confessed, "I'm not looking forward to saying goodbye to everyone."

"I know you've been making friends around here."

That was true, and she wasn't ashamed to admit it. Over the past week, Wee Bit had shown her how to tie several different knots, and she'd been practicing on bits of rope at night before going to sleep. Quick Bill and Thomas had taught her the lyrics to a handful of sea shanties. She'd even spent an entire afternoon with Pigeon at the helm, listening intently as he'd explained the basics of navigation and sailing. Now, she told Journey, "It's going to be hard to say goodbye for good when you take me back to Kinsman."

He didn't respond to that, and the uncomfortable way that he shifted his gaze away from her gave her pause. Before she could question it, however, Lucien and Dallion arrived at the bow, and Dallion snatched the spyglass out of Journey's hand to set it to his own eye. Lucien warned, "We shouldn't get much closer than this. There are too many ships with Commercial Horizon flags in these waters."

"We'll take the longboat the rest of the way," Dallion decided. He handed the spyglass back to Journey and turned to face Lucien. He said gravely, "You need to protect this ship with your life while I'm gone. She's our livelihood."

"And the love of your life," Lucien grinned. "Stop worrying and be on your way. You're wasting daylight."

Dallion, Journey, Saige, and Tawny Paul all piled into the longboat and set off for the coast. Journey and Tawny Paul each took up an oar to row, while Dallion sat at the rear of the little boat and watched as his beloved Jubilee grew smaller and farther away. Saige perched herself at the front, her excitement growing. She asked no one in particular, "What is Claymill going to be like?"

"Dirty," Tawny grunted between strokes with his oar. "It's full of ceramics factories. Beautiful stuff, but it makes everything filthy."

Saige frowned at that, but it did little to dampen her eagerness to get there. They stepped onto dry land a little under an hour later, and Saige instantly found herself overwhelmed with wonder. She took in all the sights of the port with wide eyes, trying to see everything in at once. Claymill was smaller than Kinsman, but she saw that Tawny Paul hadn't lied about how dirty everything was. Smoke from the factories had left a dark film of dust over most surfaces. The air was hazy with it, and it caused a tickle in the back of her throat. The streets were organized in a grid pattern that was easy to navigate, and although the people they passed on them didn't look rich, they weren't starving, either. The factories must have paid decent money. Old, stone buildings boasted storefronts with attractive displays in their windows: clothing, pottery, cutlery, and even books were laid out for passersby to view. The exterior of the buildings may have been coated with factory grime, but the glass windows revealed interiors that were clean and well-organized.

Saige could have spent the entire day exploring the little town, but Dallion hurried their group into a nearby tavern. It was a two-story building made of gray stone that sat on the corner of two main streets. The large, wooden sign on the front of the place declared that it was called The Crawling Crocker. Inside, they found that it looked like any number of other taverns in the region. A long, wooden bar stretched the length of one wall, and much of the rest of the open room was occupied by sets of tables and chairs. There was a small stage in one corner, and a sign above it informed patrons that someone named Lovely Livy performed three nights a week.

The place was nearly deserted, and Saige assumed that the locals were hard at work in the factories at this time of the afternoon. A pair of old men with only a half a head of hair left between them were sitting at the far end of the bar, drinking what were likely their third or fourth glasses of ale for the day, already. Three young men occupied one of the tables near the center of the room, and their style of clothing and fancy hats suggested that they were merchants who were just passing through. Two of them eyed Saige with a hunger that the three men with her knew all too well, and Dallion gave them a scowl that made them look away after only a few seconds.

The bartender was a middle-aged man with a sullen look on his face, but he brightened as Dallion slapped a small stack of marks onto the bar and announced, "We need your best room for today and tonight, and a good bottle of rum to go with it."

The man made the money disappear beneath the counter with impressive speed. There was a row of four small, metal hooks on the wall behind him, and he selected one of the keys hanging from them. He handed it to Dallion and instructed, "Last door down the hallway upstairs. The sheets were just washed this morning."

Judging by the dust on the counter and the dark grime in the corners of the windows in the wall, Saige doubted that was true, but didn't say so. Instead, she followed Dallion and the others up the stairs on the far side of the room and down the hallway to the last door. They filed inside to find a small, cramped room that featured nothing more than a bed with a lumpy mattress and a dresser that was missing one of its three drawers. Tawny grumbled, "If this is their best room, I'd hate to see the others."

Saige went to the room's only window and swept the curtains open to reveal a beautiful view of the street below. It ran all the way down to the docks, where the masts of a number of ships stood tall and proud. Saige sat on the sill and took in the sight with that excited sense of awe that she'd had since their arrival. She only pulled her attention back from it when Dallion began to lay out instructions for everyone.

"Tawny, here's the money to buy us all some new clothes. Think of a trustworthy, respectable, not-likely-to-rob-you-blind look. Journey, you and I will split up and start asking around for anyone leaving for Runes tonight or tomorrow sometime. The sooner, the better. Find out how much they'll charge for four passengers."

Saige asked, "What will I do?"

Dallion gave her a patronizing wink. "You're going to stay here. Let the boys handle all the business."

She glared, and Journey and Tawny Paul were secretly thankful that they were not on the receiving end of the fury behind those pretty eyes. She surprised them, however, by simply saying, "Okay. I'll just get some sleep while you're gone. I've missed having a real bed."

Perhaps they were naïve, or maybe they were too focused on the tasks ahead of them, but all three of them believed her without hesitation. They headed out the door, Journey reminding her to lock it behind them, and then Saige was alone. She went to the door and turned the lock, hoping that they would hear its telltale click out in the hall. Then she waited. The part about having missed a real bed to sleep on hadn't been a lie, and she had to admit that the tan and brown blankets and pillows looked inviting, but she had no intention of sleeping during a time like this.

She went to the window and watched for Dallion and the others below. Before long, they stepped out onto the street and into the afternoon sunlight. Journey and Dallion headed for the docks, but Tawny Paul went right, off to purchase their disguises. Saige waited until all three of them were out of sight before heading for the door, herself.

She had all of Claymill to explore.

Chapter Twenty-One

THE entire island of Claymill was owned by a trio of businessmen who had managed to turn it into a prosperous, bustling place. Some of the finest porcelain in the Realm was made in the kilns and factories here. Saige learned this and much of the island's history from a kindly old man who ran a porcelain shop on one of the town's main streets. In fact, nearly everyone she met that day could be described as kindly. Business on the island was booming, and Claymill's inhabitants looked like they were doing well for themselves. Even the lowliest kiln workers were better off than many of the poor folks of Kinsman Lane.

She wandered the streets for hours, meeting new people and visiting nearly every shop that was open. When she stumbled upon the main market, she was amazed to find that although the town was much smaller than her hometown, this market was nearly twice the size of the one she'd grown up with. Booths here sold everything she could have imagined, and even a few things that she couldn't. Fish, vegetables, clothing, pottery, leather, guns, live chickens and goats, and a few types of fruit that she'd never heard of lined the streets. She marveled over the wares. Near the end of one of the market's many rows of booths, she came across an elderly man who was selling jewelry. The wooden walls and shelves of his booth were covered in beautiful bracelets, necklaces, earrings, and rings. Saige spotted a tiara that she could imagine a storybook princess wearing. It was flanked by a pair of gem-graced bracelets.

The old man invited her into a corner of the booth, where he held up a fine, silver necklace. A small, white pendant hung from it. It was in the shape of a bird she didn't recognize, with a long, graceful neck. Saige marveled at the detail in each little feather. The man explained, "It's a type of water bird, called a swan. They don't live in these parts, but there's plenty of them up north a ways. They're smart, beautiful, graceful…all things that I suspect are true of you, too, miss."

Saige couldn't help but smile. "Have you seen one?"

"I have. Back in my younger years, I traveled all over to trade, but now that I'm older, I stick to the warmer parts. Swans, now, they don't mind the cooler weather." He motioned for her to turn around, undoing the necklace's clasp, but Saige's smile fell away at once.

"I can't afford it, I'm afraid…"

"No harm in a lady trying on a pretty necklace, is there?" He stepped behind her and pulled the long curls of her hair to one side. He slipped the necklace around her neck and secured the clasp, then came around her to see how it looked.

"Just as beautiful as I'd thought," he declared. Saige felt her cheeks grow red. The man drew a tiny mirror from his pocket and held it so that she could see her reflection in it. The swan rested just below the hollow of her throat. He told her, "You can't go wrong with a swan, miss. They're fierce protectors of their young and loyal to a fault. They choose a mate and stay with them for the rest of their life. I think a good number of people nowadays would do well to be more like a swan."

"Can they be trained to stay where they're supposed to?" Journey's voice from the front of the booth startled them both, and Saige whirled to face him. He was leaning against the half wall that served as the booth's counter. His arms were crossed at his chest, but he seemed more amused to find her here than angry.

Saige undid the necklace's clasp and offered it back to the man, who tried once more with, "I can make you a good deal on it. It's the only one I have in stock. Crafted by a talented woman up north…"

"I'm sorry, but I have no money," she said, too embarrassed to meet his gaze. She gave him a quick bob that was almost a curtsy – she had no idea why, but it seemed appropriate – and retreated toward the front of the booth. She headed past Journey to start down the length of the market, weaving her way between shoppers along the busy street.

Journey caught up to her and touched her wrist to stop her, but she turned on him and pulled her hand away. "What did you think I was going to do, Journey?" she demanded, fire dancing in her eyes. "Did you really think I was going to stay holed up in the room while you three got to go exploring?"

He was thrown off by her anger, and he didn't try to hide the fact. He raised his hands in a calming gesture. "There's nothing to explore. We've all been here before…"

"Well, I haven't," she said. "I'm not going to miss out on a chance to see more of the world. Besides, Dallion has no right to tell me what I can and can't do, and neither do you."

"That's not what I'm doing. In fact, I spotted you a long time ago, when you first came into the market. I didn't tell you then that you couldn't be out here."

She gaped, and his mind reeled as he realized he'd somehow made another mistake. "Have you been following me?" she asked. "What gives you the right to act as my minder? I don't need you or anyone else looking out for me."

"Saige…"

"Do not follow me back," she ordered, and turned from him so quickly that her untamed hair swung out behind her in a pretty splay of red. She stormed off, but he knew better than to pursue her. What he didn't know was what he had done that was so terribly wrong.

Women.

He gave her plenty of time to get back to the tavern on her own before heading that way, himself. When he arrived, it was after six and the first floor of the place was packed with locals, as well as visiting traders. All of the wooden stools at the bar were occupied, as were most of the tables. Some of the people here were playing cards, a few of them were eating, and nearly everyone was drinking. Journey had seen enough of these sorts of places to know that things would likely become rowdy in another hour or so.

He spotted Tawny Paul coming down the stairs from the second floor. He was dressed in a brown waistcoat over a fine, white shirt. The two earrings that he usually wore in his left ear were gone, as were the three gold rings from his right hand. White, untanned bands of flesh circled his fingers where they usually sat. He was clean-shaven, and Journey had to stifle a laugh at the sight of him. In the two years that he had known Tawny, this was the first time he'd ever seen him looking so…clean.

He met him near the bottom of the stairs, and Tawny Paul raised his voice enough to be heard over all the other conversations in the room to say, "Your new clothes are upstairs. Dallion says we don't have to wear them, yet, but I thought, why not? When are we going to get another opportunity to look like gentlemen?"

Journey nodded toward a nearby table, where two young women were currently flirting with a few men who had paused their card game to give them some attention. Journey told Tawny, "They're all yours."

Tawny straightened his back, tipped an imaginary hat to him, and headed in the direction of the two women. Journey didn't wait around to see how things turned out for him, but went up the stairs and to their room. He found Dallion and Saige inside. Saige was sitting at the windowsill once more, and when she saw him enter, she turned away to look out at the street below. He ignored this, his attention on Dallion, who was lacing up a new pair of boots. He hadn't changed into the rest of his new clothes, yet, and he was still wearing all of his usual jewelry. As Journey entered the room, Dallion pointed to a stack of neatly-folded clothes on the foot of the bed and told him that they were his.

"Tawny did alright. He could only afford one new pair of boots, so I took them. Captain's privilege."

'Captain's privilege' was a phrase that Dallion used whenever he knew he didn't have a right to something he wanted, but decided to be selfish. It was a joke that the men aboard the Jubilee tended to grumble about, but it had never been important enough for anyone to come right out and object to. Journey didn't comment on it, now, either. He leaned his back against the wall beside the door and said, "I found a sloop heading for Runes tomorrow afternoon. They'll take us with them for five hundred marks."

"I got that beat," Dallion said as he finished with the laces on his new boots. He'd been sitting on the edge of the bed to do it, but now he stood. "I met with the captain of a galleon called the Crescent Moon. Big son of a bitch. The ship, not the captain. She sails tomorrow morning. Three hundred marks to board, and another hundred when we get there."

"What are we going to do for sleeping arrangements tonight?" he asked, eyeing the single bed in the room.

"I'm going to see if we can rent a second room. Saige can have this one, and you, me, and Tawny Paul will all bunk together in the new one." He glanced at Saige on the windowsill and suggested with a grin, "Unless you're willing to share this bed with one of us."

"I'd rather throw myself out this window," she said without turning from it, and Dallion gave a hearty laugh. He headed for the door, announcing that it was time to go downstairs to celebrate. What he was celebrating, Journey wasn't sure, but he waited until he was gone to close the door behind him. Then he turned back to Saige, who still hadn't looked his way.

"I'm sorry for earlier," he told her, although he still wasn't entirely certain what he was supposed to be sorry about. "I didn't mean to upset you."

She didn't answer, at first, but she finally said in a tone that hinted of forgiveness, "I don't like being treated like I'm helpless. I'm not a child."

"I know. We're the same age, remember? That's why I was able to pose as you for so long."

This earned him a small laugh, and he was glad to hear it. She turned on the sill to look at him, at last, and he suspected that she was merely trying to stay mad at him, at this point. She asked, "Aren't you going to go downstairs to drink with Dallion and Paul?"

"In a minute. But first, I have a present for you." He took something from his pocket and held it out to her in a closed hand.

She eyed him as she tried to determine if this was some sort of prank. She decided to trust him and left the windowsill to go to him, holding her hands out for whatever this gift could be. He opened his hand, and her eyes widened at the sight of the swan necklace that the old man had tried to sell her in the market. She brought her hands up over her mouth in surprise and said from behind them, "You have to give it back, Journey! He's such a nice man. It's not right to take this from him."

He shifted on his feet uncomfortably. "I didn't steal it," he assured her, surprised by his own embarrassment. "I paid him for it. I wanted to get you something to say thank you. I think you're underestimating how much money ten percent of your inheritance is going to be."

She smiled then, and it wasn't the feisty smile that she most often offered. This one was kind and grateful, and it was more beautiful than any he'd seen before. She turned her back to him and collected all of her hair over one shoulder to bare the back of her neck. Journey suddenly felt nervous for reasons he didn't dare try to explain to himself. He fumbled with the necklace's clasp for a moment, and once he'd gotten it undone, he slipped the fine chain around her neck. His hand brushed the flesh just below her left ear, and it was soft and smooth. He focused on getting the clasp to close, and once it had, he stepped back from her quickly.

She turned to face him again, and he was pleased to find that the little swan looked right at home on her, sitting just above the top of her dress. She ran her fingertips over it as she said, "Thank you. I don't know what else to say. It's lovely."

This wasn't the first time he'd gifted jewelry to a woman, and it wasn't even the most expensive. But out of all the times that he had given similar items to Caresse Beaumont, he couldn't recall her ever being so sincere in her gratitude. He shrugged his shoulders, unable to hide a bashful look. "It isn't a big deal. I'm going downstairs. Coming?"

"I'll be down in a little while," she agreed, and watched him go until he had closed the door behind him.

Chapter Twenty-Two

JOURNEY hadn't been wrong when he'd predicted that the tavern might get rowdy. Conversations grew louder as more drinks were consumed and men lost or won money in their card games. There was almost a fight when someone slapped the butt of a young woman who had come in here tonight with her husband from one of the merchant ships. There was a second bartender on duty tonight – a hulk of a man with several tattoos covering his muscled arms – and he managed to deescalate the situation before fists could fly. The argument left a tenseness in the room, however, and that only got worse when Lovely Livy came on stage. The top of her dress bared so much cleavage that Journey expected her breasts to fall out of it at any moment. She pranced around on the stage in heels that made her at least six inches taller. Her routine was to sing and dance, and she was relatively decent at dancing. Her talent for singing left much to be desired, however. She crooned on about a lost lover who had left her to pursue a fortune on the sea, and Journey ordered another drink. He was going to need it.

He noticed movement on the stairs out of the corner of his eye, and when he looked in that direction, his breath caught at the sight of her. Saige had donned the new dress that Tawny Paul had gotten her. He had guessed the size perfectly, from the look of it. It was royal blue with white details. The lace on top complimented the swan necklace that Journey had given her. It wasn't something so nice that a baroness might wear it, but it was much nicer than the simple, brown dress she'd worn from home.

She reached the bottom of the stairs, her red curls bouncing in the pins she'd used to style it. She spotted Dallion, Journey, and Tawny Paul at one of the tables not far from the stage, and she started toward them at once, oblivious to the gawks she received from the men she passed along the way. They had saved the fourth chair at the table for her, and as she reached them, Journey stood to politely move it for her. She thanked him, flattered, and sat down.

Dallion hadn't noticed her until now, and his wide eyes and slack jaw said that he was suddenly smitten. She ignored his stare from across the table and said to Tawny Paul, "My dress is wonderful. Thank you."

"Who knew I had such good taste?" he mused, and then turned his attention back on Lively Livy as she began to belt out another song. Neither Dallion nor Journey were able to do the same, however; they couldn't take their eyes from the woman at their table.

Dallion's gaze made her uncomfortable, so she joked, "Are you going to buy me a drink, or just keep staring?"

He laughed, unashamed to have been caught, and immediately headed for the bar to fetch her something.

She got through her first two drinks okay. They were a fruity mixture that barely tasted of alcohol. Halfway into her third, however, she realized she was drunk. Even so, Dallion kept them coming, matching her sip for sip. Tawny Paul and Journey weren't all that far behind them, and at some point that evening, Lovely Livy actually began to sound good, via the miracle of booze.

A young woman who was advertising herself in a short, tight dress got Tawny Paul's attention, and it wasn't long before he'd disappeared into some other room with her. Dallion was lured away by three card players who were looking for a fourth to continue their game. That left only Journey and Saige, and he couldn't look away as she laughed and cheered for Lovely Livy along with her drunken fans of the male persuasion. Livy was joined on stage by another woman who looked enough like her to have possibly been her sister. Together, the two sang a comical duet about a sailor who fell in love with a mermaid. When Saige reached for her fifth glass, she bumped it with her hand and spilled the small amount of alcohol that was still in it. She merely laughed some more, and Journey joined in, even as he righted the glass for her. Their eyes met over the table, and for a moment, they both stopped laughing. The raucousness of the bar around them continued, but they forgot all about it.

Saige's lips were tilted in a smile, and she asked rather shyly, "Can I ask you something, Journey?"

In answer, he left his chair across the table and sat down in the one to her right, where Dallion had been sitting. They leaned close to one another so that she could speak quietly amongst the wailing of the two women on stage. She said, "I've been wondering what a guy like you is doing with a bunch of pirates. I mean, I like Dallion, Tawny Paul, Wee Bit, Lucien...I just don't think that you're much like any of them."

"I'm more like them than you'd think," he muttered, reaching for his drink. It was empty, and he set it aside with a sigh.

Saige pressed, "You grew up in a good home, you had lots of money, a happy childhood..."

"Do you have me figured out so well?"

She shrugged. "Not yet, but I'm trying."

There was a commotion two tables away, where a large man in a typical potter's uniform threw his ale on the floor and began scuffling with one of the men he'd been playing cards with. The other two men at their table joined in. The girls on the stage attempted to keep going with their song, but their voices were quickly drowned out by the ruckus of a fight that was about to spread. The tattooed bartender came at a run, but he was too late, this time. A card player from another table broke a glass over the head of one of the fighters, and it erupted into utter chaos. Men from all over the room joined the fray, and the few women here ran for the stairs, squealing in excitement and fear.

It took mere seconds for the first chair to be thrown, and then the entire first floor of the tavern was the arena for one big brawl. Journey looked for Dallion, but couldn't find him in the commotion. He felt a hand touch his arm, and he turned to find Saige looking frightened. It may have been his drunkenness, or it could have been a sense of chivalry that Jubilee had tried to instill in him as he'd grown up, but an urge to keep the young woman safe overtook him. He grabbed her hand and pulled her to her feet. She followed closely as he led her toward the wall to their right, where there weren't currently any fighters. There was a door here, and he threw it open to lead her out into an alleyway. He closed it behind them, and when he turned to face her once more, he found that she was laughing so hard, there were tears in her eyes. He wanted to call her crazy, but then he was laughing, too. Perhaps they had both lost their minds.

She rested her back against the cool stone of the building and tried to calm herself with deep breaths of fresh air. She still had a hold of his hand, and she gave it a small tug toward her. He didn't object, and he moved close to her so that she was between him and the wall. He placed his free hand on the back of her neck, but didn't kiss her, yet. Instead, they both stood very still, looking into one another's eyes. He saw some fear in hers, but there was mostly a sense of desire that matched his own. Her flesh felt good beneath his hand, and her lips parted slightly in invitation. His heart was racing, and he was certain that if he were to cup one of her breasts, he would feel hers fluttering against his palm.

"Saige," he whispered, but he had nothing more to say than that. Instead, he leaned closer, slowly bringing his lips within inches of her own, close enough to smell the sweet scent of fruity drinks on her breath, almost close enough to taste her lips...

The door beside them was thrown open, and Dallion stumbled through it. He was laughing and still holding a half a glass of ale in one hand. Journey let Saige go and stepped back so quickly that he nearly tripped over his own feet, but when Dallion turned to him, he showed no sign of being aware of what he'd just interrupted. Dallion's bottom lip was bleeding from a hit he'd taken inside.

"I thought I saw you two come out here," he said, his words slurred by alcohol and injury. "I got us a second room upstairs. I think it's about time for bed."

Journey didn't look at Saige, afraid of what he'd give away if he did, but he saw out of the corner of his eye that she was avoiding Dallion's gaze by staring down at her feet. She agreed, "I think that would be a good idea."

A commotion around the other side of the building said that the brawl had spilled through the tavern's front door and out onto the street. Dallion laughed again, as if this were somehow a joke that he found especially funny. He slapped Journey on the shoulder and said, "You seem halfway sober. Be a gentleman and lead the way for Saige. We've got to get upstairs without getting killed on the way."

Journey muttered for her to stay close, but didn't offer his hand, this time. She followed both men back into the unruly tavern. All the while, she wished she was sober enough to handle the thoughts and feelings now swirling within her.

Chapter Twenty-Three

DAWN came far too soon for any of them, but they somehow managed to haul themselves out of their beds. Journey couldn't help but laugh when he saw Dallion readying to head to the docks: black waistcoat over a white shirt, only a single ring on his fingers, and a clean shave. He had removed the rest of his jewelry, save for the shark tooth necklace, which he tucked into his shirt to conceal. Even his earrings were gone. They'd left small, round holes up the side of his ear, which he covered by allowing his freshly-washed hair to hang loose. Saige scrounged up a pair of scissors from somewhere in the tavern and carefully cut a few inches off so that it hung just even with his shoulders. Dallion had never looked so well-groomed and presentable.

For Journey, putting on his new clothes was like stepping back in time. Two years ago, he had owned a similar coat to the dark green one he now donned. His hair was much longer than he'd used to wear it, but he washed it thoroughly and pulled it back in a braid. He completed his look with a silk kerchief around his neck, and as he considered himself in the reflection of the water in the basin, he realized that he looked very much like Landon Travert. It wasn't a realization that brought him any joy, but he would have been lying to himself to say that it wasn't nice to look like he could fit in with more respectable people than pirates again.

They found the Crescent Moon easily enough at the docks, and all four of them stared up at the monster of a ship in wonder. Saige asked the others, "What kind of ship is this?"

"She's a galleon," Journey answered, admiring the length of her hull, which must have been somewhere north of a hundred and seventy feet. Three of her four masts were graced with square sails that Journey didn't doubt could fetch her at least seven knots, if not eight. He observed, "She's flying partnership flags for both Commercial Horizon and Western Straights. Whoever owns her is doing well for themselves."

"Have any of you ever been on a ship this big?"

All three men shook their heads. Saige considered the look of awe on Dallion's face and asked him, "Do you wish you could own a ship like this one?"

Dallion scoffed, as if her suggestion had been something obscene. "I'd take the Jubilee over this old whale any day. The Jubilee is a lot faster, for one thing, and I can sail her in shallower waters. That's important when you need to outrun monsters like this," he said gesturing to the massive ship before them. "Besides, the Jubilee is mine. She isn't bound to any company, so we can sail anywhere and do whatever we want. I guess you could say she's..." He shrugged his shoulders, unable to come up with the right word.

Journey supplied, "Freedom."

Dallion grinned. "That's right. The Jubilee is freedom."

"Well, this ship means money," Saige said, starting for the gangway. "Let's go get what we came all the way out here for."

Journey, Dallion, and Tawny Paul all followed her without further prompting. They filed up the steep gangway, where they were greeted by a man with a gray, curated beard that stretched nearly to his navel. He stuck his hand out in an offered handshake to the newcomers and said in a gravelly voice, "I'm Horace Webb, first mate. Welcome aboard the Crescent Moon."

As the mercantile world was more of Journey's territory, he stepped forward and shook Webb's hand. It was time for the lies to start flowing, and Journey and had prepared plenty on the way here. "I'm James Terrance. This is my sister, Saige, and our two business partners, Dorian Romy and Perry Taylor. We're hoping for passage to the Isle of Runes for business."

Webb didn't bat an eye at the lies. Instead, he said, "I've been told you've already discussed the price with Captain Mercier. Is that correct?"

Journey nodded to Dallion, who took the agreed amount of money out of an inner pocket of his waistcoat. He handed it over to Webb, and they were all amused to note that he was too polite to count it in front of them. Instead, he placed the money in a pocket of his own and motioned for them to follow him. Sailors in crisp uniforms were readying for the ship's departure from port, but they were careful to step aside as their first mate led his new guests across the bustling deck. As they walked, Webb explained, "The Crescent Moon is one of the largest ships to operate in this region of Cruxes. She's a hundred and seventy-six feet long from stem to stern and can carry nearly two thousand tons of cargo. She was commissioned just six years ago, so everything on board is top of the line. She's equipped with guest quarters, and although you might find them to be a bit cramped, they'll afford you some privacy for the length of the voyage."

"How big is the crew?" Saige asked as she hurried to keep up with the others in the fancy shoes that Tawny had bought with her dress.

"Because she's a merchant's vessel and not intended for heavy combat, we generally get by on a crew of eighty men."

Dallion and Journey shared a glance at that out of habit – a ship of eighty men, most of whom had likely never seen any sort of fighting, would have been an easy target for a crew of determined pirates. Journey could barely keep himself from laughing at that. They may have looked like wealthy businessmen right now, but the wiliness that had kept them alive on the seas for so long would likely never leave them.

Webb led them down a staircase and a long hallway below the main deck. He stopped a door that looked exactly like the dozen they'd already passed and opened it for them. Inside, they found a small room that sported four hammocks, a round table, and two chairs. Webb told them, "If you need anything, any member of my crew will be able to point you in the right direction. I only ask that you don't disturb them without a reason."

Journey thanked him and waited until Webb closed the door. Once he was gone, Tawny Paul, who had spent the previous night on the wooden floor of their room in the tavern due to Dallion claiming "captain's privilege" over the bed, collapsed into one of the hammocks and draped his arm over his eyes. Dallion and Journey both sat down in the chairs beside the table, and Saige gaped at all three of them. She asked, "How can you want to sit around here? We have a whole ship to explore."

Dallion shook his head. "This isn't like what you're used to on the Jubilee. They're not going to want us to wander around out there and get in the way."

Saige frowned at the implication that she had been getting in the way aboard the Jubilee. Journey understood the look on her face and rescued her with, "What he means is that there are a lot more rules aboard this ship. The companies are strict about how vessels are run. The captain's word is always law, no matter what. A first mate aboard a ship like this probably fulfills many of the same duties that Lucien performs as quartermaster. I'm sure that Webb and a dozen lieutenants give firm orders and work their crew hard. There's no gambling, no negotiating, and certainly no voting. None of the crew on the Moon are going to have time to show us around."

"Sounds like torture," Dallion grumbled.

Staying cooped up in a room as small as this one for the rest of the day seemed more like torture to Saige, but she decided not to tell him that. Instead, she chose one of the hammocks and settled in to wait.

At noon, a crewman delivered hearty helpings of sausages, cheese, plantains, and papaya to their room. They all ate their fill. After that, they still had another eighteen hours left to travel, according to Dallion's estimate. They played cards for a while, took naps, and waited. And waited. The hours passed slowly with little to do to fill them. The last meal of the day was smaller than the one they'd been given at noon, but was just as good, featuring more sausages, fresh eggs, and bread. Dallion promptly passed out in a hammock after eating, and Tawny Paul wasn't far behind him. Saige fell into a light nap, and she woke a half an hour later to find that Journey was gone from the cabin, despite the earlier warnings about wandering around. She left the others to their soft snores and made her way up to the deck, where the sun had set and the stars were coming out in all their magnificence. The first night crew had just come on duty, but she stayed out of their way well enough, and no one seemed interested in asking her what she was doing out here. She spotted Journey at the port side of the ship, his elbows propped on the banister as he peered out over the dark sea. It was a calm night, and the starlight danced off of the tops of the gentle waves.

She came to stand beside him, asking once it was too late if she could join him. He nodded, but didn't take his gaze from the sea. Neither of them spoke for a long time. They ignored the noise and conversations of the men working on the deck behind them and focused on the endless expanse of sea all around. Somewhere out there, life on the two islands of Stonewell and Kinsman was going on as usual. Francis Moore was getting ready for bed. Abigay Laval was finishing her chores for the night and ensuring that her uncle had everything he needed before retiring to his room. Caresse Beaumont (or whatever her last name was, now) was climbing into bed beside her husband, possibly in the very room that Landon Travert had been murdered in, or maybe the room that Journey had called his own for the first twenty years of his life. All of those people and things seemed so far away that they may as well have existed in another Realm. Out here, there was only the sea and the light of the stars upon it.

When Saige finally spoke, it was exactly what Journey had hoped she wouldn't mention. "What happened in the alley last night...well..."

"I'm sorry," he said immediately. "I'd had a lot to drink, and I let it get the better of me."

"I didn't think you were that drunk," she said, her voice quiet and tinged with something that may have been hope. "I know that I wasn't that drunk."

He still didn't look at her, knowing very well that if he made the mistake of doing so, he would continue what Dallion had interrupted last night. Saige gave him a minute to answer, and when it became clear that he wasn't going to, she placed her elbows on the banister and rested her chin in her hands. A short distance away, a pair of dolphins broke the surface of the water for a moment before disappearing below it once more. In the starlight, their wet flesh had seemed to sparkle. Saige gave a contented sigh.

Journey decided to wish her a good night and head down to their cabin, but before he could do so, she said, "Tell me about my real parents, Journey. Please?"

He lifted his shoulders in a shrug. "I'm not sure how much you really want to know. Landon wasn't a very nice man. He could be kind when he tried to be, but that wasn't often. Jubilee was his opposite. She had a good heart. She was gentle, loving, beautiful..." He paused, then added, "You get your red hair from her."

"I was ashamed of my hair when I was a little girl," she confessed. "I didn't know anyone else like me. Then my mother...Winnie...told me that my great-grandmother had red hair. She said that up until she'd died, she had been the most beautiful woman on Kinsman because of it." Her lips turned up into a smile, but there was some embarrassment in it. "After she told me that, I started thinking that maybe, just maybe, I would grow up to be the most beautiful girl on the island, too."

"You are," he whispered. She looked at him, startled, and found that he had finally taken his gaze from the sea. Their eyes met, and even the light of the stars was enough to reveal the blush that darkened her cheeks.

She was the first to look away, and she told him, "I think you should know that I don't blame you or Jubilee for what happened. I don't blame anyone. I didn't have a big, fancy house or servants to take care of me, but I grew up knowing I was loved by Winnie and Francis. I wouldn't trade that for anything in the world. And Jubilee rescued you from being an orphan, so how could I be upset about that? Now, you've found me to help make sure that my adoptive father and I don't have to worry about where our next meal will come from, or what we'll do if his bad hip keeps getting worse. This changes everything, Journey. I can't thank you enough for what you've done." She nudged his arm with hers, smiling. "If Jubilee really was as kindhearted and good as you say she was, then I'm sure she would be proud of you for setting everything to rights. You're a good man."

He didn't answer, and when she looked at him again, there was a look of near panic on his face. She replayed her words in her head, worried that she had said something that had inadvertently upset him. Before she could ask him what was wrong, he said, "I'm going to go get some sleep. We should get to Runes tomorrow morning. Goodnight."

She spoke his name, but he didn't pause in his retreat toward the main hatchway. She watched him go and wished she knew what she'd said that was so wrong.

Dallion was still snoring in one of the hammocks when Journey returned to their cabin, but he woke as he shook his shoulder. He turned his face away from him, grumbling about being woken up, but Journey shook him again. He shoved Journey's hand away and growled, "What?"

"We need a new plan," he said. Dallion rubbed the sleep from his eyes and sat up to get a better look at him. In the light of the single lantern in the room, he could see the determination on his friend's face, coupled with a generous dose of something that may have been guilt. His first thought was that Journey had done something to the girl that he shouldn't have, but he dismissed that in mere seconds. He knew the young man better than that. This was something else.

"What's wrong with our current plan?" he dared to ask.

Journey had been sitting on the chair that was closest to Dallion's hammock, but now he stood. He felt the urge to start pacing, but this room was far too small for that. Instead, he stayed where he was and said, "It isn't right, Dal. We can't just leave her somewhere and take off with all that money. She'd never be able to get back home on her own, and even if she could, it's not right to take everything from her and sail off."

Dallion gaped at him for a moment, dumbfounded. Then he began to laugh – deep, wild laughter that caused him to rock back in the hammock and slap his knee. It woke Tawny Paul, who loosed a loud yawn and rolled onto his feet, muttering something about needing to find whatever served as a toilet around here. He headed into the hall outside their cabin, and Dallion's continued laughter followed him out. Once Tawny was gone, Journey crossed his arms at his chest, unamused, and demanded, "What's wrong with you?"

Dallion managed, "I should have seen this coming! I should have known when I saw the look on your face the first time we laid eyes on her on Kinsman."

"What are you talking about?"

Dallion reined himself back in, but had to wipe a stray tear from his cheek that had escaped during his fit of laughter. He was still grinning, but at least he was otherwise serious again. "You've gone lovey-dovey for the girl, and now you feel bad about taking her money. That's all this is."

He knew that arguing that would only convince Dallion that he was right. Instead, he tried, "She's grateful that we tracked her down for this. We can ask her for twenty percent, after all, and I think she'll give it to us. We'll let her keep the rest."

Dallion's grin had disappeared, and the first sign of anger touched his face. He said sternly, "Here's what we're going to do: we're going to get the girl to Horizon, like we said we would. She'll get the money. We'll take her back to Claymill with us and meet up with Lucien and the Jubilee. We'll take her to Port Kelsey and drop her off there. We'll leave her with nothing, just like we planned. That money isn't hers, Journey;

it's ours. We're the ones who thought up this whole idea, and we're the ones working for it. She's just a tool that we needed to use to make this happen."

"You're willing to leave her broke and alone in Port Kelsey, of all places?" he asked. "She's never done anything to deserve this. I can't just stand by while…"

"Stand by?" he demanded, getting up from the hammock. In such a cramped space, they were only a few feet apart, and Dallion's raised voice was very loud in here. "We came up with this plan together! You were perfectly happy with it before, and now your conscience is having a fit about it? Are you even thinking about anyone else? I can't believe that you're willing to fuck over me and the rest of the crew as soon as some cute brunette bats her eyes at you."

It took Journey a second to understand his error. He groaned, "You colorblind son of a bitch! It isn't like that, alright? This has nothing to do with you or the crew."

Dallion lowered his voice so that no one beyond the door of their cabin could overhear and spat, "I've promised everyone on the Jubilee a lot of money, and they're going to expect every bit of it. You know damn well what could happen if I turn up empty-handed after all of this. I'm not willing to risk my position as captain just because you feel sorry for some farm girl with a sad story. Get your head on straight, Prince. We've got more important things to worry about than whatever the hell you're feeling for this girl."

Fighting was against the rules aboard the Jubilee, and that was strictly enforced by Lucien. But they weren't on that ship, and Journey had never wanted to hit this man more strongly in the two years he'd known him. He clenched his hands into fists, and everything in him screamed for him to swing. Then a more rational part of him told him that it would likely scar their friendship forever, as well as risk his own position as part of the Jubilee's crew. Somehow, he managed to force himself to turn his back to him and headed for the door. As he left, he hissed over his shoulder, "Whatever you say, Captain Romilly."

The last two words were dripping with acid, but Dallion didn't try to stop him. As soon as Journey closed the door behind him, Dallion let out a furious roar and punched the wall beside him. It promised bruised knuckles, but he felt a little better. For a moment there, he'd thought that things were going to come to blows.

Chapter Twenty-Four

JOURNEY didn't return until well after midnight. By then, Dallion, Saige, and Tawny Paul were all sleeping. He climbed into the vacant hammock to wait for morning, doubting that he would get any sleep tonight. He was wrong; he slept for a few hours, only to dream about that fateful night aboard Landon's sailboat. Over and over, he saw Landon raise the gun to shoot him, and over and over, the bullet found his shoulder and sent him over the side. Then the worse part came: the splash that signaled Jubilee's corpse being tossed in after him. The dream was so vivid that he could feel each wet strand of her hair as he hid beside her body in the water. He could taste the salt of the sea and hear the splash of each oar as Landon started his return trip home.

He escaped the nightmare as he woke just after dawn. Dallion was gone, but Tawny Paul was snoring in the hammock beside his. Saige was sitting in one of the room's two chairs. When she saw that he was awake, she told him, "You were talking in your sleep. You kept telling someone you were sorry for leaving them. Are you alright?"

"I'm fine," he answered, his tone perhaps a little too stern. She didn't ask any more questions. Journey was glad.

He and Dallion avoided each other that entire morning. Tawny Paul likely noticed what was happening, but he didn't comment. By eight o'clock, the Isle of Runes was spotted on the horizon. Journey, Saige, and Tawny Paul found one another on the deck and gathered near the bow to watch as the land grew steadily closer. There were several other ships in the area, likely all traders who were coming or going. This was the heart of Commercial Horizon, and Journey doubted that the surrounding waters were ever void of ships for any significant length of time.

Dallion was standing beside him before he knew it, but neither man spoke to one another. Instead, Dallion asked Saige, "You still have the letter as proof, don't you?"

She nodded, placing her hand in the pocket on her dress to grasp the slip of paper. "I hope they don't think it's forged. I don't have any other way to prove who I am."

Tawny Paul warned her not to jinx it by saying things like that, but Journey hardly heard the conversation. He was lost in thought as he watched the isle grow closer and closer. He was trying to convince himself that he would be able to go through with Dallion's plan once they reached Port Kelsey, but the more he thought about it, the more he knew it was impossible. Perhaps if they only took some of the money before abandoning her, or if they took all the money, but returned her safely to Kinsman Lane...

His thoughts were interrupted when crewman's voice called out from somewhere atop one of the masts, and a murmur swept over the deck. Off the starboard side, a ship they didn't recognize was approaching quickly, and it seemed to be on course to intercept the Crescent Moon. As she grew a little closer, they saw that she was a frigate fitted for battle. A red Commercial Horizon flag flew from her topmast. Captain Mercier, a crotchety man who may have forgotten how to smile years ago, ordered his men to slow the Moon down, but the frigate adjusted her course accordingly. There was no doubt that she meant to intercept them, and that only became more obvious when two small sloops drew in close behind the Moon, as well. They sported flags that matched the frigate's own.

Mercier called for his men to bring the Moon to a stop. Journey spotted Webb among the crewmen who had gathered on this side of the ship, and he slipped between two sailors to post himself beside him to ask lowly, "What's going on?"

"I don't know," Webb replied without taking his eyes off of the approaching ships. "It may be a misunderstanding of some sort. Whatever it is, you have nothing to fear. Everything about the Crescent Moon is aboveboard and up to the appropriate standards. If the frigate's orders are to board us for some reason, then we'll welcome it without a fuss and get things straightened out from there."

Journey left him there without comment and returned to the others. Saige was watching the frigate with more curiosity than concern, but that changed when Dallion took hold of her arm to guide her toward the main hatchway. Journey and Tawny Paul followed closely behind, all three men ignoring Saige's question when she asked what was wrong. Dallion told her to be quiet, and she bit back any more questions. They shut themselves inside their cabin, and as soon as the door was securely closed and the lock bolted, Saige demanded to know what was going on.

"I don't know," Dallion told her, "but whatever it is, we need to stay out of the way."

"I've got a bad feeling about this," Tawny Paul said as he sat down in one of the hammocks. "It's one thing to go into a snake's nest if they don't know you're coming, but it's something else when they come swarming out to meet you."

"What do you mean?" Saige asked him. "I thought we were coming here to meet with the Horizon people, anyway. Why does it matter if they come to us, first?"

"Because they don't just board someone else's ship for a friendly visit," Journey muttered. He was sitting on one of the chairs, and Saige now sat down in the other one. Her eyes were wide with fear, and he was tempted to reach over the small table between them to grasp her hand to comfort her. With Dallion here to see it, however, he didn't dare.

They were silent for a while, and the minutes spun out around them in the tiny room. When Saige started to speak again, Dallion shushed her. Eventually, a sound that he hadn't wanted to hear reached his ears through the closed door: a commotion of stomping boots and barked orders down the hall. Journey heard it, too, and he reminded everyone in a tight voice, "Stick to the names we gave Webb and Mercier."

"I don't think that's going to help," Dallion said, and as if to prove him right, the door burst inward as it was kicked from the other side. The lock snapped easily, and then they were staring down the barrels of two guns. The soldiers behind them were wearing red and black Commercial Horizon uniforms, and from the sound of it, they had more than a few friends with them out there in the hallway. They began shouting orders for Dallion and the others to get on their knees. Saige screamed, and Journey reached for her hand, after all. At this point, it no longer mattered.

Journey didn't put up a fight as a dozen armed soldiers hauled him and the others up to the quarterdeck. He was shoved unceremoniously to his knees on the deck, where he laced his fingers behind his head when ordered to do so. He was quickly joined there by Dallion and Tawny Paul. The soldiers kept their guns aimed at their chests to keep them from going anywhere. Dallion kept assuring them that there had been some sort of misunderstanding, but Journey ignored his useless attempts to talk them out of this and focused on Saige. The soldiers were a little gentler with her as they led her out onto the deck, but not by much, and she was soon forced to sit down beside Journey. She wrapped her arms around herself in a frightened hug, and Journey silently willed her to be brave.

The Moon's crew were gathered around to watch what was happening, but they scurried out of the way as Mercier and another of the Horizon soldiers marched to the center of the quarterdeck. Mercier appeared angry, but the soldier with him had a smug look of victory on his face. He came to stand before his captives and announced for the gathered crewmembers to hear, "My name is Commander Blakeshire. This ship has been stopped so that we might apprehend four pirates who posed as respectable merchants to board this vessel." He asked Dallion directly, "Are you Dallion Romilly?"

"There's been a mistake," he answered, feigning meekness. "My name is Romy, not Romilly. We paid good money to be passengers on this ship..."

"An employee of Commercial Horizon recognized you on Claymill. He heard that you were looking to buy your way onto a ship that was headed here. He sent word ahead that you were coming. And now you're saying that it's just a happy coincidence that one of the ships that was docked at Claymill yesterday morning happens to have a man matching the description he gave? How stupid do you think I am, Mr. Romilly?"

"Pretty damn stupid, you company stooge," he replied. It was all over, now, so it hardly mattered, but from his left, Tawny Paul let out a defeated groan.

Blakeshire scowled. He told his men to get iron cuffs on them, but before they could obey that command, Saige was on her feet. The soldier tasked with guarding her reached for her arm, but she slipped nimbly from his grasp and approached Blakeshire, her cheeks flushed and her eyes afire. Before Blakeshire could tell her to sit back down, she reached out with one hand and slapped him across the cheek. Some of the surrounding men drew in sharp breaths, but Blakeshire merely stared back at her, clearly stunned.

"How dare you!" Saige cried. "How dare you accuse me of being in cahoots with pirate scum, sir! Do I look like a pirate wench to you? Do I?"

Blakeshire raised an eyebrow. "You're traveling with a known pirate…"

"I hired this man to get me to the Isle of Runes," she said, pointing at Dallion. "If he's a pirate, I had no idea. He offered to get me here for a price I couldn't refuse. I've come all this way from Kinsman Island to speak with someone from Commercial Horizon about my family inheritance. My father was Landon Travert, a partner with this company. I have a letter proving my heritage. What do you think your superiors will say when they find out that you've shackled and shamed the daughter of one of their most valuable partners?"

Blakeshire hesitated at that, studying the young woman's face for any sign that she was lying. He must not have found any, for he said, "Ms. Travert, I'm very sorry for the assumption…"

"As you should be," she assured him. "I've never had to deal with such incompetence in my life."

Despite everything that was happening, Journey had to conceal his pride for her. She was playing the part well, and no matter what else happened today, if she could save herself, then he wished her all the best. Blakeshire asked with a tinge of embarrassment, "Are these other men with you, miss, or did you hire them, as well?"

"That one," she answered without hesitation, pointing at Journey. "He's my half-brother. He wouldn't let me leave Kinsman Lane without coming along to look after me. He said he wanted to protect me from pirates." She gave him an ironic look. "Clearly, he failed."

Dallion and Tawny Paul gaped as Blakeshire ordered his men to let Journey go. He didn't move, at first, certain that it couldn't have been that simple, but Saige and Blakeshire were both looking at him expectantly. He got to his feet and kept his hands out before him where the armed soldiers could see them. He needn't have bothered, however; they had taken their guns off of him and were aiming them solely at Dallion and Tawny, now.

"Again, I apologize for the misunderstanding," Blakeshire told Saige. As he said this, a pair of soldiers began placing heavy, iron cuffs around Tawny and Dallion's wrists. Tawny struggled against them at first, earning him a knock on the head from one of the soldier's rifles, but Dallion let them do as they would. His gaze was fixed solely on Journey, and there was raw betrayal in his eyes. Despite everything in him screaming to do something to stop this, Journey stood aside with Saige as the soldiers forced their two prisoners to their feet.

Chapter Twenty-Five

DALLION and Tawny Paul were moved to the frigate, which would carry them to the Isle of Runes. Before they left, Saige asked Blakeshire what would happen to them, and he explained that the pirates would be put on trial by a tribunal that specialized in charges of piracy. If found guilty, which he seemed certain they would be, Dallion and Tawny Paul would be hanged within the next day or so. Saige successfully feigned indifference to this information. Inside, however, she was nearly giving in to panic.

The Crescent Moon was allowed to continue on her way into port. As soon as the soldiers were gone from the ship, Journey and Saige retreated to their cabin. The broken door would no longer stay closed on its own, so Journey braced it shut with one of the chairs. As soon as it was secure, Saige burst into tears. She moved to put herself in Journey's arms, and he held her as she cried against his chest. A million thoughts raced through his head, but the one that trumped all others was the sight of the betrayal that had been in Dallion's eyes. But what could he have done?

For now, he took on the task of calming Saige down, and after a few minutes, he got her to sit down on the cot that wasn't against the door. He sat down beside her, and he didn't object when she twined her fingers with his. There were still tears in her eyes, but she'd managed to stop crying. She asked him, "There's hope for them, isn't there? Do you think Dallion can convince the tribunal that he's not who they think he is?"

Journey knew enough about such "trials" to know that they were generally over within a few minutes, and they nearly always resulted in a guilty verdict. Considering how much money Horizon and their partners had lost to Dallion in the past, it was not going to end well for him. Saige must have read this in Journey's silence, for she began to weep again. She rested the side of her head against his shoulder and whispered, "I couldn't save them. They already knew who Dallion was, and I thought it would be too suspicious if I told them that I was related to both you and Paul. I didn't know what else to do."

"You did everything you could," he told her, resting his head against hers. "You didn't have to save me, but you did. I owe you."

"Then why do I feel so guilty?" she asked, but Journey didn't have an answer for that. He was struggling with the same feeling.

Chapter Twenty-Six

BEFORE long, Webb sent a sailor to their cabin to let them know that they were about to enter one of the three ports that the Isle of Runes was so famous for. Journey made his way to the quarterdeck with a heavy heart, Saige in tow. They found the entrance flanked by massive, stone pillars that were carved with ancient runes, the meanings of which could only be guessed at, these days. The pillars loomed more than two hundred feet above the shoreline they were perched upon. They had been left here by some ancient civilization, and under better circumstances, Journey would have marveled over their size and age. The only emotions that he was capable of feeling now, however, were grief and guilt.

Webb emerged out of the commotion of scrambling sailors who were getting the ship ready to dock, and he approached Journey and Saige with an apologetic look on his face. As he joined them on the quarterdeck, he said gently, "I'm sorry for all the trouble you've experienced aboard the Moon. Captain Mercier once fell victim to a pirate scam, himself. I hope this hasn't entirely dashed your business plans. A deal is a deal, however, and we're still owed another hundred marks for your passage here."

Journey reached into his pocket and took out fifty marks. It was the last of his own money, as he'd spent everything else he'd had on the swan necklace for Saige, but he offered it to Webb, saying, "Unfortunately, the pirates were carrying the rest of our money in their pockets."

He accepted the cash with a look of pity that Journey didn't much care for, but certainly needed. "Pirates are excellent fraudsters, if nothing else. We'll call it even with this. After all, we're only delivering half of the agreed passengers to port."

Journey muttered that he was grateful as Webb retreated up the length of the deck with the money. Saige asked, "Was that really the last of the money?"

He didn't want to worry her by telling her the truth, but he also didn't feel like lying to her. Instead, he opted not to respond and waited in silence as the Moon maneuvered gracefully into port.

They stepped off the ship to find an island that was unlike any Saige had ever imagined. All of the walkways and streets here were smoothly paved, and they were teeming with people, horses, and fancy carriages. There were bustling shops that catered to visitors and locals alike, taverns advertising affordable rooms and cold drinks, and street vendors selling everything from clothing to bouquets of flowers. A pair of regal-looking horses trotted by, pulling a wooden carriage that was decorated with elegant ribbons, and Saige marveled over how wealthy its passengers must have been to afford such luxury. This was a place of profit and affluence, and everywhere she looked, she found a myriad of new and enticing things to gawk over.

She reeled herself in and forced herself to focus on the mission they had come here to accomplish. Journey's steps were quick and determined as he led her away from the docks, and Saige hurried to keep up with him. As she did, she asked, "Where do you think they took Dallion and Tawny Paul? Are they somewhere close by?"

"They're probably on the other side of the island," he answered as he paused on a street corner to get his bearings. Saige marveled over a storefront that boasted shelf after shelf of leather-bound books. She'd never seen so many in one place before.

Journey got moving again, and Saige pressed on beside him. As they passed through the busy streets, however, a towering structure came into view above the other buildings, and Saige's steps faltered as she struggled to grasp what she was seeing. It must have been nearly three hundred feet tall, and its walls were made of iron-reinforced stone that reflected the sunlight off of their smooth surfaces. She'd never imagined something so big and could only guess as to how many floors were inside it.

Journey paused when he noticed that she'd fallen behind, and he returned the short distance down the street to her to urge, "We should keep going, Saige."

She pointed to the massive building and dared, "There?"

Journey nodded and offered his hand to her. She took hold and gave it an excited squeeze. He led her down a few more streets, until they found themselves in the shadow of the building they needed. It loomed over them at such a height that it made Saige dizzy to look up at it. The doors were made of some type of dark metal that she didn't recognize. Journey led her through one, and they entered a lobby that would have been lavish enough for royalty. Everything was made of either marble or glass. High above them hung a chandelier made of sparkling crystal. Saige came to a stop as she reached the center of the stunning room. Men and women in expensive clothing bustled past her, going about their business here, but she hardly noticed any of them. On the far wall, above a long, marble desk, there was a massive painting of a square-rigged ship. Along her side were the words Commercial Horizon. Saige had never seen such beautiful artwork.

She realized that Journey had made his way to the marble desk, and she hurried to join him there. There was a young woman sitting in a tall, black chair behind the desk, and she offered them both a practiced smile. "Welcome to Commercial Horizon. How may I help you?"

"My name is James Terrance," Journey answered, reflecting that smile. "We'd like to speak with Audrey Dumont."

"I'm afraid Ms. Dumont doesn't accept visitors without an appointment. You're welcome to schedule a time to return next week."

Journey launched into a lengthy explanation of why their business was more urgent than that, but Saige hardly heard any of it. She'd been distracted by the sound of burbling water, and she searched the expansive room to spot its source: a beautiful fountain that stood nearly twice her height. It featured three bronze statues of mermaids resting on slabs of stone. She found her feet drifting toward the fountain in awe, and as she arrived, she saw that the rectangular basin was filled with dozens of live fish. Their scales glimmered prettily in the water as they swam in lazy circles. The reality of how extravagant this place was sank all the way in, at last, and Saige recalled Journey telling her that she was underestimating how much ten percent of her inheritance was going to be. Just how rich was she about to become?

Journey called her name, and she pushed through her astonishment to return to him at the marble desk. The woman behind it stood and offered her hand over its surface. As Saige shook it, the woman told her, "It's a pleasure to meet you, Ms. Travert. I can schedule you to speak with Ms. Dumont tomorrow morning. Company partners are always our highest priority.

May I suggest a few nearby restaurants that you might like to visit for dinner? Only the best, of course."

"Of course," Saige agreed, and she hoped that she didn't sound as dazed as she currently felt.

They stepped outside again less than twenty minutes after going in. Having nothing but time to waste, at this point, Saige set about exploring the unfamiliar streets. Journey followed her, his thoughts on so many things besides the jewelry, fabric, and pottery that Saige fawned over. He had to do something about Dallion and Tawny Paul – that was the foremost matter on his mind. But before he could consider taking any action related to that, he needed to make certain that Saige was safe. He had no money with which he could pay for a room. He wouldn't have minded sleeping in an alleyway somewhere...but one look at Saige in her pretty, blue dress and the childlike look of joy on her face convinced him that he didn't have it in him to ask the same of her.

Saige came to a stop in front of a store that sold ceramic dishes and vases, and she gazed at the wares through the large, glass window. Journey joined her there, and he was surprised when she asked, "Why did you and Dallion agree to just ten percent?"

His heart felt as if it skipped a beat as he had to wonder how close she was to figuring him out. When he looked at her, however, she was smiling at him. She pressed, "Well?"

He feigned apathy. "It seemed fair."

"You could have pushed for more, and I wouldn't have known any better."

"Do you want to go inside?" he asked suddenly, motioning toward the door of the ceramics shop. Saige hesitated, perhaps trying to decide whether or not to let him shift the conversation. To his relief, she started for the door, and he followed her in. He found himself surrounded by tall shelves that housed countless cups, plates, bowls, and vases. They were all made out of fine porcelain, and their hand-painted designs were some that he could imagine Jubilee liking, if she'd still been alive. He was always surprised by the little things that still made him miss her.

The shopkeeper immediately approached Saige and began showering her with compliments and suggestions of what she may like to look at. Journey waited patiently as the man whisked her around the end of one of the shelves to show her some of his fancier pieces. Once they were out of sight of the door, Journey slipped through it and joined the bustling crowds on the streets once more. Dallion and Wee Bit had taught him how to pick pockets over the past two years, but he wasn't especially good at it. It took him a long time to find a target that he felt confident about. It was an older man in an expensive suit. While the man stood in a crowd on a street corner and watched a juggling act, Journey relieved him of the marks in his pocket. He held his breath as he retreated, expecting the old man to cry out that he was a thief, but nothing of the sort happened. He waited until he was around the corner of a nearby building before counting the money, and he was glad to find that it would be enough to cover a room for the night, and possibly even something for dinner.

Relieved that he'd only had to do that once, he returned to the shop he'd left Saige in…only to find that she was no longer there. His heart sped up with concern – she had no experience in a place like this, and he was certain that he wasn't the only pirate on this island who was bold enough to take whatever he wanted. He went back outside and scanned the busy street for her. There were so many people, so many other places that she may have ventured, so many dangers her on her own...

At last, he spotted her, peering through the window of yet another shop up the street. Relief swept through him, and he realized for the first time just how worried he'd been. He'd told himself that he wouldn't start falling for the girl, and here he was, nearly frantic because he'd let her out of his sight for a little while. He could almost hear Dallion's voice telling him to get his head on straight, and that was exactly the type of advice he needed right now.

As he joined her in front of the shop's window, Saige merely told him, "I was wondering if you'd gotten lost somewhere."

"I don't know why you didn't stay there to wait for me," he said, and his tone was a little sharper than he'd intended.

She looked at him, the sunlight shining in her fiery hair and her perfect lips turned up at the edges, and he knew that it was too late to keep reminding himself not to fall for her. She teased, "Were you worried about me, Journey?"

He shrugged. "You're an adult and you can take care of yourself, Saige."

"That's true, but were you worried about me, anyway?"

He leaned toward her, intending to whisper a smart comeback in her ear, but he breathed in the scent of her hair as he got close, and it dismissed all thoughts from his head. In that moment, he had to have her. He needed her like he needed to breathe air or like sails needed the wind. He sensed that she was holding her breath in anticipation of his words or touch, and something passed between them, something good and exciting and a dozen other things that he didn't have names for.

He said nothing, but stepped back, not allowing himself to meet her gaze. He could feel her eyes on him, curious and disappointed, but all he said to her was, "We should go find somewhere to stay before they rent all the rooms for the night. We'll get something to eat, too. I'm starving."

She agreed, although the butterflies in her stomach had dismissed any hint of an appetite. As she let him lead her down the bustling street, she wondered if she had the courage to make the first move, if he wouldn't.

Chapter Twenty-Seven

THE inn they chose was called Second Home, and it was so cozy and welcoming inside that the name fit. Even the tavern downstairs was comfortable and nonthreatening, with signs posted on the walls that said that anyone caught fighting or gambling would be made to leave immediately. All of the rooms were rented except for one, and Journey was glad to find that the cost was within their budget. The tavern downstairs was serving cod and fresh vegetables, and they both ate their fill. Then they headed upstairs and to the last door on the right. The room was small, but cozy, with a canopied bed and heavy curtains over the window. Saige sat down on the side of the bed with a sigh.

"What are we going to tell Lucien and everyone else?"

He didn't want to think that far ahead, yet. Instead, he went to the window and moved the curtain to look out on the street below. He said without turning, "I'm going to go see if I can hire a place on an outgoing ship for tomorrow. We should get out of here as soon as we're done meeting with Audrey Dumont."

He heard something in his own voice that he thought she might not trust, but hoped she hadn't heard it. She was silent for a moment before asking, "Do you want me to go with you?"

"No," he said, probably a little too quickly. He turned from the window and offered her a disarming smile. "Get some rest. I won't be gone long."

She only nodded and watched as he left, off to do something that almost certainly wasn't what he'd claimed.

Dallion sat in a dank jail cell that was only one in a row of over a dozen. Some of them were empty, but most of them contained men who had done something to earn the wrath of Commercial Horizon. There were a few torches on the wall outside of the cells, but none of them were lit. Instead, the only light in here was from the tiny windows near the very top of some of the cells. The one in Dallion's cell was only about a foot long by half a foot tall, and even that small of a space was reinforced with metal bars. It did little in the way of providing airflow, and the stench in this place was almost unbearable. His cell was a four-by-four-foot square with a stone floor and a small pile of moldy straw in one corner. It was cold in here – he hadn't stopped shivering since his arrival – and he wondered if he might freeze to death before they managed to hang him. He almost hoped so. At least it would steal away the bastards' satisfaction of watching him swing.

Tawny Paul was in the cell beside his. Both men sported injuries they'd received during their trip here. Tawny's ribs were sore, and one of his eyes were swollen so badly that he could barely see with it. Dallion's left cheek was bruised and tender, and he'd been punched in the stomach so many times that he'd vomited twice. The first round had occurred when he and Tawny had decided to try to fight their way off of the galleon that had brought them here. The second bout of abuse had come just after being placed in this cell. According to the Horizon employee who had done him the honor, Dallion had killed some relative of his a year ago, while raiding a ship off the coast of Toma. Now, his body ached as he lay on his back on the cold, stone floor and stared up at the tiny slat of daylight he could see through the window. Tawny was sitting in the pile of hay in his own cell, dozing, but he woke as one of the other prisoners a few cells away began shouting for someone to let him out. No one came, and after a few minutes, the man quieted.

As if Dallion had said something, Tawny Paul assured him, "He'll come."

Dallion didn't respond. Even if Journey was inclined to find them, he had no way of getting them out of here. Their "trial" was scheduled for this evening, and there was no question as to what the verdict would be. After that, it wouldn't be long before they were led to the gallows. They'd passed three corpses on their way into this jail. They'd been hung up on poles outside. Wooden signs that simply read Pirate had been hung around their decaying necks. Dallion had always known that such an end to his life was possible, but he had never imagined that it would be because his closest friend would leave him to die while he got away with the money, the girl, and all the freedom one could ask for.

He took the shark tooth out of the top of his shirt and turned it over and over in his fingers, twisting its twine necklace first one way, then the other. For the first time in quite a while, he wondered where Katria Laurent was. Had she married? Were there children? If so, did they share her dark, inquisitive eyes? He wondered if she'd thought of him at all over the years, pondering where he might be and how he was doing. After this long, did she even remember him, at all? After this, would anyone?

"He's coming," Tawny told him again, taking his continued silence for a rebuttal.

"He bailed," Dallion said, at last. He didn't take his gaze off of that unreachable slat of freedom above him. "He'd be a fool to try anything here."

"Everyone knows that you and Teach are like brothers. He won't just let you hang."

Dallion grunted, but didn't argue further. He recalled their argument aboard the Crescent Moon and knew that if Journey didn't come for them, he couldn't blame him. Either it was because he was in love with the girl, or Dallion's accusation that he'd betray him and the others for her had been a betrayal in itself. It didn't matter which one was true. With any luck, Journey was boarding another ship at this very moment, Saige at his side and his adopted father's money stowed safely in his pockets. Dallion envied him for the life that was laid out before him.

He said to Tawny Paul, "At the trial, tell them that I forced you into piracy because you're a good navigator. I'll say it's true. Maybe they'll show you some mercy. It's worth a try."

"He'll come," Tawny muttered, and Dallion only wished that he could believe it.

CHAPTER TWENTY-EIGHT

JOURNEY returned to the room at the tavern just before nightfall. He'd asked the right questions of the right people, and their answers had led him all the way to the other side of the island, where only Horizon personnel were supposed to be. The prison there was a squat, stone building that he'd been told housed suspected pirates, thieves, and conmen who had been captured by the company's galleons. He hadn't been able to get close, as the place had been swarming with people who would have known that he didn't belong there. His only chance would be to return after dark, and even then, the odds of being able to get anywhere near that building without getting caught were slim.

But there was something else that he needed to do first. When he came into their room, he found Saige asleep on the bed. One hand was lost in the curls of her hair on her pillow, but the other hand was clasping the swan pendent on her chest. The room's single lantern cast a warm glow over her, and mysterious shadows danced over her pretty face. He wondered what could have been between them in another life, but then squashed the thought. What would a good, honest woman like this want with a cheap pirate like him?

He sat down on the side of the bed and spoke her name, but she didn't stir. He simply watched her sleep for a little while as that warm light played tricks in her hair. Her chest rose and fell with her gentle breaths, and her eyes moved beneath their lids as she dreamed. He reached out and brushed a red curl from her forehead. A goodbye had never been this hard.

He spoke her name again, and this time, she woke. She opened her sleepy eyes, and immediately brightened at the sight of him. She got into a sitting position with the bed's numerous pillows propped between her back and the headboard, and she asked, "Did you find a ship?"

He didn't answer, staring down at his hands in his lap. She repeated her question, and he finally said, "Saige, there's something that I need to do. I'm not going to be able to go with you to see Audrey Dumont tomorrow. You're going to have to do that on your own."

"If you're going to go help Dallion and Paul, then I want to go with you," she said without hesitation.

He looked at her, surprised. She shrugged. "That's more important to me right now. We can come back to see Audrey once they're safe."

"No," he said, his voice so stern that it took her off guard. "If you do anything that might make them think you're associated with Dallion, you'll never see your money from this company. All they'll want to give you is a rope. You need to stick to the plan and go see Audrey Dumont in the morning. Show her the letter that Winnie wrote. Don't throw everything away over a couple of worthless pirates."

"And what are you doing?" she asked in disbelief. "You're throwing away the ten percent that I promised you. And if you're going to call them worthless pirates, what does that make you, Journey?"

"I don't pretend to be anything better," he said, but there was sadness in his voice. "I know who I am, Saige. You need to figure out who you are and what you really want."

Without warning, she leaned forward, taking hold of the top of his waistcoat, and pressed her lips against his. There was no hesitation on his part; his hands went instantly to her hair, and he ran them through her curls as he returned her kiss. Her soft lips parted as her tongue met his, and she didn't care how far he wanted to take this. If he wanted her completely, she would allow it. She certainly wanted him.

But after only a few seconds, he broke their frantic connection and pulled away to get to his feet. She let him go, but whispered his name as he walked to the window. He stood there for a while, his back to her and his eyes on the darkening street below. He took a few seconds to get his thoughts under control. Finally, he said without turning, "In another life, I would leave with you tomorrow and never look back. I'd beg you to marry me. I'd be faithful and kind, and I'd thank every star in the sky for you. But this isn't another life, Saige. I owe it to Dallion to try to save him. He took me in when he didn't have to, when I was just a rich brat of very little use. I can't betray him."

"They'll hang you, too!" she cried, fighting back tears that threatened to fall. "If you get caught, they'll hang all three of you together. Is that what you want?"

"What I want doesn't matter. Dallion's like a brother to me. I can't leave him here to die, no matter what." He paused, then added softly, "No matter whom."

She groaned in frustration. "What are you talking about?"

"I'm not the kind of man you think I am," he said, and now there was anger in his voice, as well as sadness. He still hadn't turned to her, but she saw his hands curl into fists at his sides. "Dallion and I had a plan of our own. We were going to maroon you somewhere and take off with all of the money. I thought it was a good idea, at first...but then I found myself falling for you, and I couldn't go through with it. The last conversation I had with him was an argument about it. He thought I was betraying him for you. I can't prove him right, now."

She said nothing, and when he finally turned to look at her, he found a mixture of hurt and fury on her face. In the light of the lamp, that fury looked more like hatred. He said quickly, "I wasn't going to go through with it, Saige. That's what I told Dallion..."

"You were going to go through with it," she hissed, and those tears she had been fighting back finally broke free. "You meant to cheat me out of the money and leave me all alone on a beach somewhere, until your conscience got the better of you. Tell me the truth, Journey: did you really decide not to go through with it at all, or were you going to wait until you'd bedded me?"

"It wasn't like that..."

"Then tell me what it's like!" she cried, leaving the bed to get shakily to her feet. "I don't know why I let you trick me into thinking that you might be a good person. You knew how poor my family is, and you still wanted to take me for everything I had. You don't care about my father, or our home, or even me! You don't care about anyone but yourself!"

"Saige..." he said, taking a step toward her, but she moved away from him, backing herself into the far corner. "Get out, Journey. If you don't get out, I'll go downstairs and tell anyone who'll listen that you're a pirate. We'll see how long you last up here after that."

He had no idea if she meant that or not, but he did know that it wouldn't be wise to test her. Still, he took his chances and approached her, his hands before him in a calming gesture, and he was glad when she didn't flinch away. She let him hug her, and as he pulled her close in his arms, her shoulders began to hitch with silent sobs that broke his heart. He brought his lips to her ear and whispered, "I'm so sorry. I thought I'd be able to go through with it, but then I got to know you, and I changed my mind. When you told me that you didn't blame me for having to grow up in poverty while I had everything I wanted...I can't tell you how sorry I am. For everything."

"I thought you were different," she said, struggling to keep her voice from breaking. "I thought that you were a good person."

"I'm sorry that I'm not what you thought I was," he breathed, squeezing her tighter. "All I want is for you to be happy. Meet with Audrey Dumont in the morning. Get what's rightfully yours. Let her buy you out of everything except one of the Twins – it'll be enough for you to live comfortably off of for the rest of your life. Hire good people from Kinsman Lane and pay them fair wages. Take care of Francis, find a good man to marry, and have children that you can raise without having to worry about how you're going to keep them fed. And if you ever think of me, I hope you can remember that here at the end, I only wanted you to have a good life and to be happy. Will you remember that?"

She brought her lips up to his ear, where her breath tickled his skin, and whispered, "I hate you, Journey. I hate you, and I love you."

He placed a soft, lingering kiss on her cheek and tasted her tears. He had a dozen things that he wanted to tell her, not the least of which was that he loved her, too...but the words were stuck in his throat, and he knew that he had to leave before she decided to forgive him. He had nothing to offer this young woman but more grief, and he cared for her too much to allow that to happen.

He let her go and started for the door without looking back. Saige's teary voice sobbed once more that she hated him, and the words stabbed his heart like hot knives. He left her there, closing the door behind him, and Saige sank to the floor beside the bed, her hands over her face to catch her tears and muffle her sobs.

Chapter Twenty-Nine

DALLION sat in the moldy pile of straw in his cell with his back against the cold stones of the wall behind him. He couldn't sleep, and what was the point of doing so, anyway? He only had a few more hours to live. The trial had been just as swift and biased as he'd known it would be, and it had taken them less than five minutes to decide that he was guilty. Tawny Paul's pleas for mercy had fallen on deaf ears, and he was scheduled to hang beside his captain at daybreak. If this was to be the last night that Dallion spent alive, he only wished that he could have spent it with an attractive woman and plenty of alcohol. It was a waste to squander his final hours in this cold, damp cell.

He'd thought that Tawny Paul was asleep, but his voice sounded from the darkness in the cell beside his, making him start. "Who do you think will be the next captain?"

"Pigeon, maybe," Dallion muttered. "But then they'd be losing the best sailing master any of them have ever seen. Horus or Quick Bill would be a smarter choice."

"Not Lucien?"

Dallion gave a dry laugh. "Lucien doesn't want it. Can you blame him?"

Tawny didn't answer, and after a little while, the soft sound of his snores told Dallion that he really was asleep, this time. Dallion rested the back of his head against the cold stone behind him. He could imagine his crew out there on the open waters, securing the Jubilee in case this rain shower became something uglier. The thought of any of them in command of the Jubilee was enough to make him angry. He cared more for that ship than he cared for himself.

He thought that he'd imagined it the first time his name was whispered in the darkness. Then it came again, and he sat up away from the wall. It sounded like it had come from two cells down, just on the other side of Tawny Paul's. The torches in here still weren't lit — he wondered why they even bothered keeping the things down here — and the rain clouds outside blocked most of the moonlight that might have otherwise come in through the small windows.

The whisper came again. The man in that cell was asleep, and his snores nearly drowned the sound out, but Dallion heard it. He got to his feet, somehow certain that he'd fallen asleep, after all, and this was a desperate dream of some sort. He backed up until he was near the gate of his cell, then crossed the short distance to the stone wall in two quick strides. He leapt, scrambling up the uneven stones of the wall with his boots, and caught one of the bars in the window with his left hand. He found tiny ledges between the stones to brace the toes of his boots in, and it was just enough to keep himself up here for the time being. He thrust his free hand between two of the bars, out into the rainy world outside. He snapped his fingers a few times, hoping that it was loud enough to get the whisperer's attention without also alerting any nearby guards.

After a few seconds that felt much longer, a hand gripped his on that side of the bars. The person's flesh was cold and wet from being out in the rain for a long time, but they squeezed his hand in greeting, and the silhouette of a man appeared in the gloom out there. He leaned close to the bars, and there was just enough light from a distant lamp in the window of the next building to reveal some features of his face. Dallion nearly barked laughter in relief of seeing him here, but managed to keep quiet, instead. His boots were threatening to lose their grip and slide down the stone wall, but for now, he stayed where he was and squeezed Journey's hand hard enough for it to hurt.

"I thought you'd bailed, you son of a bitch," Dallion whispered, unable to conceal his relief.

"I thought about it," he lied, but the grin that Dallion could barely see told him otherwise. "Is Tawny in there with you?"

"He's in the next cell over. We're going to need either keys or a miracle. Which one did you bring?"

"Neither of those, but I made an after-hours stop at a shop on the way here." He let go of Dallion's hand to give him one of the things he'd stolen. Dallion recognized the feel of a gun in his hand well enough to know what it was without having to see it in the darkness. He slipped it between the bars and clasped it against his chest so that he could feel along the sides of it with his fingers. It was one of the newfangled types that were slowly trickling into Cruxes from places like Withix and Dosk. It would be able to fire six bullets before needing to be reloaded.

"You lied," Dallion whispered through the bars. "This is a miracle."

"It'll be loud," Journey warned. "We'll need to make a run for it."

That was alright with Dallion. Even if he didn't make it out of here alive in the morning, at least he now had a way of putting up a good fight. One thing was certain: no matter what happened at daybreak, he wouldn't meet the noose. That was good enough for him.

The sound of a door closing somewhere in the next building reached their ears, and Journey whispered, "I'll be nearby." With that, he was gone, and Dallion was left with only the soft pitter-patter of rain on the muddy ground outside the window.

He let his boots slide down the wall to the floor, wincing at how loud the sound was as he landed. It was enough to make the prisoner in the cell beside his wake from whatever sleep he'd been managing to get, and he grumbled something about letting a man enjoy his last night alive. Dallion ignored him and went to the other side of his cell to squat down beside the bars. He reached between them and found Tawny Paul's shoulder in the wet straw. He gave him a shake, and Tawny woke with a start.

"It's me," Dallion whispered, squeezing his shoulder. "When they come for us in the morning, be ready."

He saw the dark blob that was Tawny's silhouette nod its head, and Dallion was glad that he didn't ask any questions. He let him go and returned to his own pile of straw. He had bullets to count to make sure the gun was full and ready. He also had a few hours to wait until it was time to use them. The most important thing that he now had, however, was hope.

Outside, there were several stacks of wooden barrels beneath an awning behind the next building, and Journey spent the rest of the night there, sitting between two of the stacks of barrels in the mud to stay hidden from sight. The rain continued to fall, and it drummed lightly against the awning above him. The sound threatened to lull him off to sleep. He didn't want to doze, afraid that he would miss signs of approaching guards before it was too late. He was also afraid that he would dream of Saige, and that wasn't something he was prepared to deal with, yet. It was going to be a long, painful road to forgetting her, and he would have to begin the trek down it if he happened to survive whatever happened in the next few hours.

On the other side of the island, Saige stood at the window of her rented room, watching the rain run in gentle waves down the other side of the glass. Her head was aching from all the tears she'd cried, but she was too anxious to sleep. She tried to imagine Journey out there, skulking through the rain on his search for his fellow pirates. She decided that she would do as he'd suggested with the islands and return to her adopted father with promises of a safe, secure future. They had everything to gain and nothing to lose.

So why did it feel as if she had lost something more important than any of the money and security that was now within her grasp?

Chapter Thirty

BEFORE the sun had cleared the horizon, the guards came into the prison to retrieve the hangman's first victim for the day. It was a middle-aged man with a mouthful of rotting teeth and very little hair on his head. He cursed the guards and spat on their boots as they dragged him from his cell, clamping irons around his thin wrists as they went. Dallion and Tawny Paul watched them drag the man down the corridor and out the door at the end of the room. Then there was a heavy silence about the place, and the rest of the men in the cells looked around at one another with wide eyes as they wondered who would be next.

The gun that Journey had brought here was stashed within the straw in Dallion's cell. It was only a few inches away from his hand, but his fingers longed to hold it. Soon. He didn't know where Journey was or if he'd be able to give him much help once the bullets started flying, but he had restored faith in the young man that he considered his closest friend, and he didn't doubt that Journey would do everything he could.

The bang of the trapdoor in the gallows was so loud that he heard it down here. The sound sent shivers down his spine, and he could almost feel the burn of a rope pulling tight around his own neck. It was the fear of every pirate on the seas, no matter how daring or reckless. There were rumors that sometimes, when a pirate was particularly hated by a company, the executioner was sometimes paid extra to ensure that his neck didn't break, making for a longer, painful death by strangling.

He didn't know if that was true, but deep down, he feared it was. He continued to fight the urge to hold the gun.

After a few minutes, the same three guards returned and made their way past the other cells. They came to a stop before his and Tawny Paul's, and one of the guards growled, "You two are next. Be men about it and don't try to make a scene."

They didn't answer, and the guard took out a set of keys. There was a moment when Dallion thought that he was going to open his cell up first, which would have thrown his entire plan out the window...but then he placed the key in the lock on Tawny's door and opened it up.

Tawny cast an anxious glance toward Dallion, and he gave him the slightest nod of his head. Tawny stood very still as two of the guards stepped into his cell and began putting a pair of iron cuffs around his wrists. They were so tight that they hurt, but Tawny didn't flinch. He followed the guards out of his cell and stood to the side, where they told him to wait. Then the guard with the keys reached for the lock on the next door, and Dallion braced himself. His hand inched toward the gun, but it wasn't time to take it out, yet. He waited as two of the guards came into his cell, one of them holding the metal cuffs out toward him.

"Time to go," he said, and Dallion grinned. It certainly was.

The gun was in his hand before any of the three guards realized what was happening. The sound was deafening in the stone basement, and Dallion's ears began ringing so loudly that it was all he could hear. The man with the cuffs stared at him, dumbfounded, as a bloom of red appeared and began to spread across the front of his chest. It stood out in stark contrast to the white material of his uniform shirt. His comrade was gaping at the gun in Dallion's hands, and as Dallion turned its deadly barrel in his direction, he let out a panicked shriek and scrambled toward the door of the cell. It was too late; Dallion pulled the trigger again. The bullet caught the man in the shoulder, and he fell to the floor with an agonized scream. Dallion fired a third time, and this one found the back of the man's head. He collapsed in silence, at last.

The third guard had recovered from his shock a little quicker, and he had managed to get his rifle off his back and into his hands. He raised it as Dallion was ending the life of the second guard, and he would have had him, if not for Tawny Paul. He brought his bound hands up and over the guard's head to slip the chain that connected the two cuffs beneath his chin. He pulled, tightening the chain against the guard's throat, and his shot went high. The bullet whizzed over Dallion's head and ricocheted off of the stone wall behind him. Dallion crouched, but the guard wasn't able to get off another shot. Tawny yanked him backward, making him stumble and almost fall down. He dropped the rifle to dig frantically at the chain across his throat.

Dallion was out of his cell in a few quick steps. To save his few remaining bullets, he turned the gun around and brought the hard, metal grip down against the top of the guard's head. The man cried out in pain before going limp in Tawny's arms. Tawny let him fall to the floor at Dallion's feet. There was a ruckus on the other side of the door at the end of the room, and Dallion started in that direction, his aim steady and his heart racing. The ringing in his ears hadn't stopped, but he could hear the shouts of at least two more guards through the door.

They threw the door open and came into the room with guns of their own in their hands. Dallion took out the one with the rifle first, catching him in the middle of his chest. He went down in a heap. The second guard had a pistol, and he squeezed off two shots before Dallion could take aim at him. The first one missed, zinging off a set of bars to his right, but the second one found its mark. Hot pain lit up the side of Dallion's neck. He cried out, going to his knees, and squeezed the trigger. The bullet struck the guard in the left ankle, and he howled in pain as he stumbled against the bars of the cell beside him. He fired his gun, but the bullet went wide, and then it was Dallion's turn again. He pulled the trigger, and the bullet caught the man in the forehead. He slid slowly down the metal bars beside him until he was a puddle of a corpse on the floor before it.

The other prisoners in the room were begging to be let out, but Dallion didn't hear them. It wasn't the ringing in his ears – that was bad, but not bad enough to block out their shouts and cries for help – but the sound of his own heartbeat in his head. Blood was pouring from the hole in the side of his neck and soaking the shoulder of his shirt. He clapped a hand over the wound, but that wasn't going to do much. It wasn't helping that he was breathing hard, as if he'd just run a mile. He took a few deep breaths to try to calm himself down, even as he struggled up from his knees and onto his feet. His legs felt rubbery. Worst of all, he was out of bullets.

There was a firm hand on his shoulder, and he realized dazedly that Tawny Paul was here. His hands were no longer cuffed together, as he'd scrambled to use the dead guard's dropped keys to free his wrists. Now, he held up a rifle that one of the guards had dropped, and he stepped past Dallion to start for the door, motioning for him to follow. Dallion did so, one hand still pressing against the wound in his neck. The blood continued to flow.

No guards appeared at the top of the stairs as they started up them, but Tawny paused as he heard a series of four gunshots somewhere outside. Dallion shoved him forward with his free hand, muttering, "It's Journey. Move!"

He got going again, and Dallion followed close behind. They arrived on the ground level to find the building empty. The front door was open, however, and the legs of a fresh corpse were blocking it from closing. They made their way to the door and stepped over the body, only to find two more dead guards in the small yard in front of the building. The rain was mixing their spilled blood into the mud on the ground around them as their unmoving eyes stared up at the morning's dark clouds.

There were shouts coming from all directions of the surrounding cluster of buildings, but only one of them registered in Dallion's ears: Journey's voice calling his name from between two nearby buildings. Tawny Paul started in that direction, running with his head low as his boots splashed through the mud. Dallion followed, but at a much slower pace. He wondered if he was going to bleed to death as his boots sloshed through the mud beneath him. Each step was a struggle to take, and he didn't know how much farther he would be able to go.

Just before he reached the gap between the two buildings, there was an arm around his waist, and then Journey was helping him. Dallion put his free arm around Journey's shoulders, and they hobbled into the relative safety of the space between the buildings. Behind them, a half a dozen guards arrived in the rain-soaked yard and filed into the prison building, calling out for their fallen comrades inside. Tawny Paul was already at the other end of the buildings, peeking out from around their corners. Journey said in a hushed voice as they reached him, "The edge of the island is a rocky cliff. There's enough cover there to stay out of the way of their bullets."

Tawny nodded in understanding and rushed out from the cover of the two buildings. There was only a row of small warehouses between here and the cliffs that were their destination, but just before he could safely reach the first warehouse, three shots rang out in rapid succession from somewhere further down the row. One of them found Tawny, and it delved deep into his right side. He threw himself across the short distance remaining before the corner of the warehouse, and once he was safely behind it, he writhed in pain in the muddy grass there as he clasped his hands over the new hole in his side.

Journey pulled Dallion back away from the corner of the building they were behind, and Dallion nearly fell down as his feet tangled together. Journey let him go and motioned for him to stay where he was. Behind them, the guards were coming back out of the prison building and were calling for reinforcements. It would only be a matter of seconds before they found them here.

Journey closed his eyes, forcing himself to be patient, and listened as the sound of footprints approached from wherever the man who had shot Tawny had been hiding. He was coming at a run, doubtlessly convinced that he'd successfully downed his mark. When Journey stepped out from around the corner, his pistol raised and his steps calm and measured, the guard wasn't ready for him. He skidded to a halt and tried to get his own gun up in time, but it was too late. Journey fired twice, and both shots struck the man in the chest. He went down in a wheezing mass in the mud.

Dallion got moving again without Journey's help, and they both darted across the gap before the warehouses to join Tawny. He had managed to get to his feet, but it was clear from the way that he was doubled over that he wasn't going to be able to move very quickly. That was alright – the first large boulders that lined the edge of the cliff were less than thirty yards away from here. Journey got a shoulder under one of his arms and half-dragged him toward the rocks. They would have to try to make a stand once they got there. Journey wasn't sure how many rounds Tawny's borrowed rifle could hold, but he knew that his own gun had one bullet left in it. There were six more in his pocket, and he would need some time to load them.

They'd almost made it when bullets began to ricochet off of the boulders as guards and soldiers opened fire behind them. Journey felt a bullet pass so close that it fluttered air against the side of his head. Dallion reached the rocks and turned to raise one of his hands in the air in a catching motion. He called, "Give me a gun!"

Journey tossed him his own, and Dallion managed not to fumble it. He fired toward the Horizon men, but the gun only loosed its single bullet before giving a series of dry and pointless clicks. Dallion roared in fury and threw the empty gun to the ground at his feet. It had worked, however – the shot had frightened the guards and soldiers into retreating around the sides of the warehouse. It bought Journey and Tawny enough time to get behind the boulder, and then all three of them leaned against it, breathing hard.

"What next?" Tawny panted as he squatted down beside the boulder. Journey saw that the blood from his side was pouring out at an alarming rate that was even worse than Dallion's wound. He didn't doubt that Tawny was in terrible pain, but he'd made it this far, and that was something. Journey continued to lean tiredly against the boulder and told him, "That was it. That was my whole plan. I was hoping that one of you would have an idea about where to go from here."

Dallion swayed a little, and Journey cussed under his breath. He tore a strip of material from the bottom of his shirt and folded it into a makeshift pad. He handed it to Dallion, who moved his hand away from the hole in his neck just long enough to place the material over it. He held it there as he tried to slow his breathing so that his heart would stop pumping the blood through the wound so hard. As he did, Journey retrieved the gun he'd thrown down at his feet, and he got to work loading his last six bullets into it.

The Horizon men's bravery must have returned, for they began shooting once more. Their bullets shattered small flakes of stone from the edges of the boulder. Journey guessed from the sound of it that more soldiers had joined the others on that side of the warehouses. It wouldn't be long before they worked up the courage to storm the short distance to their temporary refuge. Journey scanned the edge of the cliff on either side of them for any possible escape route, but everywhere he looked, it was a sheer drop to the sea below. He noticed Dallion's gaze over the edge and realized what he was thinking. Journey stepped up to the edge, as well, and peered over. The ocean was nearly fifty feet below them, and the waves that were crashing against the stony side of the island promised injuries and likely death. Journey and Dallion looked at one another, and Journey shook his head firmly.

"Not a chance. Not with the shape the two of you are in."

There was an explosion on the other side of the boulder as some sort of grenade went off. The entire boulder shuddered, and the ground beneath their feet quaked with the shock. Tawny panted, "We don't have much time."

"You two can stay up here if you want to," Dallion told them as he bent to unlace one of his boots with the hand not pressed against his neck. "I'm going to swim for it."

"Swim for what?" Journey cried, sweeping an arm out toward the expanse of ocean before them. "The next island is at least thirty miles away, Dal! Is drowning really any better than taking a bullet?"

"I guess I'm going to find out," he chuckled, and Journey wondered if the man had lost his mind.

There was another explosion, and this time, it showered them with chunks of stone and a spray of mud. Tawny began taking off his boots, as well, and Journey understood that the decision had already been made. He took off his own boots, then helped Dallion take off his second.

"Lead with your feet," Tawny croaked as he tossed his boots aside. "As soon as you're in the water, swim away from the rocks. If you surface too soon, the waves will just throw you up against them."

"We've all gone insane," Journey informed them, but then came the sound they had feared the most: the thunder of two-dozen boots stomping across the mud and rock between here and the warehouses. Their time was up. Dallion clapped him on the shoulder, offered one of his most arrogant grins, and took a running leap over the edge. Tawny followed. Journey brought up the rear, and his feet left the edge of the cliff just as the first soldier rounded the boulder. He fired two shots at him, but his aim while running was wild, and both of them missed.

Journey kept his feet pointed toward the water, as Tawny had advised, but it still felt as if he'd crashed through a stone wall as he hit the surface. He shot through the salty water like an arrow, and he had to fight against his instincts that screamed for him to start swimming toward the surface. Instead, he swam away from the cliff with all his might. He swam until he thought his lungs would explode, and then he swam some more. The memory of the night he'd escaped Landon's attempted murder flooded his head, but he pushed it away and focused on staying alive. Just as the first wave of dizziness swept over him, he finally let his head break the surface.

He gulped salty air into his tortured lungs, but above the sound of the crashing waves behind him, he could hear small splashes to his right and realized that they were bullets. He took another deep breath and dove back down into the water. He swam as far as he could, then surfaced once more. There was more space between him and the cliff, but it still wasn't enough. He dove again, and then again, and yet again. Each time he surfaced, he spared a second or two to look for Dallion and Tawny, but there was no sign of either of them. He kept going, and after a time that seemed like an eternity, he decided that he was far enough away to allow himself a rest. The soldiers and guards atop the cliff were no longer shooting, and he watched as the small dots that they had become left the top of the cliff in a hurry. They were going to alert one of the ships to come out here and collect the escaped prisoners, he didn't doubt. There was little that he'd be able to do to escape them.

He scanned the surrounding water for Tawny and Dallion, and his racing heart skipped a beat as he couldn't find either of them. They'd both been injured, and it had been foolish for them to make the jump and expect to be able to survive that swim...

The surface of the water broke to his left, and Dallion's head appeared for a short moment. Then he was under again, and judging by the flailing of his arms, it wasn't by choice. Journey swam the dozen or so yards to him and wrapped one arm beneath Dallion's own and across his chest to grip his opposite shoulder. He used all his strength to haul him back up above the surface. Their heads broke water, and Dallion gagged on the little bit that had made its way into his lungs. Journey helped keep him from sinking as he coughed the water up. As he did, Journey told him, "You're a crazy son of a bitch, Dal."

"That's me," he agreed between wheezed breaths. "Do you see Tawny Paul?"

Journey didn't answer, but that was enough. He looked all around them, searching for anything that could help them, but there was nothing to offer any hope. He stifled a laugh at the fact that things had circled around and he was in almost the exact same predicament he'd barely managed to survive two years ago. Instead of a crazy ex-father trying to kill him, though, there were dozens of soldiers headed this way on a ship. Dallion was so weak from the bullet wound in his neck that he wouldn't be able to swim much farther on his own, and Journey didn't know how far he'd be able to take him like this. Only a fool wouldn't have thought that all hope was lost. For only the second time in more than two years, Jubilee Travert's voice spoke up in his head, telling him that this wasn't finished. If that was true, then he wished that she would also tell him just how in all the worlds he was supposed to get both himself and Dallion out of this one.

Around the edge of a mass of stone that jutted out from the rest of the cliff to the south, a shape appeared that was so unbelievably lucky, he couldn't believe his eyes. It was a small fishing boat, and as Journey watched, the tiny shape of a fisherman appeared near its bow. It was in the opposite direction from which Horizon's ship would come. It was too good to be true, and yet it somehow was.

"We need to swim," he told Dallion. "If we don't get out of here before they send a ship out to pick us up, we're dead."

"I'm halfway there already," he said, but there was little fear or worry in his voice. He was looking up at the sky above them. The rainclouds had finally started to clear, and the sun was shining through them in long, beautiful shafts of golden light. "If I die, now, it's alright. I'll die a free man."

Journey let him go, forcing him to tread water on his own, and he managed to keep from going under. Journey shoved him with hand in the direction of the fishing boat, saying, "After everything I just went through to save your ass, you'd better make it to that boat."

Chapter Thirty-One

SAIGE sat in a small lobby on one of the highest floors in the Commercial Horizon building. The view out the window made her dizzy, so she focused on the fancy paintings on the walls, instead. There was also a mirror on one of the walls, but she'd already made the mistake of looking into that to see the dark circles beneath her eyes. They were evidence of how little sleep she'd managed to get last night. She'd spent hours staring up into the darkness above her bed, instead, while her heart had turned from feelings of betrayal to sadness and back again. She hated Journey, yet missed his presence. She was glad he was gone, but still longed for his touch.

The door on the other side of the lobby opened, and a woman with blond hair and business attire stuck her head out. "Ms. Dumont will see you, now."

Saige stood on legs that felt weak and headed through the door. The blond woman stepped aside, and Saige found herself in a large office that seemed to be all mahogany and glass. The far wall was one big window that gave a view of the surrounding island. It threatened to make Saige's head spin. Before the window sat a desk made of flawless wood. The woman sitting behind it stood from her chair to reveal a long, slender body clad in a tailored suit, the likes of which Saige had never seen a woman wear before. Her brown hair was pinned up in a tight bun, and her red lipstick matched the color of her earrings. She offered her hand across the desk, and Saige crossed the room to shake it, even giving a slight curtsy as she did so.

"Ms. Moore, it's a pleasure to meet you," Audrey Dumont said as she let go of her hand. Her grip had been firm, and Saige hoped that the woman hadn't felt how badly she was trembling. Dumont motioned to one of the two chairs on that Saige's side of the desk. "Have a seat and tell me what I can do for you."

She sank deep into the chair's cushion. She was nervous – this woman was practically a queen in her own right – but when she spoke, she was pleased to find that her voice didn't show it. "I recently learned that you've changed the inheritance bylaws for company partners," she said, reciting the words exactly as Journey had coached her. "I also understand that the changes can be applied retroactively, up to one generation."

Dumont's painted lips turned toward a grin. "And they told me that you were from some backwater port town in the south. You sound like a well-educated woman, Ms. Moore. And you're right: I have changed the bylaws concerning inheritance for this company. It's about time Commercial Horizon got over its obsession with whether or not someone has a penis in their pants, don't you agree?"

Saige was surprised into a laugh, which she quickly blushed about. It made Dumont's grin widen. "A woman has every right to her family's wealth and standings as any man does. However, I've been told that there's been some confusion about your bloodline. Is that accurate?"

"There was," she admitted, "but that's been cleared up. I was adopted by another family as an infant, but I have a letter from my adopted mother that explains what happened." She took the letter from her pocket, unfolded it, and offered it across the desk.

Dumont took it from her and read Winnie's neat printing on the page. When she was finished, she set the letter aside on the desk and folded her hands before her. Her brown eyes were sharp, and they studied Saige so penetratingly that it made her uncomfortable. She said, "I know that it's not great evidence, but..."

"You don't have to sell it to me," Dumont said. "I believe you. There are records indicating that Landon Travert alerted us to the plot carried out by his wife and adopted son. He reported it immediately after learning the truth, as he should have. There was also a sworn statement given by a man named Manton Laval that backed up Mr. Travert's claims. We knew there was a biological daughter out there, but had no idea where she could be. You showing up with this letter wraps everything up nicely, doesn't it?"

Saige wasn't sure how to read the woman's tone, so she remained silent. Dumont sat back a little in her chair, heaving a sigh. "The only issue is that we haven't encountered anything like this before. So far, all of the other women that this new bylaw has affected have had the backing of the rest of their family. There are birth records and witnesses willing to testify that they are whom they say they are. But you..." She shook her head. "You've come out of nowhere. Both of your biological parents are dead, your adopted mother is dead, and the young man who posed as Landon's son has been on the run for Jubilee Travert's murder for years, now. Frankly, it's a mess that Commercial Horizon is hesitant to get involved in."

"But you're already involved," she argued. "This company took things that are rightfully mine. Whether it's messy or not, it's the truth."

Dumont raised a calming hand as her grin returned. "All that is to say that we could drag this out for years, if we had to. But we won't. When I became president of this company, I vowed to be fair and honest. You're right about the Travert family's holdings being yours." She opened a drawer on that side of the desk and took out a large, blue folder. She dropped it onto the desk before her, where it made a heavy thud as it landed. It was at least two inches thick and looked to be crammed full of papers. Dumont set a hand on top of it and explained, "This contains records of all the holdings you're to inherit. Your father was a respectable businessman, and he was doing well for himself, right up until he was murdered by pirates. I'm prepared to surrender all of this to you, but we will not be compensating you for any of the profits we've made off of it since Landon Travert's death. However, I'm willing to offer you a buyout option, in which Commercial Horizon will pay you a sum equal to the worth of the market value of everything in this folder, and all assets will then remain under our ownership. The choice is yours to make."

Saige took a deep breath and told her what she wanted.

Chapter Thirty-Two

TO Journey's relief, the two men aboard the fishing boat heard his calls for help and turned the boat toward them quickly. The wind was in their favor, and before long, the fishermen were hauling Dallion out of the water. Journey came next, and they both collapsed onto their backs on the floor of the boat, panting hard. Journey turned his head to get a look at Dallion and make sure he was still breathing. He was pale and looked half-dead, but he'd somehow made it.

The younger of the two men looked to be around Journey's age, and he was firing off what may have been dozens of questions in rapid succession. The older man shouldered him aside, however, and growled, "Leave them alone for a minute, Edmund. Let these boys catch their breath."

If Journey had to guess his age, he would have placed him in his early fifties, but decades spent out on the salty water and unforgiving sun had weathered his face beyond his years. He was dressed in a loose, white shirt beneath a leather apron, which was typical for fishermen in these parts. There were no signs of company insignia on his clothing or on his boat, from what Journey could tell. The spark of hope that he'd allowed himself to feel started to grow.

"Where do you think they came from, pa?" Edmund asked.

"A mermaid's ass, for all I know," the older man grumbled. He squatted beside Journey and offered him a metal canteen. Journey took a sip of it and felt the warm burn of alcohol make its way down his throat. He coughed a few times, and the man grinned. "Brother-in-law makes it, himself. It'll warm you up quick after a swim in the water."

"Thank you for pulling us out," Journey panted, keeping his face turned toward the sun. It had never felt so good on his skin. "Our boat sank and I'd thought all hope was lost."

"Fishing boat?"

"That's right." He forced himself into a sitting position. His muscles thrummed and ached from the swim and everything else before it. He set a hand on Dallion's shoulder and squeezed. Dallion didn't open his eyes, but he gave a slight nod – he was alright.

"I'm Walter Lear," the older man said. "This is my son, Edmund. You boys are lucky we came along. I wasn't even planning on being on this side of the isle today. Must be some kind of providence."

"You've saved our lives, Mr. Lear. If you drop us off on shore, we'll be out of your way."

Edmund said, "We were about to cast out another net, so if your friend isn't in too bad of shape, we'll wait to take you in until after that…"

"We need to get back to shore right away," Journey objected. He cast an anxious look in the direction that they'd come from. Rounding the edge of the island, a small sloop came into view. A Commercial Horizon flag graced the top of her single mast.

Walter followed his worried gaze and understood more than Journey would have liked him to. The older man studied the two strangers carefully, and after a moment, he pried, "Fishing boat, you said?"

Journey nodded again, but Walter raised an eyebrow. "The two of you are dressed like you're off to sell your finest wares at market. I'd be willing to bet tonight's supper that neither of you were out here casting lines or nets. Besides, I've been fishing this side of the isle since I was nine years old, and I've never seen either of you two out here before." He nodded toward Dallion, who was still unmoving. "I'd also bet that hole in his neck was put there by somebody who wants him dead. Now, you can either start telling me the truth, young man, or get back over the side and swim for the little sloop that's headed this way. Something tells me they'll be glad to see you."

Dallion spoke up, at last, confessing, "They're pissed off because I escaped execution by hanging this morning, and they don't mean to let me go that easily."

"Hanging?" Edmund asked him. "What for?"

"Piracy. We've cost Horizon more money than they'd like to think about, and they want us dead for it."

Journey winced at this, afraid that such a blunt dose of truth hadn't been the best route to take, but Walter surprised him with a broad smile that revealed every last tooth in his mouth. "That's more like it. Let me tell you boys a story: my granddad raised three sons and a daughter on the money that Horizon used to pay him for his hauls. My old man raised me and my brother the same way. But me? A few years ago, Horizon started driving unfair prices and putting restrictions on fishing around here. I'm earning half of what my granddad used to, and it's for twice the weight in fish. If you ask me, it isn't right. Whatever money you've cost them, they probably owe me for all the perfectly good fish they refuse to pay full price for, anymore. To hell with Horizon. Let's get you boys to shore." Journey eyed the vanishing distance between them and the approaching sloop. "It's too late for that."

Walter gave an unworried shrug. "Well, we'll have to deal with these jokers, first. Edmund, help me with these nets.

This isn't going to smell great, boys, but it'll keep you out of a noose. Lay flat and stay still."

Journey did as instructed, laying on his back beside Dallion, who still hadn't moved much. Walter and his son got to work piling heavy, wet nets on top of them, and Journey could only hope that such a simple ploy would work.

He shouldn't have underestimated the power of simplicity. He stayed silent as the soldiers aboard the sloop drew close and signaled for Walter to bring his boat up beside theirs. He did so, until there were only a few yards between them. From beneath the pile of nets and a small tarp, Journey listened as one of the soldiers called down to the smaller vessel, asking if the fishermen on board had seen two men in the water. Walter looked the man directly in the eyes and lied through his teeth, claiming that he'd been out here for the last few hours, and he hadn't noticed anything but the sound of gunfire from farther up the side of the island. The soldier thanked him and then did something that none of them had dared to so much as hope for: he told Walter to take his boat back to shore so that he was out of the way of the continuing search. Walter gave a cheeky salute and told him he had absolutely no problem doing that. With Edmund's help, he got the little fishing boat away from the sloop and back toward the shore.

They put in at a handful of docks that the local fisherman shared amongst one another, and Walter and his son moved the nets to free their stowaways. Dallion had lost consciousness at some point, but Journey was able to rouse him, and Edmund helped him move the half-dead pirate from the boat to a small, wooden shack that Walter's family had long used to store their nets and other supplies in. They crowded inside and got Dallion into a sitting position with his back resting against one of the walls. His breaths were shallow, and when Journey asked how he felt, he gave no answer.

"The boy needs a doctor," Walter said, shaking his head in pity. "Don't know one, but my wife's patched up more than a few holes in me in our twenty-four years together. My daughter, too. I'll go fetch one of them and send them down here to you."

"You've done more than we could have asked you to," Journey told him. He stood and offered his hand.

Walter shook it, looking slightly bashful, and warned, "You two should get as far away from Runes as you can. Do you have a way out?"

"One step at a time," Journey muttered. He sat down beside Dallion. His eyes had slipped closed again, and Journey couldn't tell if he was still conscious or not.

Walter considered something for a moment before saying, "My wife's cousin has a boat. He runs passengers out to Breakers Bay on Miquelon every now and then. He might take you."

"Would he be willing to take us to Claymill?"

Walter took off his hat and wiped sweat from his brow. It was warm inside the little shack, and it didn't help that there were four grown men gathered inside it. "That's in the opposite direction, but he might be willing, so long as you can pay him. Do you have any money?"

"No," Dallion responded, answering Journey's concerns about his consciousness. "The Horizon bastards took it when they searched me."

"They call themselves businessmen, but they're really just thieves in fancy clothes," Walter chuckled. "Let me talk to Matty – that's my cousin – and I'll see what he can do. In the meantime, you two wait here with Edmund, and I'll send one of the girls down to take a look at that neck."

Journey thanked him once more, and then Walter was gone, leaving the door open only a crack to allow some light in. Edmund squatted down before Journey and Dallion and asked with honest curiosity, "Since you guys are pirates, shouldn't you have your own ship?"

Dallion began to laugh. It was a deep, ironic sound that had no business here in this shack, especially under these circumstances. After a few seconds, however, Journey found that it was contagious, and they laughed together as a look of bemusement came to poor Edmund's face.

Journey kept a watchful eye on Dallion, who dozed off and on as they waited. Eventually, there was a knock on the door, and Journey answered it to find Walter's nineteen-year-old daughter with an armload of supplies. He introduced her to Dallion, who came around enough to flirt with her as she worked, pretending to be delirious and calling her an angel sent to rescue him. His antics earned him the young woman's giggles and even a kiss on the cheek. She treated the wound with some sort of paste she claimed was made from leaves and herbs, then sewed it closed and bandaged it. With that done, she left them in Edmund's care again, although the young man had long since fallen asleep in a slump in the corner. Journey didn't wake him. When Dallion slipped back into the mysterious land of unconsciousness again, he didn't bother him, either. A few hours later, Walter returned with good news: his wife's cousin knew a man who was scheduled to set sail for Claymill in the morning, and they were welcome to come along, as long as they didn't mind spending the trip on a ship full of goats and sheep. They agreed that they didn't.

Walter left them each a serving of bread and cheese before heading home for the night, Edmund in tow. Once they were gone, Journey coaxed Dallion into eating at least some of the food. When it was finished, Journey rested his back against the wall on the opposite side of the shack as Dallion, whose eyes had drifted closed once more. Journey closed his own eyes to try to sleep, but before he could do that, Dallion spoke, his voice hardly more than a whisper in the dark.

"We have to go back to the Jubilee empty-handed. No money, no girl, and no Tawny Paul. I'm in trouble."

Journey didn't respond. Dallion was lucky to be alive, but that didn't mean he couldn't be disappointed in everything that had been lost. Tawny had been a good friend and an even better sailor. He'd been popular among the rest of the crew. They wouldn't take kindly to the fact that this entire excursion had not only proved fruitless, but had cost them all the money that they'd pooled together to send along with Dallion to cover costs for the trip. Journey thought that Dallion might get Lucien's sympathies, but the rest of the crew was bound to be furious. There was a good chance that they would hold a vote over whether or not to allow him to continue serving as captain. Given all the promises he'd failed to make good on lately, the outcome wasn't likely to be in his favor.

Dallion asked, "What happened to Saige, anyway?"

"She met with Audrey Dumont, as planned," he said, rubbing the bridge of his nose with one hand. It had been a long day, and he was tired. "She might already be heading back to Kinsman, for all I know."

Dallion laughed, but it was a sour sound. "At least somebody made out alright in all of this." He paused, then mulled, "Do you think she's the one who ratted on us on Claymill? Blakeshire could have lied about that when he boarded the Crescent Moon."

Journey shook his head, though it was too dark in the shack to see him. "No, Dal. Saige didn't trick us. We were the only ones who were lying."

Dallion muttered something about hunting her down after all of this was over, anyway, but Journey ignored him. Instead, he closed his eyes again and rested the back of his head against the wooden wall behind him. He waited for sleep to come.

Chapter Thirty-Three

EDMUND accompanied them to a ship called Jaded Heart the following morning. Dallion was feeling a little better, at least enough to be able to walk on his own, but he tired quickly and needed occasional rests. Journey wondered how much blood the man had lost and decided that he didn't dare to know the answer. The docks were so busy with ships being loaded and unloaded that they were able to stay hidden in the crowds, even from the few Horizon soldiers who were patrolling the area. The Jaded Heart was a medium-sized schooner that had been outfitted for transporting livestock. Two dozen goats and a handful of sheep were crowded in a pen on her deck. The captain was named Baroux, and they found him to be a jolly, round mass of a man. The Heart ran on a skeleton crew under his command, but he promised to offer what hospitality he could to his two passengers.

As the schooner moved away from the dock and headed for the open sea, Journey cast one last glance back. There, climbing a gangway to board a brigantine that was flying a Commercial Horizon flag, was Saige. She was wearing a yellow dress that she must have purchased since he'd last seen her. Her red hair was pinned up at the back of her head, allowing some of the longer curls to dangle and bob as she walked. Behind her, a man in a Horizon uniform was carrying a small stack of luggage for her. There was no doubt that she'd gotten her money. As the Heart slipped past the dock, Saige took her eyes off of the gangway beneath her feet and looked in that direction.

She caught sight of Journey on the deck of the schooner, and her steps faltered as she came to a stop, nearly causing the man behind her to run into her. Just above the top of her dress, the swan pendant rested against her pale flesh.

They merely watched one another for a moment, neither of them able to look away. Journey raised one hand to chest height in a hesitant wave. Saige didn't move to do the same…but she did raise her hand to the top of her chest, where her fingers gently caressed the swan. Journey felt a sudden and commanding urge to leap from the deck of the schooner and swim to her. He would confess his love and beg for her forgiveness, and if she would have him, he would be hers forever.

He did none of those things. He watched her for a moment longer, and then he forced himself to turn away and fixed his gaze upon the blue sea before him. On the gangway, the man behind Saige urged her to continue up it, and she did so, not allowing herself to look after the departing schooner.

Sometimes, he decided, crossed paths were fated to diverge.

Chapter Thirty-Four

THE Jubilee was waiting for them off the coast of Claymill when they arrived the following morning. Although the Jaded Heart wasn't equipped with a longboat, she did have a small dinghy, and Captain Baroux was kind enough to have one of his crewmen row them to the Jubilee in it. Journey took Lucien's offered hand and let him help him up onto the Jubilee's main deck, where he found the majority of the crew gathered to celebrate their success. Instead, Journey focused on helping Dallion climb aboard, and as soon as his boots were on the smooth wood of the deck, he set off toward his cabin with nothing more than a curt order for the crew to get the ship moving. Before Journey could follow him, Lucien gripped his shoulder and pulled him in close so that he could say into his ear without the gathered crewmen overhearing, "Math isn't my strength, but I know we dropped four people off, and now there are only two of you. What happened?"

"There were complications," Journey muttered, and shook Lucien's hand from his shoulder. He made his way after Dallion, and when he stepped into his cabin, Journey found him already sprawled out on his back on the bed. Journey collapsed into one of the chairs at the backgammon table and let out a sigh of relief. After everything they'd been through over the last few days, it was good to be home, no matter what else lay ahead. He asked Dallion, "Where do we go from here?"

Dallion didn't answer, but continued to stare sullenly up at the canopy above his bed. Journey didn't press. He soon felt the Jubilee turning with the wind as the crew out on the deck got her moving, as ordered. That was good. The more space they put between themselves and this terrible place, the better.

Before long, Lucien entered the cabin without bothering to knock. He closed the door behind him and then simply stood before it with his arms crossed at his chest. Journey braced himself for the slew of questions that he was bound to ask, but Lucien surprised him by not speaking for a while. After an entire day and night of sheep bleating in his ears, he was thankful for the silence. When Lucien finally shattered it, he did so to ask, "Tawny Paul?"

"Dead," Dallion answered from the bed.

"Saige?"

"Sailing away on a Commercial Horizon ship with more money than she's ever going to know what to do with."

Lucien shook his head in clear disbelief. "What the hell went wrong?"

Dallion let out a humorless laugh, then said simply, "Everything."

Journey broke it all down for him, starting with Dallion's arrest aboard the Crescent Moon and ending with their passage to safety aboard the Jaded Heart, surrounded by flea-ridden sheep and goats. He spoke in a flat, unreadable tone and left out any mention of his feelings for Saige. When he finished, Lucien sat down in the chair opposite Journey's and said nothing for a while. Journey could tell by the slump in his shoulders that he'd come to the same conclusion that he and Dallion had about what would happen next. After a long time, Lucien verified this by warning Dallion, "The crew isn't going to be happy about this."

"Nobody's happy about this," Dallion muttered.

"They're going to want me to hold a vote about you."

Dallion raised both of his shoulders in a careless shrug that Journey didn't believe. He and Lucien shared a worried glance as Dallion said, "They won't vote me out. This is the first time I've ever failed them. I'll come up with a new plan to pitch, and they won't be as pissed off, anymore. It'll be alright."

Lucien gave him a doubtful frown at that, but suggested, "We could run down the Horizon ship that Saige is on. We know where she's headed."

Journey's blood ran cold at the idea. He bit back the objection that wanted to spring from his lips, however, and let Dallion think it through. To his relief, Dallion said without taking his gaze from the canopy above him, "It's over. Let her go."

Journey wasn't sure if he was talking to him or to Lucien, but either way, he knew he was right. He sat back in his chair and stared down at his hands in his lap. Lucien didn't argue Dallion's decision. Instead, he stood and said in resignation, "I'll go break the news to the crew."

There was, in fact, a vote held to determine Dallion's fate. He stood by and watched as the men who had gathered on the main deck raised their hands to cast their votes. In the end, the count was close, but it was decided that he would remain their captain. He had no doubt that he had Journey and Lucien to thank for that, as both men had advocated hard for him to keep the position. As soon as the vote was decided, he slunk back into his cabin and shut himself up inside. He had a lot of thinking to do.

That night, he and Journey sat in his cabin, halfheartedly playing a game of backgammon. Dallion was too distracted by thoughts of how to make up the recent losses to the unhappy crew to pay much attention to the game. Journey also seemed unable to focus, and Dallion didn't doubt that his thoughts were on Saige. They'd both lost a great deal and almost everything else. He supposed they should both feel lucky to be alive, and although he was glad to have escaped the hangman's noose and drowning, he couldn't seem to escape the feeling of gloom that hung heavily in the air around him.

He moved one of the checkers on the board before saying, "You were right about her."

Journey didn't respond as he pretended to mull over his next move. Dallion pressed, "You were right about Saige not ratting us out on Claymill."

"It doesn't matter."

"If she'd wanted to turn us in, she could have done it when she spotted you boarding the Jaded Heart. She could've collected the bounty on my head and gone home with even more money. I don't know why she didn't."

Journey rolled the dice on the board, but then he gave up on the game and pushed back in his chair, his shoulders slumped. He said quietly, "She's a good person, Dal. Most people are, if you give them a chance. We're the broken ones."

Dallion snorted at that, but he didn't have a real argument against it. He didn't object as Journey wished him goodnight and left the cabin. Once he was alone, settled into his bed to think about ways to restore the crew's faith in him.

Over the next two months, that's exactly what he did. Under his command, the Jubilee raided and sank three Commercial Horizon ships: two schooners and a small frigate that they managed to sneak up on around Windway Island. These were risky excursions, but as each one paid off and lined the pirates' pockets, Dallion found that their attitudes toward him warmed. By the time winter arrived, things were back to the way they had always been before the Isle of Runes debacle...mostly.

One afternoon, Dallion approached Lucien while he was alone near the bow of the ship. He'd been inspecting a few lines on the foremast that Brain had said were due to be replaced, but he stopped what he was doing as Dallion told him, "We need to do something about Journey."

Lucien looked around the deck for the man in question, but Dallion shook his head. "I sent him below to help Old Rube with something. I didn't want him to hear us talking about this."

"What's wrong?"

Dallion threw his hands up in exaggerated exasperation. "He's been moping around here for months, now. You can't tell me you haven't noticed. Ever since the whole mess with the girl, he's been miserable, and it's driving me crazy."

Lucien's brow furled. "He's miserable, and somehow that's something that he needs to fix for your sake?"

"Not just for my sake. Look, Pigeon and Thomas say that he hardly ever plays cards with them at night, anymore. He just sulks whenever we play backgammon. Brain says he hasn't been trying to teach him to read lately. And when was the last time you heard him singing along to the shanties?"

"I don't know what you want me to do about it," Lucien shrugged. "None of those things are duties that he has to carry out."

"This isn't about duties; this is about him pouting over Saige. It's been months, now. I think we should tell him that he needs to get over her..."

Lucien held up a hand to stop him and said gravely, "Leave him alone about it, Dallion. You told him to choose between the girl and this ship. He made his choice and saved your life in the process. What else do you want from him?"

Dallion started to respond, but found that he couldn't think of anything to say to that. Finally, he admitted, "I just want things to go back to how they were before."

Lucien merely shook his head to signal that he didn't think that was possible. Dallion refused to admit that he might have been right.

On a bright and sunny winter day, Journey found some peace and quiet in his hammock below deck. Most of the crew was in Port Kelsey, celebrating the recent raiding of a brigantine laden with winter wheat, but he'd volunteered to stay behind to help mind the ship. They had spent the last few weeks in these waters, where the Jubilee could stalk easy prey in small merchant ships heading north with supplies for islands that saw snow this time of year. Such easy pickings were great fun for the majority of the crew, but it had done little to lift Journey's spirits. He'd found that there wasn't much that could to that, these days.

He'd just started to drift into an afternoon nap when Thomas clambered down the stairs and called his name over the rows of empty hammocks. He was anxious about something, judging by his quick pace and wide eyes, and Journey would have given almost anything to not have to deal with whatever issue had arisen, now. Any hope of that was dismissed as Thomas told him, "Lucien says he wants you up top. There's a schooner on her way here. She's headed right for us."

"Is she flying any flags?" he asked as he sat up in the hammock.

Thomas shrugged. "It's a green one that we don't recognize. We're on a skeleton crew right now, and if she wants a fight…" He didn't have to finish that sentence; Journey already understood what sort of trouble that could mean.

He got moving and followed Thomas up the stairs and onto the main deck, where bright sunlight assailed his tired eyes. He shaded them with one hand and spotted Pigeon at the helm, eagerly awaiting orders. Dallion and Lucien were trading Lucien's spyglass back and forth nearby. Journey followed their gazes to find a medium-sized schooner approaching from the south. The Jubilee was anchored only a hundred yards off the coast of Kelsey, and although there was an unspoken agreement between pirate crews not to attack one another in these waters, it wasn't a rule that everyone could be trusted to follow. As Journey and Thomas joined them at the helm, Lucien nodded toward the approaching schooner and said, "She was flying a green flag we don't know, but then she ran up a white one. We're not sure we can trust it."

"Why not?" Journey asked, nudging Dallion's arm in a request for a turn with the spyglass.

Dallion didn't surrender it to him, but told him, "We've used that trick before. It was before you joined up. Fly a white flag to keep their guard down, then get in close and start firing. Works like a charm."

"And now you see why that's not a good idea," he grinned as he nudged his arm again. "There's no such thing as trust, anymore."

Dallion handed him the spyglass, at last, and Journey found the ship through it. None of her cannon ports were open, from what he could see, but that could change in a matter of seconds. He didn't recognize it as one of the many ships that wintered in this area. He passed the spyglass to Lucien and shrugged. "There's only one way to find out what she wants."

"Or we can shoot first and ask questions later," Dallion muttered, but didn't give any such order. Instead, he snatched the spyglass back from Lucien and peered through it once more, telling him, "Get the cannon ports open and have the boys ready, just in case."

Lucien swatted his shoulder with one hand and started off to pass along his orders, growling over his shoulder, "Don't snatch things out of my hand, boy."

Dallion ignored him and kept his eyes on the schooner. Behind him, Pigeon asked, "Should I turn her?"

"You know what that'll look like," Thomas warned, and Journey knew that he was right. The Jubilee was sitting at just enough of an angle from the schooner that she couldn't fire her cannons in that direction. If they turned her while also opening the cannon ports, the schooner would assume they meant to fire.

"Don't turn her, yet," Dallion decided. "But if they so much as flinch in either direction, Pigeon, be ready to do the same."

The captain of the schooner must have anticipated their anxiety, for he made sure his helmsman kept her nice and straight. The ship slowed as she grew closer, and before long, they had a good view of the men on her deck. One of them had a second white flag on a short pole, and he was waving it furiously from the bow. Their cannon ports were still securely shut, and Dallion told Pigeon to let her come up alongside the Jubilee. Pigeon grumbled about the idea, but he obeyed.

"Ahoy, Jubilee!" one of the sailors on the schooner called. "We have a message for Captain Romilly!"

Journey and Dallion shared a bemused look at that. What sort of fool would commission a ship just to send a letter? Dallion raised an arm and motioned for them to send someone over. The deck crew on the schooner scrambled to get a longboat in the water, and a few hands aboard the Jubilee hoisted a man up from it with a rope. Journey, Dallion, and Lucien met him on the main deck as Quick Bill and Thomas hauled him over the banister.

Once he was on his feet, he gave Dallion a salute that was very out of place here and dug deep into an inner pocket of the coat he was wearing. He produced a sealed envelope and offered it to him, saying, "Captain Romilly, I've been charged with delivering this to you. It took us weeks to find you, but we heard rumors that you often come to Port Kelsey this time of year…"

He continued with the story of how he'd found them, but Dallion tore the envelope open without bothering to hear him out. His eyes skirted over the words printed on it, and although Journey couldn't read it from where he was standing, he noted the grin that slowly stretched across Dallion's face. The few hands on board had gathered around to see what was going on, but once Dallion finished reading the letter, he refolded it and announced, "This is nobody else's business! Get back to work!"

They hurried to do so. Journey and Lucien remained, however, along with the messenger from the schooner, and Dallion asked him, "Do you work for her?"

He shook his head. "She hired my captain to track you down and deliver the letter."

"Who is she?" Journey asked him, and there was something in his tone that said he had his suspicions about the mystery woman's identity, already.

Dallion thanked the messenger and told Thomas and Quick Bill to help him back down to his waiting longboat. As they did that, Journey asked again, "Who sent the letter, Dallion?"

"I think you know damn well who sent the letter," he grinned, and slapped the paper against Journey's chest. His nose registered a slight hint of perfume still on it. Journey unfolded it to read the flowing script that filled most of the page.

Captain Romilly –

I'm very happy that this letter has found you well. I've had these long months to settle into my new life, and I think you'll be glad to know that I'm also doing well, thanks to you. My father, Francis, taught me as a child that it's important to keep your word, however, and we had a deal. Despite whatever intentions you truly had for me, I agreed to give you ten percent of my inheritance, and I still owe you that. After all, you did deliver me to the agreed destination, and I'm now rich because of it. I invite you to Stonewell Island to collect your share. I think you'll find it more than worth the trip, and so will your crew. This isn't a trick or some petty attempt for revenge, you have my word. Let the past be the past, and I hope that we can settle this debt once and for all.

Saige Moore Travert

P.S. – if Journey is willing to come with you, please tell him that I have something that belongs to him, and I will gladly hand it over when he gets here. Thank you.

Dallion didn't wait for his response, but told Lucien, "Send Thomas and Old Rube ashore to round up everybody else. We're leaving as soon as everyone's on board."

"Where are we headed?" Lucien asked him.

"Stonewell," he said through a triumphant smile, and started down the ship toward the helm to inform Pigeon of their destination. Journey hurried after him, refolding the letter in his hands, and as he caught up to him, Dallion asked, "Excited?"

"We agreed to write this one off as a loss months ago," he objected as he offered the paper back. Dallion didn't take it, but he did stop walking, and he turned to him with an incredulous look on his face.

"Do you have any idea how much money we're talking about? Of course you do – you, of all people, should know how much we're talking. You read what she wrote: a deal's a deal, and she owes us that money."

"Look, I can assure you that whatever she really wants, it's not just to hand over a small fortune to a bunch of pirates."

"I know," Dallion agreed, and then threw his head back and laughed.

Chapter Thirty-Five

JOURNEY was even more withdrawn during the trip than he had been before, but it was clear to him that Dallion was pretending not to notice. He and Lucien had a few meetings behind the closed doors of Dallion's cabin, and Journey minded his own business. He kept his head down, got his work done, and somehow kept himself from going crazy. He didn't want to return to Stonewell, after the terrible things that had happened there, and he definitely didn't want to see Saige again. He'd spent the last few months trying desperately to get her out of his head. He saw her red hair in every fiery sunset, smelled her scent on the ocean breeze, felt her touch in his deepest dreams. He decided that he would stay behind on the Jubilee while Dallion and the others met with her. It would be best for all involved.

They reached Stonewell in exactly the amount of time that Brain predicted for them. When the little island appeared on the horizon, Journey couldn't help but look out over the bow to see it. It had been two long years since he'd last seen the place that had been his home for most of his life. It was just a green and gray speck in an ocean of blue, but it was also something more. This was where Jubilee had taught him to read, where he had run and played as a child on the eastern bluffs, and where he had expected to live out the rest of his life, caring for a family business that he'd turned out to have no right to, after all. He supposed that no matter where he roamed, this place would always be what he thought of as home.

Dallion was beside him before he heard him coming, and he gave Journey a warm clap on the shoulder. As if reading his mind, he asked, "Never thought you'd end up back here again, did you?"

"Be quick about this, Dal," Journey muttered, his eyes still on the island ahead. "Let's get out of here as soon as we can."

"If I start reminiscing with her about the good old days, you can tell me to shut up."

Journey shook his head firmly. "I'm not going with you. I'm staying here. Horus needs help with the outer jib, and I told him..."

"I don't care what you told him," Dallion said, grinning in a way that said he wasn't taking no for an answer. "You and I are going ashore to meet her. Everyone else can stay here. Horus has plenty of guys who can help with the jib."

"Dallion..."

"Are you going to make me give you a direct order in front of everyone?" he asked, and there was just enough of an edge to his voice to let him know that he meant it. "Do you want me to threaten to have Lucien break out the cat o' nine if you refuse?"

Such a thing happened so rarely aboard this ship that Journey doubted Lucien would be willing to do anything of the sort over something so frivolous, and Dallion wouldn't truly ask him to, in the first place. But Journey didn't have any doubt that Dallion would ridicule him about it in front of the rest of the crew, and then he'd never hear the end of it.

Journey's shoulders slumped in defeat, and Dallion laughed, clapping him on the shoulder again. "Don't act like it's the end of the world. She knows us better than she knows anyone else on board, and we all know she fancies you. I'm just trying to get as much money out of her as possible. This is the best way to do it."

Journey wished that he could believe that, but he'd known Dallion long enough to be sure that the man always had an ulterior motive for his actions. He could only hope that he wouldn't make things more awkward between him and Saige than they were already going to be.

Gravel crunched beneath Journey's boot as he stepped off of the dock and onto the island that he'd sworn he'd never set foot on again. From the look of things, Saige was doing well for herself. Two dozen workers were busy unloading a small brig, and there were outgoing stacks of barrels ready to depart on the same ship. The docks and warehouses had recently been repainted, and the road leading up the hill to the mansion sported fresh gravel. Dallion set a comfortable pace in that direction, Journey in tow. It felt strange to be back here, but not quite as strange as he'd expected. In fact, it almost felt like he was meant to be here.

As they reached the top of the hill, they saw that Saige was standing outside the mansion, waiting for them. She was wearing a powder blue and pink dress that would have been fitting for any socialite of admirable wealth and influence to wear. Her red hair was in curls that cascaded over her shoulders. Journey had tried to brace himself for this moment, but it hadn't worked; she took his breath away, and his heart felt as if it was being torn from his chest. He refused to let his steps falter, however, and he kept up with Dallion. Before they were within earshot of her, he reminded him, "Let's make it quick."

"Relax," Dallion soothed. "We're all friends again, remember?"

He didn't respond, and as they drew closer to her near the mansion's front steps, Saige wouldn't look at Journey.

Instead, she greeted Dallion with a smile that both men would have done anything for. For a moment, none of them spoke. They simply took one another in beneath a clear, blue sky and the flitting birds it hosted. The sound of the sea crashing against the island was a distant thing, and the breeze up here was light and warm. Journey realized that he was happy for her. She was where she'd deserved to be all along, and by the look of things, this new life was treating her well.

Finally, she said, "I've been watching for the Jubilee for weeks, now. I'm glad my letter got to you."

"We were in the area, anyway," Dallion lied. His smile matched her own, and he opened his arms in an offered hug.

Saige crossed the short distance between them without hesitation, and Dallion put his arms around her and squeezed. He placed a loud kiss on her cheek, making her laugh, and told her, "You're gorgeous, Saige."

"You've looked better," she said as she eyed the scar on his neck, but then placed a gentle kiss on his cheek, as well. Her painted lips left a small, red smudge amongst the scruff of a cheek that hadn't seen a razor in the past three days. Then she stepped back, but she still didn't look at Journey. Instead, she said to Dallion, "I'm glad you got away from Horizon alright."

He looked around, admiring the statuettes along the edge of the paths in front of the house. "Are you working for them, now?"

"No," she said with unhidden pride. "I told Audrey Dumont that I wanted Stonewell Island, both of the Twins, and just one of Landon's cargo ships. I let her buy the rest of my interests in the company. I'm not partnered with Horizon, Whitefish, or anyone else. It's just me, so I can do whatever I want." She cast her first glance at Journey, who was standing silently beside his fellow pirate, but when she spoke, she directed it to Dallion once more. "I took some advice I was given and hired locals from Kinsman Lane. I'm paying the highest wages any of them have ever earned. I can get and keep the best people that way. Besides, I'm not trying to make a huge profit. I'm just trying to help out people who aren't as fortunate as I am."

"People like us?" Dallion teased. As if in answer, the front door of the mansion opened, and a man in a servant's uniform came outside. He was carrying a wooden chest, and Dallion's eyes lit up at the sight of it.

Saige saw by the look on his face that he knew what was in it, and she nodded. "I promised you ten percent of everything I'm worth. Hopefully, it makes up for all the bad things that happened."

The servant came down the stairs and set the chest on the ground before Dallion. Then he bent and opened the lid. Inside, neat stacks of marks were sorted by value. Dallion rubbed his hands together, clearly pleased. "Saige, you're a good woman."

"A deal is a deal," she told him, but it was easy to see that it brought her joy to give this to him. "I'm here because of you. Francis and I can finally have a good life, and that's worth more to me than any money I could ever have."

The servant retreated back toward the house, and Dallion squatted before the chest to paw through the stacks of cash. As he did that, Saige finally turned her attention to Journey. Neither of them spoke, but there was a novel's worth of thoughts and feelings in their eyes. Saige was the first to find words, and she told him, "I've had a few months to think about everything, and I want you to know that I forgive you. It's been awful to know that one of the last things I said to you was that I hate you. That isn't true."

"You have every right to hate me," he said, and was surprised by how much more pain his heart could feel. "I'm sorry."

She reached into some hidden pocket of her dress, and when she held out her open hand to him, the swan necklace was coiled in her palm. He searched her eyes and found sorrow in them. She said in a voice that threatened to break, "I didn't feel right keeping this. Besides, it's worth a pretty coin, so I thought that maybe you'd want to sell it to get your money back."

Journey reached for it, but instead of taking it from her hand, he gently closed her fingers over it. Her flesh was as soft and warm as he remembered. He didn't let her go as he said quietly, "It was a gift that I don't regret giving. Besides, I can't have it back. If I had it to remind me of you every day, I'd go insane from missing you."

Tears had been collecting in her eyes, and now they spilled over her long lashes. She laced her arms around the back of his neck and stood on her tiptoes to kiss him. He put his arms around her as their lips met, and he breathed her in. Dallion closed the top of the chest and stood back up, beaming at the sight of their kiss. He stuck two fingers between his lips and whistled in praise of it, then laughed and clapped his hands. They ignored him as Saige's hands explored Journey's hair and his arms held her close. Journey was desperate for just one more moment of this, and then a minute, and then years and all eternity.

But he knew that it wasn't meant to be. He broke their kiss and rested his forehead against hers, still holding her close. His eyes were closed, but he didn't need to see her to know that there was a dangerous look of hope on her pretty face. He whispered, "I'm sorry, Saige."

She knew that he wasn't talking about the things that had happened before, but what had to happen, now. She squeezed her own eyes shut against the tears and breathed, "I understand."

Letting her go was the hardest thing he'd ever done, but he made himself do it, anyway. He stepped back from her with a freshly-broken heart. She wiped at her wet cheeks, leaving streaks of makeup across them, and wouldn't meet his gaze. To Dallion, she said, "Take care of yourself out there, okay?" She didn't bother waiting for his response, but turned and went quickly up the stairs to the front door. Journey and Dallion watched her go, and once the door was closed behind her, Dallion let out a heavy sigh.

Journey stared at the large, wooden door that had taken her from his sight. He would never be the same man he'd been before he'd met her. He knew that, now. He just hoped that the pain would someday go away.

Dallion hefted the chest onto one shoulder and started back toward the downhill slope that would take him to the dock. Journey turned away from the mansion to follow him, but he kept his gaze on his feet. He concentrated on keeping them moving, one step at a time. If he could make it to the ship and keep from looking back as they sailed away, he thought he might be alright...

After about thirty yards, Dallion stopped and turned around to face him. Journey was still watching his feet, and he almost ran into him. He met Dallion's gaze, and he shook his head in disapproval.

"What the hell is wrong with you?" Dallion asked.

Journey wasn't sure what he meant, and there were so many thoughts swirling in his head that he couldn't even guess. All he knew for sure was that he needed to get back on the ship before he started allowing himself to want impossible things.

With the hand not keeping the wooden chest steady on his shoulder, Dallion pointed back toward the mansion and said sternly, "Go."

"What are you talking about?"

"I didn't come all the way out here for the money," Dallion said, but then added with a grin, "Although that's nice, too. I came here to drop you off."

Journey's thoughts only whirled some more, and some half-dazed part of him suspected this was some sort of test. He assured him, "I'm not going to walk out on the Jubilee for some girl, Dal. I thought I already proved that."

"You'd be an idiot not to."

Journey looked at him as if he were crazy, and maybe he was. Dallion was still grinning, and he set his free hand on Journey's shoulder. "I'll keep the first mate position open for you, just in case you need it. But I doubt you will."

"I...I can't..." He fumbled for words that wouldn't come because he had no idea what to say. Dallion waited with a patience that wasn't much like him, and Journey finally managed in a rough whisper, "Are you sure?"

"Go," he urged again, and that was finally enough. Journey threw his arms around him in a hug that was so tight, he nearly knocked the chest off of Dallion's shoulder. Dallion laughed, hugging him back with his free arm, and said, "Get out of here, you lucky son of a bitch. The girl isn't going to wait forever."

Journey gave him one more squeeze that was hard enough to hurt, then let him go to start back toward the mansion at a jog. Dallion laughed some more as he watched him go, and he called out after him, "I get to dock here anytime I want! This is a safe port for me, Prince! Anytime!"

Journey didn't answer; he was too focused on reaching the front door. Dallion adjusted the heavy chest on his shoulder and started down the slope toward the dock again, humming a merry tune as he carried his riches away.

Acknowledgements

I'd like to thank Line by Lion Publications for taking a chance with me, as well as my developmental editor, Ian Jedlica, who helped me polish a story I care so much about. And special thanks to Jenny Fick for pushing me to get this done. I love you, mom.